COLD CASH

DAN YOKUM

Life is always a Thriller. You never know what's coming next.

You can follow Dan Yokum at
www.danyokum.com

Chapter 1

"We're already a half hour late," Roy Collins said. "We're never going to get there."

Ethan Racine ignored him and slowed the car down a touch.

They passed the snow-covered *Leaving Adirondack Park* sign and Roy said, "We're only at the park border. Maybe we should turn around." He dug his phone out of his coat pocket and looked for the bars. Like the last time he checked, still none.

"Stop looking at your phone. You can't call 'em so chill out." He took a hand off the steering wheel and gave Roy a gentle poke "They'll wait for us. Nobody's leaving in this mess."

"Just keep your eyes on the damn road. I thought winter was over. And now this."

"It's all good, man. No worries. A few more hours and we'll be all done. Three pounds of the best cannabis. We'll double our money by next week."

"If nothing goes wrong."

"It won't, man," Ethan said. "I have it covered. Don't I always have it covered? Those dudes are solid. That last haul was awesome."

The wind blew the snow with enough force to cancel most of their visibility and the old station wagon's headlights barely made a dent in the swirl and darkness. A few hundred yards ahead, a county snow-plow truck with orange flashing lights dumped salt and sand on the road. The truck kicked up even more snow and Ethan kept his distance. Following any closer would surely have made driving impossible.

The car's old heater fan functioned with two choices: on full or completely off. Every few minutes, Ethan flicked the control from one to the other in an attempt to balance the blasting heat with the icy cold. He drove with one gloveless hand on the wheel, the other tapping out some rhythm on the side of his seat to a scratchy song struggling to reach the radio. When for a few moments the song found a better connection, he shook his upper body and head, swinging his long brown hair from side to side, doing what he called his ten-second seat dance.

He turned the heater fan off and Roy, parka zipped tight, hat pulled over his eyebrows, said, "Leave it on. I don't want to freeze."

"Well then fix the damn thing like I've been asking you all winter."

Roy picked a brown duffle bag off the floor, pulled out a large, unsealed envelope, and set it in his lap. He removed a loose stack of ten- and twenty-dollar bills and began counting them.

Ethan asked, "How many times have you counted that?" Roy didn't answer. Ethan continued, "Seriously, Roy. This will all work out. These guys are okay."

Roy let out a sigh. "Yeah, I guess you're right. It's nice dealing with Canadians. René and Norm are good guys, aren't they? A hell of a lot nicer than those creeps from downstate we bought from last time."

"That's for sure." Ethan gave a small laugh. "But Norm's American so you still have to watch out for him."

The radio connection devolved to an annoying rumble and Roy turned the dial, searching for a new station. He settled on something coming from somewhere in Quebec, on the other side of the border. A woman's muffled voice, speaking in French, faded in and out.

A minute later Roy asked off-handedly, or what he hoped sounded like it, "How's your sister doing?"

"My sister?"

"Uh, yeah. You know? Her name's Betsy? Last time I checked, she was your sister.

"Man, you are so transparent. You're obviously way into her. And she's much too young for you."

"She's sixteen, gonna turn seventeen, and I just turned eighteen so what…"

"Don't even think about it. You're not her type."

"Oh yeah? Well, what is her type?"

"Not somebody like you."

"You're such an asshole," Roy said.

Ethan sighed, loud and dramatic, then said seriously, "That *was* kind of assholish of me but Betsy really isn't your type. She's always been kind of different, right? You know what I mean. But lately, she's been a lot different. I mean, I'm all about the outdoors and all that but she's been taking it to a whole new level. You know the old camper thing in our driveway that's on the back of the dead pickup truck? She's been sleeping out there. The window hardly closes and there's no heat."

"Wow. How come?"

"When my Grandpa moved in with us, we were short a bedroom so I offered to switch off and on sleeping on the couch. We did it for a while and then, about a month ago, she took all her stuff and moved it outside. Said she likes to hear the animals at night."

"How much does she know about all this, you know, dealing weed?"

"Uh, not much." He hesitated. "It's like this. I don't ever talk to her about it. I know she's happy we have some money coming in so she acts like she doesn't know. But this deal we're about to do? She'd be so pissed if she knew about it."

"Why?"

"Just don't ever tell her."

A half-hour later, they turned into a small nearly empty parking lot next to a metal-walled warehouse. One floodlight made a vain attempt to break through the snow and darkness and brighten the un-plowed lot. Ethan barreled in—snow tires and all-wheel drive, he always said, will take you anywhere—and parked next to a company cube van. He picked up the duffle bag and hurried around the corner of the warehouse to a door at the front.

Roy followed but turned back to the parking lot. "I have to take a leak," he yelled. I'll be right in."

"I'll wait for you," Ethan yelled back.

While Roy peed, he absently looked at the side of the van and read the words, Matrox Imports, Montreal PQ and LaFrond, NY. He started back around the corner of the building, stopped, and turned his head. The front of another vehicle, a black SUV with a New York license plate peeked out from the other side of the van. The plate holder read, Bridgely Auto Sales, Yonkers, NY.

"I'm going in," Ethan yelled.

"Wait! No. Hold on."

It was too late.

***

Ethan went through the door and into a dark entry room filled with cardboard boxes. Some of the boxes were opened, and arms or legs of dresses, pants, and blouses hung out over the edges. An overhead light shone a dim path through the boxes to a set of double doors on the far wall. He pushed his way into another poorly lit room, this one much larger, with a chipped concrete floor and a high ceiling. It was filled with racks of clothes, packing tables, more packed cardboard boxes, and an old forklift.

About fifty feet away, a floor lamp illuminated two men standing next to one of the tables. Both wore long black woolen coats, and one had on a fur hat. Stacks of shoebox-size packages crowded the tabletop and surrounded a small pile of something white. A large propane heater stood next to the table.

"Hey Norm, René," Ethan said, walking forward. "Is that you?"

It was René, sitting on a chair, his hands in his lap.

Ethan stopped. "You okay?"

Just as Roy crashed through the door, Ethan saw the guns, both pointed at René.

One of the black coats swung around and fired toward them. Roy dove into the clothing and hit his head on the hard metal base of one of the racks. As the other black coat aimed at Ethan, he also pitched into the racks, dropped the duffle bag, and knocked over a rack that fell on top of him. He hit the floor and his deceptively stylish glasses, without which his vision was a blur, flew off and out of reach. Three shots whizzed over his head.

René pulled a gun out of his jacket, shot one of the black coats in the stomach, and slid down behind the table for protection. Bleeding, dying, and in extreme pain, the black coat picked up his duffle bag and tried to run. He made it halfway to the door and fell on the floor, dropping the bag and sending his gun skittering into Ethan. René lifted his gun but the fur hat got him first and René's shot hit the propane heater, putting a hole in the supply line. The fur hat calmly put another bullet into René and headed toward the door. As he passed by the other black coat, he poked him with his foot, picked up the duffle bag lying next to him, and continued toward the front entrance.

The fur hat hesitated and sniffed the air. He turned back to the heater, crouched down, and sniffed some more. He pulled a dress off one of the racks, draped it over the heater, took a lighter from his pocket, and lit the dress on fire. Then he turned back toward the door, this time moving a lot faster.

He passed by Ethan, twenty feet away and covered in clothes. Ethan picked up the gun that had slid into him and fired.

The fur hat fell and Ethan jumped up and ran to Roy. Blood covered Roy's hair and face and pooled onto the surrounding floor, and he lay there, unmoving.

"Aw no, man." Ethan cried.

He ran back to the fur hat who was now sprawled on the ground, moaning.

The fur hat tried to stand. "You little shit. You shot me in the leg."

"You killed him!" Ethan screamed. "I'm gonna kill you now." But he couldn't do it. He couldn't bring himself to pull the trigger.

Ethan picked up the duffle bag and ran out the door into the blizzard. He scrambled into his car, threw the bag on the seat, rummaged through the glove compartment for a pair of back-up glasses which were thankfully there, and drove off.

The duffle bag. In his pumped-up escape, he didn't notice how much heavier it was than the one he had brought in. He tried to lift it off the seat. It had to weigh four or five times as much as before. It wasn't his, wasn't the one he and Roy had brought. It couldn't be.

He drove for ten minutes, having no idea where he should go or what he should do. He pulled onto a dirt side road and did a U-turn. He hoped he wouldn't be seen by a passing car and could spot the fur hat if he came that way. He unzipped the duffle bag and tried to reach his hand in but wasn't able to because the bag was full. He pulled out a bundle of bills and attempted to examine it in the darkness. He felt the thick crisp rough-textured paper and the band of tape holding the bills together, and when he put the bundle up to his nose, smelled the distinctive fragrance of new money. He couldn't make out the denominations, but when he put his hand back in the stuffed bag and touched a few more of the bundles, he did grasp that, whatever was in there was an unimaginable amount of money, more than he or anyone he knew had ever come close to having.

A large black SUV crept by but didn't stop. Ethan couldn't bring himself to kill the fur hat but the fur hat would have no problem killing him. He hopped out of the car, opened the trunk, and re-arranged a few things. He pulled out the winter gear he always stored there: extra clothes, better boots, backpack, one-person tent, low-temp sleeping bag, freeze-dried food. He debated snowshoes and decided they weren't worth it. As bad as the snow was coming down, it didn't seem that deep. *Helps to be an outdoor type.* In five minutes, he suited up, filled the backpack, and left.

***

The fur hat, whose name was Walter Lazrove and who was well connected with the big city drug trade, picked up the duffle bag next to him, shook it, unzipped it, and pulled out the envelope with Ethan's and Roy's money. "What the hell," he yelled. "This isn't my bag. That little shit took my money."

He hobbled out the door, still carrying the wrong bag, the money still in it, and threw it in the snow. He pulled himself into his SUV and followed the tracks out of the lot and onto the road. Blood covered his pants and his leg hurt so much that he had to fight to keep from passing out. But no way was he going to lose his money.

A few minutes later, he spotted the station wagon parked on an unpaved farm road. The kid didn't do a very good job of hiding it. He would sneak up on the little shit and take him out. He continued past the car, did a U-turn in the middle of the road, and pulled over about a hundred yards from where the kid was parked.

Lazrove figured the kid still had the gun, but he wasn't worried because he had already seen that the kid was a wimp about using it. He limped up to the car, dragging his bad leg through the snow, yanked open the front door, gun drawn, and looked in. The kid and the duffle bag were gone. He opened the rear door and crawled inside. Nothing there, either. He leaned over the back seat, and tried to evaluate the rear cargo area but couldn't tell much because the light was too dim. He squirmed back out and opened the rear hatch. Nothing there but a blanket and a pair of snowshoes.

He screamed and swore into the howling wind. He attempted to run down the farm road, trying to follow the path of the already disappearing footsteps, but he could only manage a slow, stumbling gait. After a few hundred yards, the footsteps took a dramatic turn up a steep embankment and into thick woods. He grabbed onto saplings and rocks, pulled himself up the embankment, and kept going. At a tiny, nearly frozen stream, the footsteps disappeared. He used the flashlight on his cell phone and trudged, first upstream, then downstream, but found nothing. The snow fell so fast that his own footsteps, his breadcrumbs leading the way back, were also vanishing. He finally gave up and slogged back to where he had started.

When he came to the kid's car, he fought the urge to empty his gun into it. Instead, he took another look inside, made it back to his SUV, and stormed out of there.

Chapter 2

Seventeen Months Later....

"Hey Pepe," Betsy Racine called from the kitchen, "You want a cup of coffee?" He had almost finished his lunch and would want coffee but she always had to ask. He banged on his metal TV tray one time, signaling a *yes*. She loaded up the coffee maker, turned it on, and went into the living room. She pointed to a rusting woodstove and said, "That thing's too big for this little trailer. It's too hot in here." Pepe shook his head and hugged himself to show he was cold.

He sat in an easy chair, watching an old western on the TV, the volume up too loud, and slowly slurped and chewed the last of the tomato soup and sandwich Betsy had made for him. While he ate, she checked the oxygen tank next to him, and with her fingers, traced the clear plastic breathing tube ending in his nose to make sure there were no kinks.

"I'm going outside for a minute," she said. "Your coffee will be done soon."

The property was not much more than a muddy clearing hacked out of the woods. In the rutted and potholed driveway sat two vehicles: an ancient, badly rusted pickup with a detachable camper on its bed, and a ten-year-old sedan that Betsy shared with her mother. A fresh pile of firewood and a tree stump with an ax slammed into it ornamented the edge of the driveway. The trailer was nearby, it's underside skirting falling off in many places and the front steps a season away from rotting through. Nearly hidden, Ethan's old station wagon, no longer driven but still registered and insured, peeked out from behind the far end of the trailer.

Yet all around their small parcel, rolling hills covered with maple, oak, birch, and beech trees gloriously showcased the vibrant beginning of their changing colors. Behind the trailer, a thick stand of pines and spruces acted as a cover for a small path that followed a rocky stream ending at a large pond. Also, although their land wasn't large, on either side of them were vast tracts Betsy hoped would never be developed. The nearest neighbors were far enough away that she always had the feeling she lived far out in the wilderness. Their living situation was rough and minimal but she never stopped appreciating the seclusion.

Even though the mid-October temperature was in the low fifties, she went out barefoot, wearing only jeans and a tee-shirt. She crossed the driveway, climbed into the camper and turned on a battery-powered lantern hanging on the wall. A bed piled with blankets took up half the space. Crammed into a corner was a small wooden end table, its top covered with milk crates filled with neatly-folded clothes. Blouses, shirts, and a few coats hung on hangers on a clothesline strung across the back wall. On the floor next to the bed were a pile of books, and on the wall hung a framed picture of Betsy and her brother, Ethan, at the top of a mountain, a spectacular view behind them.

She pulled on socks, hiking boots, and a fleece with a hoodie over it, and briefly checked out her face and hair in a small handheld mirror. Good enough for now. Except for the strange blemish thing on her cheek. She usually ignored it, but today it bothered her. Maybe it was the lighting. She pulled a small box out from under her bed filled with various types of makeup and found something to touch up the blemish.

She picked up a tube of red lipstick, examined it, and dropped it back in the box. When was the last time she had put on makeup? Or worn a nice dress? She used to love prepping for a night out before…before Ethan disappeared. When her life still had some semblance of fun and normalcy. When she had dreams of doing something with her future. It seemed so long ago, like a different life that belonged to somebody else. The chaos of the final months of her high school junior year took it all away from her. And, as the sympathy and support of friends and teachers faded away and her home responsibilities spiked beyond something nobody her age should have to deal with, her senior year delivered a whole new life. Barren and lonely. Somehow, she'd made it through, graduating but not attending the ceremony.

She hopped down from the camper and stood in the driveway for a minute, looking around in all directions. The trailer was such a messy contrast to the woods. She did the best she could with it, tried to stay on top of things, even though some disaster always hovered in the background, waiting to make an appearance. The day before, she had replaced a shut-off valve under the bathroom sink, hopefully fixing a badly dripping faucet. She had then worried all night that, if there were more problems beyond what she could learn to repair from YouTube videos, they would need a plumber. And where would that kind of money come from?

When she reentered the trailer, the comforting coffee aroma greeted her, and she brought a steaming cup to Pepe and set it on the tray. "Careful, it's really hot."

Pepe grunted and pointed to the TV.

"You want me to change the channel?" she asked.

He nodded.

She spent the rest of the afternoon cleaning the bathroom and kitchen, doing some laundry in the rusted washing machine, hanging the wet clothes on drying racks in the kitchen, and splitting firewood for the woodstove. When she finished, she said to Pepe, "I have to go find Mom. Do you need anything before I leave? Should I help you to the bathroom again?"

He shook his head.

She pointed to a small box with a large red button on it, connected to a phone wire. "You remember what to do if something happens. Just push the button."

Pepe waved his hand at her, signaling her to go and not worry.

"But only if something's really wrong. You wouldn't want the ambulance to come for nothing." She kissed him on the top of his head and walked out the door.

She started the car and drove a few miles to a roadside bar called Marcotte's Tavern. Marcotte's was one of the few left of ten or more roadside stops that had comprised a route called the River Run. The route stretched fifty miles, with a small city at each end, and as the name implied, mostly followed a river. For years, a standing challenge had been for drinkers to stop at every bar along the way and chug a shot of something wicked and powerful. Before DWI was fully embraced as a public menace, the participants in the challenge often included the drivers of the transporting vehicles. For some reason, as the other stops closed over the years, Marcotte's thrived, and on weekends, was usually packed with hard-drinking patrons.

Betsy was eighteen, not old enough to be in the bar legally, but the bartenders didn't object, knowing why she was there. It wasn't five yet, but the tavern was already half full, mostly with regulars coming in for Friday happy hour. A few gathered around the pool table and the rest sat at the bar or side tables, starting their evening of fun.

"Hey, Dewey," Betsy said to one of the bartenders, "I have to ask you something."

"Evening Betsy," Dewey said. "What's up?"

"Have you seen Louise?"

He pointed to a doorway in the back leading to another room. "She's back there. With Bud."

"Aw, damn." Betsy hurried into the back room.

Except for a few chairs and tables, the small room was empty. Louise, Betsy's mother, lay sprawled out on a ratty couch, one leg slung over the leg of a man wearing a flannel shirt and a trucker's hat and cowboy boots. A dozen or so empty beer bottles littered the couch and floor around them. Louise had crossed over to the land of the wasted and didn't notice Betsy until she jammed her hands between them and pushed them apart.

Louise gave Betsy a dazed look. "Hi Honey. You know Bud, don't you?"

"Yes, Ma," Betsy said. "I know Bud very well. Now come on. We're going home."

"Oh, no. Not yet. I'm here with Bud."

"I'm taking you home."

Her mom patted the couch next to her. "Have a seat and hang out with us for a while."

Betsy put her arms around her mom's waist and pulled her up. She could barely stand by herself so Betsy tightened her hold with one of her arms and dragged her into the other room. When Bud realized what was happening, he jumped up and tried to stop them.

"Hey, hold on. What are you doing?"

"I'm taking her home."

Bud stepped in front of them. "The hell you are." He put his hands on Betsy's shoulders and tried to push her backward.

Like a patient mother talking to a little kid, Betsy sighed. "Bud, listen to me carefully. If you don't take your hands off of me, I'm going to kick the crap out of you."

"Oh Betsy, don't be so dramatic," her mom said.

Bud laughed and held onto Betsy tighter.

Betsy yelled into the front room, "Hey Dewey. Tell Bud if he doesn't get out of my way I'm gonna kick the crap out of him." She let her mom slip into a chair next to them and grabbed Bud by the lapels, pulling him closer.

Dewey said, "She'll do it, Bud. Better do what she says."

Bud tried to push Betsy out of the way but ended up on the floor, moaning and holding his crotch. Betsy grabbed her mom's hand, pulled her out of the chair, and calmly walked her into the other room. As she passed Dewey, she said, "Next time she's in here, how about giving me a call. You have the number."

Chapter 3

Seventeen months earlier...

Roy Collins did not die on the night of the warehouse fiasco. When Ethan Racine ran out of the warehouse with Walter Lazrove's bag of money, Roy was knocked out and bloodied, but he wasn't shot and he wasn't dead. And when Walter Lazrove ran out of the warehouse with the wrong duffle bag, Roy was conscious enough to see and hear it all.

The dim light outlined Lazrove as he stormed out the door after Ethan. The dress Lazrove lit on fire and placed on the heater's leaking gas feed did its job, and with a loud pop, flames shot out to nearby clothing racks. Smoke alarms began screaming and the air rapidly thickened with smoke.

Roy pulled himself up and rushed toward the fire, trying to figure out what had just happened. Lazrove's cohort lay sprawled on his back, probably dead. But the heat from the fire was too hot on Roy's face to get closer to the table. He tore a dress off a hanger, wrapped it around his face like a mask, pulled his head down, and rushed forward. A hill of white powder sat on a mirror on the table, surrounded by piles of small packages. On the floor, somebody's legs and feet stuck out from behind the table. It had to be either Norm or René. He got a quick look and backed away, still not sure which one it was.

A wall of fire worked its way behind him and he bolted to the door and ran outside to where he and Ethan had parked. The SUV and Ethan's car had both left, their tire tracks rapidly disappearing in the blinding snow. However, the AmCan van was still there. He tried the van door but it was locked.

He ran around to the back of the building where another car, an older sedan with Canadian license plates, sat empty. Most likely René's car, which meant he had to be the one who was dead behind the table, about to be cremated by the fire. Roy climbed in, found a key on the floor, started to turn the ignition, and stopped. He couldn't do it. It was too weird being in the dead man's vehicle.

He re-entered the blizzard, pushed his way to the other side of the car, and spotted something that made no sense. Next to it, barely visible in the snow, was a depression in the shape of another vehicle, connected to a set of faint tire tracks leading away. Roy followed the tracks around the other side of the building, up a small alley, and back onto the road, going in the opposite direction from where Ethan and the black SUV had gone. Maybe from Norm? Had he left before the shooting or was he there the whole time?

An explosion in the building nearly knocked him over and flames poured out of the roof. He forgot about Norm, he had to get out of there. But how? He couldn't just run off into the woods in the blizzard. He wouldn't last an hour. He got back in René's car door, drove around the building, and headed onto the road in the direction of the mysterious tire tracks.

The snow continued to blot out the visibility and Roy kept his speed way down. He was the only one on the road, the only one stupid enough or desperate enough to still be out there. After about ten minutes, when he rounded a sharp curve, a show of red and blue flashing lights and loud sirens greeted him. It was a long line: two fire trucks, an ambulance, and two patrol cars from the county sheriff's department. Roy sped up, frantically hoping his car would not be noticed or recognized as the line passed him. However, when the second patrol car approached, it skidded a touch into Roy's lane and he overreacted. He tweaked the steering wheel a hair too much and entered a slow, quiet glide into a snow-filled gully.

He pushed the shifter into reverse and tried to ease his way out, but it wasn't going to happen. He was in way too deep, trapped.

The patrol car stopped and a uniformed officer got out. Roy twisted around in his seat, and through a slit in the snow-covered rear window, got a quick look as the officer bent down at the edge of the gully, assessing the situation.

He yelled, "You all right in there?"

It was not just any officer, it was somebody Roy knew, Deputy Sheriff Dan Reynolds.

Roy wrapped a scarf around his neck and put up the hood of his coat. He forced open the car door, pulled himself out, and climbed out of the gully.

"Evening," Roy said, meekly. "Could you get me a tow truck?"

Reynolds looked at the car, then at Roy. "You're Roy Collins, right? Margie Collins's kid? What are you doing out here in this storm? And whose car is that with Quebec license plates?

He knew was in big trouble. On TV shows, this was when you shut up and demanded to see your lawyer. But Roy didn't have a lawyer and Reynolds was a friend, sort of. Roy vaguely remembered that his mother had gone out on a few dates with him many years before. He decided he would have to tell the truth, or at least some of it, and deal with the consequences.

Roy looked at the ground. "Well, you see, I was there at the warehouse and the fire started and I had no place to go."

"And you have no place to go now, either," Reynolds said. "So, what's going to happen now is, you're going to hop right in the back seat of my vehicle and you're going to stay there until I'm done with whatever business I'm about to have. And you better be prepared for a long night because this is surely going to be one."

When Deputy Reynolds finally brought him home at four the next morning, it still hadn't sunk in that Ethan had escaped. He'd laid in his bed, unable to shut himself down, and the image of Ethan running through the snowy woods, fully dressed for the occasion, took form in his sleep-deprived nearly delirious state. It brought so much relief that he'd alternated between laughing and crying. But two weeks later, when there was no sign of Ethan, when it seemed like he'd vanished into nowhere, Roy began to believe he was dead. He couldn't have survived, and if he had, where was he? Why hadn't he just come back? Except that Roy also knew Ethan had taken the wrong bag, had taken the black coat guy's money. And he knew that it was a whole lot more than what they'd brought with them. So maybe...

Three days after the fire, the sheriff's office brought Roy in for questioning. He expected it was going to happen, and had made a plan in his head about what he would say. He couldn't escape the fact that it was drug-related, he knew that, so he immediately said that, yeah, he and Ethan had gone to the warehouse to buy some pot, like an ounce or something. Big deal. Did anybody really care? And he didn't know where Ethan went. Also, yes, he'd heard a gunshot but that was all he heard because a second later he'd tripped and knocked himself out cold. He even showed the investigator the bald spot and stitches on his head.

Except that the police had found the duffle bag, Roy and Ethan's duffle bag, with six thousand dollars in it, lying in the snow. When the investigator pointed it out to Roy, he hesitated and almost said it wasn't theirs. But fingerprints could easily change the outcome of the story so he told the truth and admitted the bag and the money was his and Ethan's. He also clarified a few times that they didn't buy anything with it.

"Maybe, maybe not," the investigator said. "We'll be following up on the details. And, I don't believe you when you say you didn't see anything else."

"Yeah, I was getting to that," Roy said.

He quickly described as best he could the black SUV and the license plate holder that read: Bridgely Auto, Yonkers, NY. And he'd had a split-second glance at a guy wearing a fur hat.

"No license plate number?" the investigator had asked.

Roy bristled. "Gimme a break. I was on the floor in the warehouse with a smashed head bleeding all over the place."

Roy skipped the part about the duffle bag mix-up, the wrong bag Ethan had run off with. It was part of his plan. If nobody could prove he'd seen something, he wasn't going to tell them. The less he talked, the less chance for somebody like the fur hat to track him down and put a bullet in his head. However, he almost slipped and mentioned the tire tracks next to René's car. Except that, if they were Norm LaMarche's, wouldn't Norm also know something about the money? Or not. It was all so confusing and he'd sat silently.

"You're thinking of something else," the investigator had said. "I can tell."

"Yeah, I am. I want to get the hell out of here."

A day later, the District Attorney's office issued a warrant for Roy's arrest, charging him with car theft and leaving the scene of a crime. Roy was certain that the investigator didn't like and had talked the DA into making him pay for his bad attitude

When the District Attorney's office first handed down the jail sentence, Roy didn't think it would be so bad. Sixteen months in a medium-security prison didn't sound so terrible and he was pretty sure he could handle it. Most of the other inmates would be like him, short-termers who were in the wrong place at the wrong time, usually for stealing something or dealing drugs. No worries about gangs or lifers who would fill every day with some form of ongoing torture for somebody like him. And no big-time mobsters like the guys in the warehouse, thank God for that. But also, no Ethan. Thinking about Ethan was the hardest part.

Once in prison, he quickly established a survival protocol, a way to be left alone. Hide in plain sight was how he described it to himself. He always did what he was told, never talked back—to the guards or any aggressive inmates—and only spoke when spoken to. He kept his hair a mess, grew his beard out, tried anything so that he'd never come across as cute, just in case it ever became a problem. And the plan had worked fairly well.

***

Now, sixteen months later, Roy could see the end. Only two more weeks and he would be out. He had finally begun to allow himself to fantasize about his approaching freedom. Everything was going so well until that asshole guard, Skeet Burke, got involved and insisted on having a private and scary office meeting with him.

Skeet Burke. Why him? What disturbed Roy the most was that he knew Skeet from the outside, knew him from growing up in the same community, knew all about him. And most of it was not good. Skeet had worked in the prison system longer than Roy had been alive and he was proud of it, often bragging about it to whoever would listen. He had a reputation inside the prison and on the outside, for being moody and unpredictable, somebody it was best to never confront or oppose.

The first meeting went okay. Skeet started by telling Roy that the reason he had transferred a few months earlier out of Sing Sing, a downstate maximum prison, was so he could be closer to his family and the North Country he loved so much. Roy could relate and the conversation put him at ease. Skeet followed up with a string of questions about the night in the warehouse. Roy gave the same answers he'd given seventeen months earlier and Skeet nodded and smiled. No pressure at all.

The second meeting a week later was a much different affair. Skeet ambled by Roy's cell, banged hard on the bars with his billy club, and barked, "Come with me."

Like a scared puppy, Roy followed him down the cell-block aisle, trying to ignore the stares, smirks, and snide comments from the other inmates. Skeet turned into his office, a small, damp concrete cubicle, and seated himself, facing Roy, at an old grey metal desk. Roy stood, silent, not sure what he was supposed to do.

Skeet stared at Roy, his square face, dark squinting eyes, and close-cropped hair reminding Roy of a drill sergeant in a bad war movie. He pointed a beefy finger at a folding metal chair and said, "Close the door. Then sit."

Roy sat on the edge of the seat and looked away from him. Skeet continued, "I'm sure you're aware of the problems we've been having with drugs, opiates mostly, being smuggled in. And guess what? Your name's come up a bunch of times as one of the problems."

Roy looked up, eyes wide, mouth open. "Huh? What? What are you talking about?"

"I'm just telling you, this is what I'm hearing. And I can let this go or I can follow up on it. But I will need a really good reason if I do let this go. Smuggling drugs inside? Not okay. You'll need to give me something good."

"I don't understand. I don't know what you want."

"Well that's a real shame now, isn't it? A real shame. What do you have left in here? A few days, right?"

"Five days."

"So maybe you want to think about doing another four to ten years in the max facility. How's that for an idea? A nice-looking kid like you? You'd love it there."

"But I don't know what you want from me," Roy squeaked.

"Information. I want information. About what actually happened in that warehouse. About what you actually saw. About your buddy Ethan Racine, about Walter Lazrove. Everything." Skeet's tone did a major change to: cheery, excited, mimicking a cheesy game show host. "Okay, here goes. I'm going to ask you a few questions, and if I don't get good answers, you're done. Number one. Why did your duffle bag with the six thousand dollars in it end up in the snow?"

"Ethan must have dropped it when he ran to his car," Roy mumbled.

Skeet slapped his hand on the desk. "Bad answer. Let's try again. Why did Lazrove bother going after Ethan?"

"All the investigators said…"

"I don't give a shit what the investigators said. What did you see?" Skeet dropped his voice to a menacing whisper. "See, the thing is, I know what you saw, I know what you heard, but I want you to verify, you know what I mean? Corroborate. I have to be sure. What was it that you never told the investigators? You got five seconds."

"God help me," Roy said. "Ethan took the wrong bag. He took their money."

Skeet cracked a huge smile. "And there was a hell of a lot of it, wasn't there?"

How does he know that? How does he know anything about any of this? "I don't know," he said aloud.

Chapter 4

It was after midnight and Betsy had had enough of the late-night show. She began the end-of-the-day routine she always followed, starting with Pepe, asleep in his chair, his head leaning back. She woke him, helped him to the bathroom, and when he was done, got him comfortably into bed. Pepe caught her hand and gave it an affectionate squeeze.

Next came her mom, passed out on the couch. She laid on her back, still dressed in a bargain store attempt at designer jeans, an old wool coat she'd done her best to keep neat and clean, and a cheap pair of running shoes. Her long straight hair, now dyed to hide hints of gray, flopped over her face. Betsy gently pulled the hair away, revealing her mom's high, distinctive cheeks, which Betsy had always thought made her beautiful, and stared. The beauty took a big hit these days. Her hair looked greasy, her pure skin had turned pale and puffy, and the outlines of her closed eyes were red and wet. Betsy pulled off her mom's shoes, covered her with a blanket, and left her on the couch.

The next morning, Betsy got up before the other two and made coffee, eggs, and toast for all of them. When she finished, she yelled, "Time to get up, Mom."

Louise responded with a moan. "No, honey. It's too early."

"It's already after eight and I have to get into town by nine. Remember? I have a meeting with Mrs. Ducette and you have to get up and watch Pepe."

"Please, honey, just let me sleep a little longer. My head hurts."

"Listen to me," Betsy said. "There's a cup of coffee here. You sit up and drink it and then you get up. I need you to get up right now because I have to go."

Louise lifted herself to a sitting position and took a sip of the coffee. Betsy continued, "Now pay attention. Listen to what I'm saying. You don't leave the house until I get back. You stay here and take care of Pepe. Give him some more eggs and toast if he gets hungry. Can you do that?"

"I'm not a kid, Betsy. You don't need to talk to me that way."

Betsy climbed into her car and turned the key. At first, the engine wouldn't start, but on the second try, it came to life with a few chugs and pops. For the next half hour, as she drove into Plattsburgh, she blasted the radio and sang along to some tunes, trying to distract herself from the anxiety of the impending meeting.

She passed through the small downtown, parked in the city lot, and hurried a few blocks to the Social Services Offices. She found Mrs. Ducette's cubicle, took a seat on a hard-backed chair next to her desk, said a quick hello, and launched into a loud update of her situation. She rambled on, first about how Pepe was doing, and then how her mother seemed to be getting worse. "She needs to go to rehab. Please, she's got to stop drinking."

Mrs. Ducette began to speak in a crisp and measured tone—orderly, like her managed hair, un-wrinkled blouse and blazer, and the papers in the two-tiered wire basket on her desk. "I'm sorry, but there is nothing we can do unless your mother comes back in herself."

"But there's no way I can get her in here," Betsy said. "She's either too drunk or too hungover. Mrs. Ducette, my monthly food money and check just aren't enough for the three of us."

"No, they're not. They're not supposed to be. But your grandfather should be getting disability, shouldn't he?"

"Something's messed up with it. No checks have come for a long time. I was hoping you could help me figure it out."

"Who's his caseworker for that?"

"I don't know. I didn't know anything about it when it was set up. I don't even know who I would call to find out."

"Your mother doesn't know?"

"I asked her that but she didn't remember. She doesn't remember much of anything these days."

"I'll check on that. I'll see what I can do."

"My mom just keeps getting worse. She needs to go back to rehab."

"Does she want to go back?

Betsy raised her voice a notch higher. "Of course she doesn't want to go back."

Mrs. Ducette stared at Betsy and didn't speak.

"I'm sorry, "Betsy mumbled. "I...I don't know what to do."

"One thing you're going to have to do is to start thinking about a job. You only have another month before your welfare runs out."

"I thought it would get re-certified for another six months."

"No," Mrs. Ducette said, "because you just turned eighteen, you don't have young children, and you're physically able."

"But I have my mother and my grandfather. I have to take care of them."

"Unless you have young children, you won't qualify. That's what the regulations say. And I want to remind you that, with what you're saying about the state of your mother's health, you're very lucky you're eighteen now because, otherwise, I would have to have your well-being as a minor investigated."

Betsy left the office in a daze, hurried back to the parking lot, and drove out of town. She fiddled with the radio dial until she found a station playing a song she liked and blasted the volume, hoping to drown out the conversation she'd just had. Oh yeah, sure, she just turned eighteen, just had a birthday. But who even remembered it? It was by far the worst one she'd ever had. She sang along with the music until her voice cracked and she almost started crying. She turned off the radio, sat up straight, took a breath, and stared ahead at the road, stone-faced.

Chapter 5

A day before Roy's scheduled release, Skeet came by his cell and told him to meet him in his office in a few minutes. Roy had no choice, he wasn't free yet, so for the next day, he had to do whatever Skeet said. And after that? He didn't want to think about it, get his hopes up. He walked through the open office door and closed it behind him, positive it was what Skeet would want him to do.

"Did I tell you to close that door," Skeet snarled? As usual, he was sitting behind his desk, tapping his billy club, an angry and threatening look on his face. Roy grabbed at the doorknob. "No, no," Skeet was smiling now. "Leave it shut." Roy stood motionless in front of the desk. "Well, sit down already, Roy. I've got some good news."

Roy sat and Skeet said, "This is your lucky day. You're getting out a day early. Go pack your stuff and meet me back here in an hour. I'll process you out and give you a ride to your mother's house."

"Why?"

"Cause I'm a hell of a nice guy."

"Can you do that? I mean, is it legal?"

"Probably not by the books, but who cares? I'm a sergeant. I can get away with things."

A few hours later, Roy lugged his suitcase, filled with all his prison belongings other than the clothes he was wearing, out to Skeet's big black pickup truck. He threw the suitcase onto the full-size rear seat and climbed into the passenger seat. He was wearing a trucker's cap and his favorite old Carhartt jacket. He pulled the hat down and pulled the jacket collar up to block the bright daylight and the stares, real or imagined, from anyone who might see him.

Skeet, still in his Corrections Officer uniform, nonchalantly hopped into the driver's side, and in a minute, was speeding through the back roads. He drove erratically, seemingly not paying attention, always about to crash, maybe hit a deer. Or a moose. Signs had sprung up over the last few years telling drivers to watch out for moose on the road, and the stories of drivers who had slammed into one were not pretty at all. Roy figured hitting a moose wouldn't be as bad as an elephant but a whole lot worse than a deer.

Skeet launched into a stream of consciousness gab about a bag of money that had to be somewhere out in the vast Adirondack wilderness. "Wherever the body is, that's where the money is. Off a cliff, at the bottom of a lake, maybe even in a cave somewhere. If we keep looking, don't give up, we'll find it."

It went on and on until, finally, there was a moment of silence. Then Skeet said, "So I'm doing all the talking and you haven't said a damn word in the last fifteen minutes. It's time for you to speak up."

Roy looked out the window at the passing houses, barns, fields, fences, and thought, *freedom! I don't have to be afraid of this idiot anymore.* He steeled himself, searched for some courage, and with clarity and a touch of defiance, said "You keep talking about *we*, like we're going to find this money and split it. I have a hard time believing that will ever happen."

Skeet slowed way down like he was going to pull over, maybe whack the crap out of Roy or something. But he kept driving and said in an almost kind voice, "Look, Roy, I know you must think I'm a real dickhead because of the way I acted around you behind the walls, but all the COs are dickheads when they're behind the walls. You have to be to do your job, you know, keep the respect going. The thing is, the rest of the time I'm not such a bad guy. And this is a two-man job, especially because you'll probably see things out there, pick up on things that could lead us to the money. So, that's what will happen. We'll split whatever we find."

"If you say so. But there is one more part of this. It might have to be a three-man job, a three-person job, because the one who would have the best idea about any of it is Ethan's sister, Betsy. If you want to find the money, you'd probably have to get her involved."

Skeet sped up and flipped his headlights on. "So get her involved. You know her. You can do it. And we can split it three ways. There's certainly enough there to take care of all of us."

Skeet dropped Roy off at his mother's home, a split level in a cul-de-sac about five miles outside of Plattsburgh. Roy's mother was still at work for a few more hours and didn't expect him until the next day. She had arranged her work schedule to take off the next day and pick him up herself. He thought of calling her but decided he would surprise her.

He opened the front door, slowly walked through the living room and into the kitchen, stood at the sink, opened the refrigerator door, and stared out the glass sliders into the backyard. It was all so familiar, unchanged, yet like a dream. He climbed the staircase to the bedroom he hadn't set foot in for sixteen months. He opened the door, folded his arms across his chest, and let his gaze slowly take it all in. It was clean and orderly, the bed made, the dresser clear, the closet door closed. The one exception was the large table filled with radios, computers, and every kind of electronic part imaginable. Mixed in were a variety of small car parts. But, although the table and its contents might look like a pile of junk to most people, it wasn't to Roy, because even that had a certain logic, a certain order he followed each time he added to the clutter.

He picked up a few things on the table, examined them, and set them back down. He opened the closet door and looked in at the neatly hung shirts, sweatshirts, and a few jackets. He knew he'd left it tidy and orderly, but not to that degree. His mother had been in there, getting it ready for his return, and he was thankful she had.

He took off his shoes, pulled back the covers on his bed, and climbed in with all his clothes on, including his jacket. He pulled the covers up over his head so only his eyes were showing. He lay there motionless until he heard his mother's car pull into the driveway. He ran down the stairs and stood facing the doorway.

A moment later, Margie Collins came through the door, and there he was, her only son, her only child. She had visited him almost weekly in prison but now she could hug him, hold him, thank God he was back. She tugged on his long straight black hair and his curly beard and laughed.

"You still look like a hippie," she said. She stepped back and checked him out. "And you're way too thin. Come on in the kitchen. I'm going to cook up a real meal. You can help me."

Later that night, when he went back to his bed, he couldn't fall asleep. The quiet was unsettling. It wasn't like he missed the noisy banging on cell bars or guards clomping down the hallways, shining flashlights in his face when they did their midnight bed check. It was just different, so different. But slowly, slowly, he embraced the comfort, the peace, the safety. He began to relax, and for a short while, he lost his sixteen months of fight or flight response.

Deep sleep had almost won the battle until a random thought flipped him back into overdrive. His thoughts spun around like circling birds until they settled on two problems. The first one was practical. He only had about two hundred dollars stashed under his mattress, and he possibly had to buy a new cell phone, or at least pay to restore service on his old phone. He also had to buy parts for his old car which hadn't been started in sixteen months. The second problem carried too much weight to focus on for more than a moment—he was nineteen years old and needed to figure out what he was going to do now with his life.

He set up a to-do list in his head. He would ask his mother if he could borrow her car the next day. He'd offer to drive her anywhere and pick her up. And he'd go to Autoland and buy the parts he needed for his own car. He could also stop by Walmart and pick up a cheap phone if he had to. He'd see how far his money went, and if it ran out, he'd ask his mother for a loan.

He would also start looking for a job, like at the auto-repair shop where he used to work before he was arrested. Maybe they would even hire him back, would be willing to look past his new status in the world as a criminal with a felony conviction.

A third item popped up and he added it to the list. He had to find Betsy Racine.

He woke early the next morning and sat for a while with his mother, drinking coffee and eating muffins. As he'd hoped, she lent him her car, and he drove her to work, bought what he needed to get his own car running, bought a temporary phone, and then went back home. He started working on his car, but couldn't get Betsy out of his mind. He needed to talk to her and the sooner the better.

Except he didn't have a number to call her. He could find Ethan's number in his old phone but he'd never had a number for Betsy. He would have to go to their trailer, show up unannounced, and hope it went okay.

He spent another hour working on his car, getting it road-ready, and then took off. It wasn't far to the Racine's, just under twelve miles, and other than the last mile that was on a small back road, mostly on the main highway. He loved getting further away from the city where it was wilder, but the higher elevation always seemed to make it colder and windier. He pulled into the driveway fifteen minutes later, stepped out of the car, and was glad he'd worn his thick knit hat and layers under his Carhartt coat. The old sedan he remembered sat in the driveway so somebody was probably home.

He caught a glimpse of Ethan's station wagon by the end of the trailer. That was a jolt. He walked around it, looked in the windows, squatted down, checked a tire and saw it needed air, reached behind the tire, and felt the brake pads and the rust on the brake rotors. He could hear the loud TV inside the trailer and firmly knocked on the door a few times. Maybe Betsy was in there and saw him through the window and didn't want to talk to him. Or she could be wandering around on the property somewhere.

The pond was the only place he could think of to look. He hurried around to the back of the trailer and zipped down the short path through the woods that led to it. He broke into the clearing and stopped, wanting at first to keep his distance so he could evaluate the situation. The bright sun bounced off the pond, creating a glare bright enough to drown out some of the details. He squinted and made out some clothes neatly piled on a towel next to the water, and on top of the clothes, a carefully placed pair of glasses. But not Betsy.

Her head popped out of the water. He froze and didn't speak. If she was skinny-dipping it would be awkward, and the last thing he wanted was for her to be uncomfortable around him.

She climbed out of the pond, and fortunately, was wearing a bathing suit. He moved closer and said, "Hey, Betsy."

"Who is it?" Her vision without her glasses was even worse than Ethan's.

"It's Roy. Roy Collins."

She picked up her glasses and put them on. "Roy. It's good to see…" She stopped, caught herself. Her voice turned gruff. "When did you get out of jail?"

"Yesterday."

He stared at her, remembering how she looked the last time he'd seen her, comparing. She still looked like her brother. She had the same full face, long dark-brown hair, wavy even when wet, and piercing golden-brown eyes, slightly distorted by similar thick glasses.

"Stop staring at me like that," she said. "You're creeping me out." She picked up the towel and wrapped it around her.

However, in one way, she was much different and Roy tuned right into it. She and Ethan had always floated through life, relaxed, chill, even when the world around them was rough and brutal. But not now. Something about her had changed in a big way. An image came to him of the professional women fighters some of the prison inmates liked to watch on the rec room TV. She was like the lightweights or middleweights, compact and fit, as if they were giants stuffed into smaller bodies. But the change he noticed wasn't so much about Betsy's physical appearance—she'd always been compact and fit—it was something beyond that. Like the fighters, it was more about an attitude that screamed, *don't mess with me*, and anybody who got too close was going to be in for some big trouble. His prison experience had programmed him to back away from people like that.

"Sorry," he mumbled. "I haven't seen anybody for a while, you know?"

"I bet you haven't. So, why did you come here? What do you want?"

He looked down at the ground. "Just to say hello."

"Okay. Hi. Is that all?"

"I was wondering how you're doing."

Her face tightened. "I'm doing great. Everything is fine." She gathered her clothes and started up the trail. He followed her.

When they were almost to the trailer, Roy asked, "How's your mom doing?"

Betsy stopped and turned around, glared. "What the hell do you want, anyway? Why are you here?"

"I have to talk to you about something."

"Well, there's not anything I want to talk to you about."

"It's important. Just give me a few minutes."

"I think you need to leave. Just get out of here."

"Please. Just a few minutes," he begged.

"Damn. Whatever." She hurried over to the camper. "Let me get some clothes on."

She hopped up into the camper, and as soon as she closed the door, Roy hurried around to the back of the trailer. A few nearly full garbage cans, an old rusted bike, and the remains of a child's swing set junked up the scrappy little yard. Nothing of interest. He examined the skirting around the trailer, spotted a hole, and peeked in, but without a flashlight, he couldn't see much.

He ran around to the front of the trailer and Betsy stepped out of the camper at the same time and spotted him. "Looking for something?"

"No, no."

"There's a bathroom inside."

Betsy opened the door to the trailer and rushed in. Roy followed, closed the door behind him, and stood there, awkwardly. The heat from the woodstove, the TV noise, Pepe and all his paraphernalia, were overwhelming. And Betsy was gone.

She shouted from the kitchen, "Pepe, you remember Roy?"

Roy did his best to put on a smile. "Hi. How're you doing?"

Pepe grunted, picked up his hand, and gave a small wave.

"He just got out of prison, Pepe. Can you imagine that? A real-life ex-con."

Roy leaned down to Pepe so he didn't have to yell, not wanting Betsy to hear. "Uh excuse me. I'm going to use the bathroom."

He walked down the narrow hall, took a quick look through the partially opened sliding doors, went past one tiny bedroom, then another, and then the bathroom. At the end of the hall, one more shut door beckoned. He slid it open a few inches and looked in. Boxes, books, clothes, a mountain bike, and camping gear filled most of the room. In one pile were two yellow helmets with lights on them and coils of rope. One of the piles cluttered the top of a small bed.

Roy slid the door shut and went into the bathroom. When he came back to the living room, Betsy was standing at the front door, about to walk out.

She said, "I have to go to the store to get some food. Bye, Pepe. I won't be long." She opened the door, looked at Roy, and said, "C'mon. We're going."

Roy followed her to the car, still wanting to talk. She turned to him, frowning, and said, "There are only two things I can think of that you'd want to talk to me about. If you want to ask me out on a date, you can forget it."

"No, it's not that," Roy said, his patience gone. "I'm not that hard up."

"Didn't think so. So then it has to be about Ethan and I don't want to talk to you or anybody else about Ethan. Or what happened to Ethan. Or what you think might have happened to Ethan."

She got in the car, started it, and began to back up. She stopped after a few feet, rolled down her window, and hissed, "As I'm sure you know, you're blocking me in here. But I am more than capable of backing around you except that, if I were to mess it up, I would dent your precious car. So, get out of here before I decide that I don't care if I do."

Her car stalled. She turned the key to restart it and it chugged and shook for a few seconds, then died again. She tried it two more times and Roy said, "Your plugs are probably bad. It's probably been five years since they were changed."

She tried it one more time with no luck. Roy said, "I can change them for you."

"I know how to change spark plugs."

"Sure, but it's a long walk to the store to get 'em."

She got out of the car and shook her head. "All right. Okay. Give me a ride to the store."

It was a five-minute drive to the new Fast-Mart gas station and grocery store, normally a quick ride except neither of them spoke, both too angry and annoyed. When they pulled into a massive parking lot, Roy tried to crack through the iciness. "This was just being built when I left. This is amazing."

"Doesn't take much to excite you these days, does it?" She hurried out of the car and into the store.

Roy followed her in and watched as she hustled around the store, filling a plastic basket with eggs, milk, bread, and a few other things. He waited until the coolers in one of the aisles blocked her view and went to the front counter. The cashier, one of his mother's friends, looked up from a newspaper. For a moment, he wanted to walk out, but he figured he'd better get used to the inevitable interaction that was about to happen.

"Roy Collins. You're out," she said. "Nice to see you."

"Thanks. You, too." He leaned over the counter and said quietly. "Hey, could you get something for me?" He whispered what he wanted. "Here's the money. Keep the change. I don't want her to see me."

She went into a back room, came out a minute later with a small box, and handed it to him. He bought a few snacks, and as Betsy walked up, quickly stuffed everything into a bag.

Betsy emptied the basket onto the counter and said, "Hey Roy, why don't you wait outside. I'll be right out."

Roy shrugged. "Yeah, sure."

***

Betsy pulled a food-stamp EBT card out of her pocket and handed it to the cashier. "Also, my car is screwing up," she said. "I need a new set of plugs." She gave the cashier the make, model, and year of her car.

"Roy already got 'em," she said with a knowing smirk.

Betsy glared at her and the smirk disappeared. Still, that was a nice gesture on Roy's part. She knew he wanted something from her, of course he did. Still…it was nice.

They sat at a picnic table, the warm sun creating a nice ambiance, and Betsy said, "Hey, I'm sorry I was such a queen bitch to you before. I do appreciate the ride. I really do. And the spark plugs. Thank you. It helps me out. Things aren't going that well right now."

"Yeah, I figured that."

"It's gotten worse and worse," Betsy said. "It all went to hell when Ethan left. My mom's a total drunk now. She's wasted all the time. I can't work because I have to take care of Pepe. And my mom. Complain, complain, right? I guess it's better than being in jail."

Betsy took the loaf of bread and jar of peanut butter out of the bag, pulled out a slice of bread, dipped her finger in the peanut butter, and spread it on the bread.

"It all sounds pretty messed up," Roy said. "For both of us."

"Want a sandwich? You can make it yourself if this is too gross."

She licked her fingers.

He grinned and said, "Well, yeah, it is pretty disgusting. But you can make me one if you want."

She handed her sandwich to Roy and took out another slice of bread.

"Hey," she said. "I just remembered something. Do you still shoot guns?

"I can't now. I'm not allowed because of, you know, prison and all that."

"You sure could shoot. You could hit anything."

"Yeah. I know," Roy said. "It was the only thing I could do better than Ethan. Other than fixing cars and stuff."

Betsy sighed and said, "Ethan was always the best at everything, wasn't he?" Then, with a touch of anger, "Sometimes it used to piss me off."

"Yeah, me too," Roy whispered.

After a moment, Betsy said, "So, what? You got rid of your guns?"

"Well, uh, let me get something."

Roy hurried to his car, poked around in a day-pack he'd brought with him, and came back holding a small pistol. Betsy scrunched her eyebrows and gave him a what-the-hell-are-you-doing look.

"Don't worry," he said. "It's just an old BB gun. I was going to go somewhere in the woods and try a little practice-shooting later on."

He pointed to a garbage can on the side of the building about thirty feet away.

"See the handle on the middle one?"

"No way," Betsy said. "You can't hit that."

Roy aimed carefully, fired, and missed, hitting the side of the can.

"One more try," he said. "I'll get it this time."

This time he started with his back to the can, spun around, dropped into a crouch, and fired again. One more miss.

He sat back down at the picnic table and stared at the ground. "Guess I'm out of practice."

***

When they got back to the trailer, Roy replaced the spark plugs in Betsy's car, had her start it and let it run for a minute, then turned it off.

"Well, I guess it's good to go," he said.

"Yeah, and thanks. You really helped me out." She hesitated, didn't speak, stared at the ground near him, then said, "I should go inside and check on Pepe."

"Uh, could you wait just a second? There's something I've got to tell you. Something nobody else knows."

She stood in front of him, hands on her hips, and stared at him. He backed away a little.

"While you were in jail, Roy, the whole time, a lot of people kept saying they knew something, saw something, had an idea about something. But they never did."

"But I was there. I really did see it."

"And you didn't tell the cops?"

"It would have made things way worse than they already were."

"For you?"

"For me, for Ethan, maybe even for you."

She moved closer to him and nearly spit the words. "Ethan's dead and you went to jail. What could be worse than that?"

"I went to jail for bullshit charges…"

She cut him off. "He's not alive. No way. He wouldn't have just left like that." She turned, hurried toward the trailer, and mumbled, "He would have come back."

She stopped, stood for a moment, then turned back around, and ran back to him. "Okay, tell me."

He revisited almost everything he could remember of that night, leaving out only a few details he wasn't sure had any meaning. He emphasized that the bag Ethan carried out of the warehouse was heavy and repeated twice what Walter Lazrove had said: "That little shit took my money."

"Oh, come on," she said. "You know what happened after he took off. You were here at the beginning. They looked everywhere. The caves, the woods, the whole fricken North Country. And nobody found a trace of him."

"They didn't know he had the money. They just thought he was scared."

"What difference would that make?"

"He could have hidden it someplace no one would even think to look," Roy said.

"So where do you think that place might be?"

"I thought maybe you would know." He waved his arms toward the woods. "You went everywhere with him out there. If anybody would know, it would be you."

She slowly shook her head. "Go home, Roy," she said. "Forget about it. Ethan's dead, and if there is a bag full of money, somebody either found it and didn't tell or it's rotting in the bottom of a swamp somewhere."

Again, she ran across the driveway to the trailer and this time didn't stop. Roy slowly walked to his car, climbed in, and sat for a while wondering what he should do. After about five minutes, he started the car and drove home.

Chapter 6

Betsy poked around in the kitchen, looking for something to make for dinner. A friend of her mom's had stopped by earlier and they'd driven off together, probably ending up at a bar. Betsy tried calling her phone, didn't get an answer, and decided, to hell with it, she'd make up a few boxes of macaroni and cheese. It would have to do.

Her afternoon with Roy would not stop replaying in her head, and although she'd found the time annoying, it had also been kind of nice. Adding to her confusion, she also couldn't stop thinking about her brother. What if she could finally learn what had happened to him? Even if they found his body, at least she would know. And what if there was money? It wouldn't be hers. She couldn't keep it, wouldn't keep it, at least not all of it, maybe just enough to bail her out of the mess she was in.

Pepe made a few grunts from the other room, nothing unusual, and then a deep painful groan. Betsy rushed in.

"What's wrong, Pepe?"

He pointed a shaky hand at the valve on the oxygen tank. She turned it both ways and he shook his head, groaned again, and pointed to the air tube. She carefully massaged the tube, straightening it.

"You were playing with it, weren't you? Just leave it be and you'll be okay."

She called her mom again and still got no answer. She looked out the window, paced back into the kitchen, clenched her hands into tight fists, and stomped back to the living room.

She said to Pepe, "I have to go out for a few minutes. I'll be right back."

She drove to Marcotte's Tavern, already filling up with another Friday night happy hour crowd, pushed through the door, and entered into the festivities. The voices, many of them already working on an alcohol buzz, roiled at high volume, competing with the music blasting from the jukebox. She wove through the crowd, working her way to the bar until Skeet Burke stepped in front of her. He towered over her and still wore his intimidating uniform, but he was polite and friendly.

"Oh, sorry," he said. "You're Betsy, right?"

"Yeah, I have to talk to Dewey."

She walked around him and had a gut feeling his eyes were following her. Old guy checking her out. Not the first time and always creepy.

She pushed her way between two men sitting on stools at the bar, deep in drunken conversation.

"Hey," one of them said. "We're talking."

She ignored them. Dewey had his back to her, mixing a drink, and she yelled to him that she needed to talk.

He walked over, shaking his head. "She's not here."

"Was she earlier?"

Dewey motioned her to follow him to the end of the bar so he could get closer to her. He leaned in so she could hear better. "She left about an hour ago."

"With Bud?"

"No, some new guy. I'd never seen him in here before."

"What?" Betsy yelled. "What did he look like?"

"He had black hair. Maybe mid-forties. He didn't look like he was from around here. Dressed kind of fancy, like a rich city guy."

"Oh no. How bad was she?"

"The usual," Dewey said.

The jukebox screamed out an eighties tune her mom liked, from the group, Abba, one Betsy also appreciated. She considered waiting a moment before she began what she was about to do. But, no, it had to happen right then. She sauntered over to the jukebox, reached around behind it, and pulled the plug. When the music stopped, the raucous voices also halted and most of the patrons turned and stared at her, wondering what was happening. She stepped onto a chair so everyone could see her.

She cleared her voice and said, "Most everyone in here knows who I am and you know my mom, Louise Racine. And you all know she's a drunk and she's getting worse every day. She's a danger to herself and everyone else. So from now on, she's cut off."

Somebody yelled, "Shut up and turn the music back on."

"No, you shut up and let me finish," she yelled back. From now on nobody ever buys Louise anything to drink. Not anything ever. Everyone got that?"

A young guy stumbled toward her, his hands in front of him like he was about to push her off the chair, and yelled, "Turn the fricken music back on."

Suddenly Skeet was between them. He put his hands on the guy's shoulders, turned him around, and gave him a gentle but firm shove.

Dewey rushed over and plugged the jukebox back in. "Okay, Betsy, you said your piece. Everyone understands. And you will never, ever do that again. Do you understand?"

She got off the chair and faced Dewey. Skeet was standing next to him. "I mean it," she said. "She's cut off."

"If she comes in here with money and isn't driving, I can't very well turn away business," Dewey said.

"You know what, Dewey," Skeet broke in. "Considering the situation she's in," and he looked at Betsy, "you certainly could turn her mom away."

Betsy looked at both of them, puzzled. Why was Skeet getting involved in this? "It doesn't matter anyway," she said, "because, from now on she's not going to have any money unless I give it to her."

***

Betsy hurried out the door, raced to her car, and instantly Roy was there beside her. She jumped back. "Damn, Roy. You scared the crap out of me. Why are you here?"

"I was driving by and saw your car so I stopped."

She raised her eyebrows, then turned away. "Well, I have to go. My mom took off drunk with some strange guy." She mumbled, barely audible, "Damn. This is not good at all. I don't know what to do."

She got in her car but Roy held the door open. She hopped back out, grabbed his shirt with both hands, pulled him close, and yelled, "What? What am I supposed to tell you? I don't know anything." She shoved him. "Just leave me the hell alone."

They stared at each other a moment, and then Betsy sighed and shook her head, trying to regain her composure.

"If we could find the money, it would change everything," Roy said gently.

"I don't care about the money. I just want, I want…" Her voice cracked and she lowered her head and choked back a few sobs.

Roy puts his arms around her. At first, she resisted but then allowed him to. He stroked her hair and she melted into him. "I know. I know. I miss him, too," he said.

It didn't last long, No more sad and vulnerable nonsense. She pulled away, took off her glasses, wiped her eyes with her hand, and stared at him. "That money," she said, "if there is any, would be bad vibes, you know? Bad drug money."

"All the more reason for someone like you to have it. Do something good with it."

"Who else knows about this? Somebody must know. What about Lazrove? He must want it back really bad."

"He'll never get out of prison," he said. "In for life."

"There's no one else?"

"Uh, yeah," His words stumbled. "One other. Listen, uh. Something happened to me in prison. I had to tell one of the guards. It was kind of a bargain thing. But he's the only one, I promise."

When Roy said *guards*, Skeet Burke's face popped into her head. *Gee, what a surprise.* "Roy, you've got to be kidding. Skeet Burke? I guess you already know what an asshole he is. There is no way in hell I would ever get involved with him for anything." She poked her finger in his chest, giving him a small push. "So, I'm telling you one more time, leave me alone." She slowly got back in her car and drove off, shaking her head the whole time. But as she drove, confusion once again gained the upper hand because… what if? What if there was money somewhere? And most important, what if she really could find out what happened to Ethan?

Chapter 7

When Betsy got home, it occurred to her that she couldn't cut her mom off financially because she didn't know anything about the household money, how it came in and where it went back out. She knew they each had an EBT card, the debit card for food the government agency replenished each month. But how were the bills paid? She found a piece of paper and a pen and wrote down all the possible bills: electric, their cell phones, cable and internet, car insurance. Maybe home-owner's insurance except there wasn't much to insure. She remembered recently seeing her mom take cash out of her purse and pay for something at the Mini-mart. She always seemed to have cash. Where did that come from? Did her boy-friends give it to her?

My God, what if these sleaze-balls are paying her to do stuff with them?

She was going to figure it out, not give up until she had all the answers, and she would start in the most obvious place. She turned on a computer sitting on a small table in the kitchen and looked through her mom's recent browsing history. Her mom liked to keep up with the news and was, in Betsy's opinion, obsessed with it, so at first, she wasn't surprised her mom had searched several news sources every day for the last month. But when she dug deeper into the history, it didn't make sense. Why had her mom viewed so many local sources from the New York City area? She was originally from the city, and had lived there until her early twenties. But why would she care about the news from Staten Island or Westchester County or New Jersey? She also found repeated search entries for Walter Lazrove and Sing Sing prison that might have made some kind of sense. But the more she thought about it, especially considering Lazrove was in prison for life, she wondered if her mom was finally going off the deep end.

She took off her glasses, laid them next to her, and rubbed her eyes. She walked to the sink and got a glass of water, still with no glasses. If her eyes were a little worse, even just a little, she would be legally blind, and she sometimes walked around the trailer and the property outside to experience what that would be like. Just in case, so if it happened, when it happened, she would be ready to adapt. Right then, she did it because it was a distraction from how angry she was.

The whole day was too much, more than she could stand. She needed something to calm her down. She opened a cabinet door next to the kitchen stove and reached far inside to the back. She found a bottle of whiskey she had taken and hidden from her mom a few months earlier, filled a small glass, and chugged it down. She was not a drinker and the familiar nausea instantly played around in her throat and stomach. Even so, she wanted another shot. But she didn't dare. Within a minute, the alcohol forced her anger to morph into a pit of despair.

She had to hide her mood from Pepe so she wouldn't upset him. She hurried by him to the back of the trailer and into the room Ethan had once lived in, still filled with all his belongings. She pushed aside some clothes and sat on the edge of the bed, looking at everything. To somebody who didn't know better, it might look like a hoarder's paradise. However, everything in the room still had a purpose for the right person. It had sat, unused, since Ethan took off, since he disappeared.

Next to the bed was a small table and on it a stack of printed photos, some matted and some not. She picked up one of Ethan sitting on top of his car, happy, smiling, ready for an adventure. She looked at two more, one of her and Ethan inside a cave wearing helmets with headlamps, and another taken right after with Ethan and Roy. She remembered the day, how they had lugged lights on tripods into the cave and tried different ways to get the lighting correct. Ethan had bought the lights and camera off of somebody, for dirt cheap, he'd said. And he loved that camera. She was fifteen then and Roy and Ethan were nearly seventeen. Just three years ago.

Another one caught her, a family shot from when she was young, five or six. She and Ethan sat next to each other and her dad and mom were like bookends on either side, holding them up like real parents would. She couldn't bear to look at her dad. He'd left when she was twelve and never come back, and she had a long way to go before she could begin to think of forgiving him. But she loved seeing her mom and how she used to look. Her long hair, much like Betsy's but darker, swirled around her gorgeous face. And her eyes, focused and fully present, stared large and dark directly into the camera.

She leafed through a few more photos, slowly, absorbing the details of each one. Underneath the photos was a large picture-filled book titled *The Catacombs of Paris*. She had bought it for Ethan on his eighteenth birthday, not long before he disappeared. The orange seventy-five percent off sticker still on the cover reminded her of how happy she'd been to get a book like that for so cheap. She had actually been able to afford it. She opened the cover and read the handwritten note on the inside: *Happy Birthday, Ethan. Let's do this before we die. Love, Betsy.*

"You wouldn't have gone without me," she whispered, "would you?"

***

In the early morning, when Louise finally returned, Betsy was asleep on the couch, slouched but mostly upright, with her clothes still on.

Louise tiptoed through the doorway and carefully closed the door behind her, but Betsy heard her and sat straight up. Louise's hair hung in a messy snarl, her makeup was smeared, and her blouse was not tucked in.

"Go back to sleep," Louise said. "It's okay."

Betsy jumped up. "It's already morning. Where were you?"

"Oh, honey. You look a mess."

"Not as bad as you look. My God, Ma. You can't do this. I can't stand it anymore."

"There's nothing wrong. Everything's okay."

"No. No, everything's wrong. Look at you. You're killing yourself. Ma, you look like shit. You smell like...Ma, my God, you actually stink."

Louise walked into the kitchen and put on water for coffee. "Stop being so dramatic."

Betsy stared out the front window, her eyes unfocused.

Louise came back into the living room and Betsy took her hands and sat her on the couch. Louis was too surprised to object.

"Ok, Ma. Listen to me. This is how it's going to work from now on. I'm controlling all the money, what little there is that comes through here. I'll be the one to cash all the checks if we get any."

Louise pulled her hands away. "Stop it, Betsy."

"And, and, I will give you money only when you tell me what you're getting and if you show me what you bought. And don't bother going to a bar because nobody's gonna serve you anymore. The drinking's over, Ma."

Louise shook her head quickly, over and over. "You really can't do this. You don't run this house and you certainly don't run me."

"I do now, Ma. It has to be this way."

"I'm going to the Post Office. And then to the store. I want a newspaper."

"You don't need another newspaper. Why do you keep getting all those papers? You don't even read 'em."

"Why do you care? They're free. You need anything at the store?"

"You're not going. I'm not driving you."

"I'm walking," Louise said.

"That's a hell of a long walk."

"I need the fresh air."

Betsy looked at a clock on the wall. "Oh, damn. It's already late. Just stay here."

"No. I have to get out."

"Goddammit. Okay. You go and you come right back. You bring any check back here. And, if you try to cash it, I'll find out."

"What are you late for?" Louis asked.

"I have to get Pepe up and then I'm leaving for a while. You come right back and stay with Pepe for the day. But go clean up first. At least wash your face and comb your hair."

Louise went into her bedroom and closed the door, and Betsy slumped onto the couch, put her head in her hands, and closed her eyes. *I just turned eighteen and I'm telling my forty-four-year-old mother what she can and can't do.*

She fought back tears and exhaustion, and a moment later, forced herself to stand up.

43

Chapter 8

Skeet Burke had hung out at Marcotte's until about ten, drinking a little too much and telling jokes to a few of his buddies. He liked to tell jokes, liked to entertain, liked to put on acts. Hell, if he had taken a different path in his life, maybe he would have even become an actor. Made a lot of money, had a good life, had not had to put up with all the damn problems that were always swirling around him these days. After Betsy's entertaining meltdown, what he'd labeled *The Betsy Racine Showdown*, he'd come up with a skit, alternately playing Betsy, Dewey, and one of the drunks, and was funny enough that a crowd of ten or so gathered around and egged him on.

At first, Dewey ignored him, but after about ten minutes had come over and whispered in Skeet's ear, "Here's a deal. I'll give you free rounds for the rest of the night if you will shut the hell up."

"What'd he want?" one of Skeet's fans asked, nodding toward Dewey as he walked away.

Skeet made a goofy fake-scared face, waved his hands and fingers around like they had a mystical power, and started in on another unrelated story with lots of drama and comedy.

He arrived home at midnight. His wife, Mary, who had recently begun a second round of chemotherapy for stomach cancer that had returned with a vengeance, had gone to bed upstairs hours ago. He wasn't in the mood to have to be quiet and knew the morning would be no different than it always was, he would be wide awake at six am., so he kicked off his shoes, laid on the couch under a quilt, and quickly fell asleep.

He woke at six, slugged down a cup of coffee still in the pot from the day before, washed his face, put on sweats and running shoes, and went out for a short run. Daylight wouldn't happen for another hour, making it dangerous to run on the roads, but he had another route to take, an abandoned and deserted railroad bed with the tracks long gone. A half-moon gave him just enough light to see where he was going and he found a fast gait he could hold for a half-hour or so. Usually, a run on the trail calmed him down and kept him away from his demons, but not this morning. He didn't feel right, something was up. He knew he'd drunk too much the night before, but he wasn't hungover. This was something else and it was making him anxious and angry, always a nasty combination.

When he returned home, he took a quick shower, dressed for a day outside, and fried up a few servings of eggs, bacon and toast. He knew Mary would smell it and come down. But whether she would be able to eat anything was always an unknown these days.

Her footsteps on the stairs announced her entry. "You hungry?" he asked.

"I'll try," she said. "Did you make enough for Shelly?"

He kept any hint of emotion out of his voice. "Shelly's not here, Remember? She went back to the facility to get better."

"I saw her eat yesterday. She probably ate more than I did."

He didn't try to correct her again. "Yeah, but at least you have a good reason, chemo and all."

"Shelly has a good reason, too," Mary said.

Skeet didn't answer. For a long time, when Mary defended his daughter's bizarre behavior, it pissed him off way too much. Now it was compounded by his wife's, or legally ex-wife's, increasingly demented reality.

An hour later, Skeet left in his pickup to round up his two new cohorts, his new allies, for the first day of their big adventure. He composed a plan for how he would act, how he'd present himself and came up with a dual role. For Betsy, he'd lean toward funny, sarcastic, a little bit cynical, and for Roy, he would deliver a big dose of fear and intimidation, what he called his *don't you dare cross me or you'll pay the price* act. The way he felt at that moment, the first persona was going to take some work. The second one? No problem at all. He laid a shotgun in the back seat and a pistol next to him in the center console. They would get the idea.

Skeet was about a mile from Roy's house when his phone rang. His phone screen showed a number but no name. Spam. He'd ignore it. He looked again and realized it wasn't spam. Not even close.

He pulled over, answered the call, and when he hung up, he threw the phone on the floor and squeezed the steering wheel with an iron grip. His whole body shook. This couldn't be happening. It was going to mess the whole thing up. He had always known it was a possibility, complex legal stuff and all that, but never took it seriously. And now, here it was. Three days ago, Walter Lazrove had been released from prison, with all charges dropped on technicalities.

What the hell! He had to pull it together. He had to. He had way too much at stake to freak out now. He needed that money and he was going to get it. He would follow the same plan as ten minutes ago. And Lazrove? If he dared show up, Skeet would do whatever it was he had to do. He wouldn't say anything to the two young ones he was about to pick up. One way or another, he needed to get every bit of information he could out of them. It was also possible, if the timing was right that, if Lazrove did show, he might surprise them when they were no longer of use and remove them from the whole situation. Do the dirty deed so Skeet would never have to think about it.

Chapter 9

When Skeet and Roy pulled into Betsy's driveway, Roy considered offering Betsy the front seat. She could ride shotgun, almost literally, except it was only a pistol that sat in the middle console between the two front seats. The shotgun, tall and proud, stood propped up in the back seat against one of the doors. Skeet was acting weirder than ever—humorless, grumpy about something, more like his on-duty prison personality. No, it was even worse than that.

Betsy stood in the driveway, waiting, a large backpack leaning against her. She would be just like her brother, prepared, always prepared. But the tense look on her face, the rigid body language, like a coiled snake ready to strike, was not promising. He envisioned a long, stressful, possibly dangerous day with two seriously out-of-sorts characters. No, not promising at all.

Roy hopped out, grabbed the backpack, and said to Betsy, "You can sit in the front." He hustled back, threw the backpack onto the rear seat, and jumped in next to it before she could get it together to complain.

She got in the front and spotted the pistol. "Are you expecting trouble, or are you going to just shoot us when we find the money so you can keep it all to yourself?"

Skeet's mood did a one-eighty shift. He turned to Roy, his face light and smiling. "She said *when* not *if*. You hear that, Roy? She's got the right attitude. We're off to a good start." He looked at Betsy. "And, Ms. Racine, my question to you is, in which cave are we going to begin our search?"

In the backseat, Roy breathed a little easier.

At first, Betsy stared straight ahead, stone-faced, and didn't answer. Then, "You do know, don't you, that every inch of the whole damn Adirondacks was already searched, right? You weren't here then and Roy got shipped away in the middle of it. And I…" Her voice dropped to a whisper. "For obvious reasons, I never went out there. Teams searched for about ten days. Not for this imaginary money, only for my very real and very dead brother."

Skeet's tone shifted again, softer, almost gentle. "I know, Betsy. And I'm sorry about your brother. I truly am. But we should at least look, give it all we've got one more time."

Roy felt bad for Betsy and wondered whether Skeet's sympathy was for real. Most likely not.

"We should get going," Skeet said.

Betsy held up her hands. "Wait, wait. There's one thing I have to ask you, Skeet. I keep thinking about this. Let's suppose Ethan did run off with Lazrove's money. Yeah, Lazrove is locked up for life, thank God, but what about his buddies. One is dead but there have to be others he borrowed from, or from his family or something. Why haven't they been up here asking me crazy stuff, putting guns to my head, making me take 'em into caves?"

Skeet didn't answer right away. Then he got his big, bright smile back. "See, that's what's so beautiful about this whole thing. All that money belonged to Lazrove, nobody else. Just him. And he doesn't have any family, at least not any family who would ever talk to him."

"Ok," Betsy said. "Sounds good. But how do you know all this?"

"Oh, come on. I'm a CO. I'm in the system. I can find out anything I want."

Betsy stared at him. "Did you hang out with Lazrove when you were working down in Sing Sing?"

At that moment, Roy's opinion of Betsy soared through the roof of the truck. He had already figured out the connection between Skeet and Lazrove. It was obvious. Yet here she was, not only with her own conclusions but unafraid to throw them right in Skeet's face. Of course, she'd never been in a prison where Skeet was a big-time sergeant who walked around with a billy club.

Skeet looked straight ahead and said matter-of-factly, "All the time. We were good buddies." Then he laughed and started the truck.

He put the pickup in reverse and was about to back up but stopped. The trailer door opened and Louise came out and hurried toward them. Betsy lowered her window and said, "Hey Ma, look who's in the back seat."

Roy's opinion of Betsy took a sharp dive, moving her back into the category of angry, nasty, attack dog. He sighed and put his window down. "Morning Louise. It's nice to see you."

She leaned in and gave him a hug. "You must be glad to be back. What are you going to do now?"

"I'm going to try to get my old job back at Trombley Auto and then maybe go to the Community College. I have a good start on that already."

"A regular college con," Skeet said.

"Skeet," Louise said. "What're you doing here?"

"Just going for a ride."

"Well, have a good day."

She turned and ran back into the trailer.

Chapter 10

They started out on the main highway, then switched to a side road with only a scattering of houses. After a few miles, Betsy said, "Just up ahead on your left. Turn there."

Skeet did a hard turn, barely slowing down, and the pickup lurched onto a thin dirt road. It was steep and rough and Skeet carefully swerved in and out of ruts and rocks.

He maintained his speed for a minute, then asked, "How long does this go on?"

"A long time," Betsy said. "Like two or three miles, I think."

Skeet kicked on the four-wheel drive, downshifted, and floored it. The truck almost bounced into a tree but Skeet yanked the steering wheel and kept it on the road. He still didn't slow down.

Puke bubbled up from Roy's gut.

It was now Betsy's turn to do the one-eighty mood flip and she shouted, "Yeah, all right. Do it!"

After a hellish ride, at least for Roy in the back seat, the road ended in a small parking lot. Betsy hopped out first, opened the back door, and said to Roy, "You okay back here?"

Roy shook his head, glared, grabbed the backpack and handed it to Betsy. "Move so I can get out.

Betsy put on the backpack, said, "Follow me," and took off on a small trail into the woods. Roy kept close behind her, watching her skip along the path, happy like he remembered her from before. It was infectious—he could smell the wet forest dirt, feel the gentle breeze, see the scattered sunlight filtering through the mix of trees. For a brief time, the woods did for him what they always did for her, calmed him right down, even from the wild ride they'd just been on. He wondered if it was having the same effect on Skeet. He hoped so.

Ten minutes later, they stopped at a massive rock face and Betsy led them to a small vertical split flanked by two large boulders. She opened the pack and emptied the contents on the ground: three helmets with headlamps, three large flashlights, and a large coil of rope.

"We won't need the rope for today's cave," she said. "Unless we discover some part I never knew about. And Skeet, I hope you brought your pistol in case some psycho tries to jump us in there. But it's okay you didn't bring the shotgun because it would be tough to shoot in such tight quarters."

"You know what, Betsy?" Skeet said. "You're a real comedian. Maybe when this is all done, you and I can do a comedy act and get famous." He looked inside the black cave opening. "How many times have you been in there?"

"A lot," Roy answered for her. "It was Ethan's favorite. I know it was already searched but it's the best place to start."

Betsy put on one of the helmets and clipped a flashlight to her belt. She also took a much smaller bag out of her backpack and strapped it to her back.

"What's in the small pack?" Skeet asked her.

"A first aid kit, compass, a few knives, lots of spare batteries."

"Impressive."

She switched on her headlamp and flashlight and climbed through the cave opening. The other two did the same.

"Stay close to me if you want. It's a little sketchy at first."

They carefully descended a steep and narrow passageway, barely high enough to stand up in, and clutched at the rough damp walls to keep from slipping. For the last twenty feet, Betsy crouched down and alternately slid on her rear or duck walked. Skeet and Roy mimicked her method. The passage spit them out into a much larger cavern about the size of a two-story house. Betsy shone her flashlight at a wall, moving it slowly along the chiseled broken rock, and upward in various directions, toward a ragged dome-like ceiling. The light illuminated a mess of graffiti and mostly crude attempts at murals that covered nearly every reachable piece of wall space. One mural, better executed than the others, depicted a passageway with struggling kids fighting to get out, and large monstrous hands pulling them back in.

Skeet pointed to it and said, "I like that one."

A fire pit filled with grayed ash and half-burned pieces of wood sat in the center of the room, surrounded by two wet and torn mattresses, empty beer cans, and liquor bottles. The smell of the char from the wood nearly overpowered that of the natural underground dampness.

"Somebody was here not that long ago," Betsy said. "The fire's not that old. Now, turn your lights off a second," When their eyes adjusted, they could see a sliver of light through the roof. "That's why you can have fires in here. It's a good chimney."

"Did you kids party down here?" Skeet asked, sounding parental for a change.

"Never. Ethan hated this part of the cave," Betsy said. "He would come through here and get all pissed off about the mess."

She pointed to another opening and said, "We go this way. Lights on because it's dark the whole way. It curves back around and ends behind us." She pointed again, across the room. "Way over there."

Betsy plunged into the next tunnel and Roy followed close behind. The passage was not as difficult to navigate as the first one, still short, narrow, and rough, but not as steep. About fifty feet in, that changed. Roy had forgotten about this next part and how much he hated it. The tunnel quickly steepened and damp algae clung to the walls, making them harder to use for support. They had to get on their hands and knees and inch down backward and a tiny rivulet of icy water seeped out of the wall and instantly froze their skin and soaked their clothes.

As always, Roy didn't like anything about being in the tunnel, but at least it was mostly dark. As long as nobody shone a light directly in his face, his expressions were not apparent, and he didn't have to put effort into faking that he was enjoying being deep inside the dark wet claustrophobic earth.

The passage flattened again and they came to a small opening off to the side. Betsy zipped through it and Roy followed, into a room much smaller than the last one. She scanned the room's walls with her flashlight, stopping at each crack, probing it with her hand, sticking her arm into it as far as it would go. The room appeared to be empty of any remains left by humans.

Where's Skeet?" Roy asked.

"Right here," Skeet said from the tunnel. "I found a quarter out here but that's it."

Roy flashed his light into a far corner that was mostly hidden by a piece of rock sticking out. "Hey, what's that up there? Is that an opening?"

"Yeah. It's another small space," Betsy said. "You almost can't see it from the ground." A large boulder protruded from the corner like a giant table. She found a slight indent and put her foot in it to help her climb on top of the boulder. She hesitated, stepped back and looked up, then pulled herself onto the boulder and shone her light at an angle, revealing a circular opening just above her head, about two feet in diameter. She set her flashlight on the boulder, stuck her hands inside the opening, and pulled herself up so that her upper body was balanced inside the hole.

Roy angled himself to try to illuminate the hole with his flashlight. "Betsy, what are you doing? Are you going in there?"

She reached her hand in, screamed, and dropped backward. She landed on her feet on the boulder, couldn't keep her balance, and fell onto the ground.

"You okay?" Skeet and Roy knelt next to her.

She stood, shook some dirt off of her jeans, and said, panicky, "There's something in there."

Skeet hooked his flashlight to his side, scrambled onto the boulder, and hoisted himself up, mimicking how Betsy had done it. The awkward position made it difficult to unhook the light again, but after nearly falling backward, he managed and flashed it around the inside of the space. He reached far inside, pulled something out, and flung it onto the ground. It was a damp sleeping bag.

"Was that Ethan's?" Skeet asked.

At first, Betsy wouldn't go near it. "I don't know. Maybe." She squatted down and lightly ran her fingers over the fabric. "Yeah, I think so." Her voice brightened. "It's from a long time ago."

Skeet pulled his large body all the way into the hole. A minute later, he tossed a book down, then scrambled back to the ground. "Is that Ethan's book?"

Roy picked it up and looked it over. The title read, *Into Thin Air*, about a climbing disaster on Mt. Everest. "This was probably his. It was one of his favorites."

"So, he was here, then," Skeet said.

Betsy pointed to the sleeping bag and book. "No, those things were from over two years ago. Somebody dared him to sleep in there and he did. But everything got wet and heavy and he left it there in the morning."

Skeet shook his head. "You know what, you kids are just plain weird. Who would ever choose to sleep in a place like this?"

"I never would," Roy said.

"Yeah," Skeet said. "But you did sleep in a jail cell for a year and a half."

Betsy couldn't resist. "So, Roy, if you had a choice, a week sleeping up in that hole or another week in a jail cell, what would you pick?"

"Go to hell, both of you," he said and hurried back into the passage.

Betsy caught up with him and took his arm. "I'm sorry. Really. That was mean. Skeet just gets me going. His assholishness rubs off, you know?"

"Oh yes, I most certainly know." He kept walking, and after a few moments, he said, "Don't worry about it. It's okay."

They crept along for another ten minutes, crouching much of the time, and came to another small room. They waited at the entrance for Skeet.

"Where is he?" Betsy asked. "I thought he was behind me."

"Maybe he went back to the big room with the fire pit. Isn't it just another minute if we keep going? Should I try to find him?"

"Sure, but let's just check this one out first."

The new offshoot was about the size of a small bedroom. Betsy flashed her light around and said, "Not much here."

A bright light blasted their faces. A scream followed. Roy dropped his flashlight and yelled back, "Dammit, Skeet."

Betsy laughed. "Good one, Skeet."

"I didn't find anything in here," Skeet said.

Roy turned to Betsy and said, "He found the money and stashed it already."

"Yeah, I did. I've got millions stuffed in my pockets."

They walked back to the main cavern and entered the tunnel that led out. Skeet turned and fired his pistol three times back into the cavern, creating a deafening blast. "I just had to hear that echo," he said.

55

Chapter 11

After Skeet dropped Betsy off and then Roy, he didn't go straight home. It was still early, only late afternoon, and he needed to figure out his next move. He wanted to believe Walter Lazrove wouldn't be stupid enough to rush right up there and want to meet with him. But he knew that was most likely exactly what was going to happen. Should he have told Roy and Betsy? Warned them? He'd kind of enjoyed himself today. They weren't bad kids if they could just find some direction in life. Hell, he wished his own daughter was more like them.

He pulled onto a little traveled back road and stopped next to a stand of trees. He reminded himself that it wasn't going to do him any good to go all soft on those two. He needed the money, and if he did meet with Lazrove, he was going to set everything up for his own benefit, even if it meant that bad things might happen to a few people.

He saw a slight motion in the trees and a flash of a white tail. Hunting season was still a few days away and he only had a shotgun, not the best for deer, but it didn't matter. He picked up the shotgun, hopped out of the truck, stilled himself to be calm, focused, and blew off a shot. The underbrush rustled and the white tail flashed a few times as the deer ran away, unharmed. Skeet didn't care. He knew he wasn't going to make a kill right then. But he loved to pull the trigger.

Chapter 12

When Betsy walked into the trailer, Louise surprised her with a cheery hello, a hug, and an invitation to eat a potato chowder soup she'd just made.

"Ma, what's the occasion?"

"Just sit. I'll serve you."

Betsy collapsed onto the couch and let out a sigh. "Thanks, Ma. This is a real treat. I didn't realize how tired I was."

Louise set up a small TV tray and brought Betsy her soup. She gave her a big soft smile and said, "Tell me about your adventures today."

"Roy wanted me to take him to that river Ethan and I used to go to. See the fall colors."

"But why with Skeet Burke?"

"I guess they got to be friends in the prison. Skeet's not such a bad guy."

The roles had reversed. Now Betsy was the one telling the lies, and she knew it. She looked at Pepe, at the pained look on his face, the slow shake of his head, but she was too tired to care. When Louise said she was going into town with a friend, Martha—whoever that was—to see a movie, and that she didn't need to worry, Betsy said, "Sure, Ma. Have a good time."

An hour later, Betsy got her energy back. She washed and dried the dishes, put the leftover food away, and walked down the hall to the bathroom. She glanced through the doorway to Louise's room as she walked by. The table next to the bed, covered with magazines and newspapers, caught her attention. A small drawer under the table was open a crack and she went in and pulled it all the way out. Inside were a few papers related to car insurance and a pile of about ten plain envelopes. She absently leafed through them, finding nothing of interest as they were all unused. Until she got to the bottom. One more envelope underneath the rest had something in it. It wasn't sealed but the flap was tucked in, and she opened it and pulled out the contents. She looked at what was in her hand, amazed, confused. A stack of money. She counted thirty twenty-dollar bills. Six hundred dollars.

She stormed out of the room, the wad of cash squeezed in her fist. Pepe had drifted to sleep and she woke him, furiously waving the bill ends in front of him.

"How did she get all this, Pepe? And why is she hiding it? I don't understand." She stood still, bent down, stared at him. "Please, Pepe. You'd tell me, wouldn't you? Are you sure you don't know anything about this?" Pepe shook his head.

She paced around the room. "There's only one way she could be getting this. I don't even want to think about it. It's got to be...Oh no, Pepe. My mom is turning tricks. She has to be. Your daughter's... Oh no."

Pepe continued to slowly shake his head. Betsy plopped down on the couch and spread the money out. She stared at it, then scooped it up into a pile.

"You know what Pepe? To hell with her. We need this money real bad, and I don't care how she earned it, I'm gonna go spend some of it. I'm going to the grocery store to buy some food. And chocolate. And expensive ice cream. And maybe even some beer. For myself. You want some?

Pepe groaned.

"They won't card me. You'll see. I can get it."

Chapter 13

Shortly after Roy arrived home, he got a text from his mother saying she wouldn't be back for a few hours and he should heat up a frozen pizza. He prepared the pizza, opened a can of beer, and went into the living room to watch TV. He surfed through a few channels, couldn't find anything to catch his attention, and turned it off. Too much activity raced through his head and he needed to sit quietly and sort it out. It was one of the few benefits he'd gotten from his prison time—learning to sit still for long periods of time to let his thoughts settle down. In prison, the practice was a method of survival, a way to stay calm, not freak out, not let inmates or guards notice him and hassle him. Now it was more of a tool to figure things out.

He reflected on the day and what it was like to hang out with Skeet for so long. The experience was pretty awful. Skeet was way too intense, and even when he tried to be funny, he was always one step away from scaring the crap out of Roy. But Betsy acted like she wasn't afraid of him at all. In fact, other than possibly finding a dead body belonging to her brother, she acted like she wasn't afraid of much of anything. Roy had figured out that Skeet must have gotten info from Lazrove about the money, how much Ethan had run off with, and who else cared about getting it back, but Roy never would have dared to shove that knowledge in Skeet's face.

Those thoughts inevitably led to the night the whole thing started. Nearly every day since that night, Roy relived parts of it. Sometimes it played back like a horror movie, with the giant haunts of René Dupuis's body and even the body of the other killer in the black coat, digging especially deep. Other times he tried to un-puzzle facets that still didn't make sense. One thing he was sure of was that he had escaped a whole lot of complications when he had first told the police he was still unconscious when Lazrove took off after Ethan. And Lazrove pretty much said the same thing—it was so dark in the warehouse, he didn't see Roy, didn't even know he was there.

Along with the first part of the story were all the bits and pieces that happened later on. The cash-filled duffle bag Lazrove had thrown in the snowbank had Roy's fingerprints all over it, and it was obvious to everyone involved in the case what Roy and Ethan had planned to buy with the six thousand dollars. But the legal folks had no direct evidence because nothing was purchased, and no drugs were found on him when Deputy Reynolds made him take off his coat and then searched the pockets. Still, the legal folks had wanted to pin something on Roy—just like they were using sketchy fire-tainted evidence to determine that the bullets that killed René Dupuis had come from Walter Lazrove's gun—and stealing a car and leaving the scene of the crime was what they used.

At first, Roy's assigned lawyer had advised him to fight the charges, had said he could plead not guilty and get off. And then, abruptly, the lawyer had encouraged—demanded—Roy to plead guilty and do the time. Roy was only an eighteen-year-old kid and didn't know what to do. What happened next convinced him to do what the lawyer wanted.

A day before he was scheduled to appear in court to make his plea, he had left his house in his mother's car, turned a few times at corners, and thought he was being followed. He had driven into a gas station mini mart, gone inside, and, when he came back out, a man was standing by his car. At first, Roy didn't recognize him because the day was frigid and the man was wearing a long coat, a scarf, and a knit hat pulled down to his eyebrows. When Roy got closer, he knew, even though it was somebody he had only met once before, exactly who it was. It was Norm LaMarche, René Dupuis's cousin.

"Hey Roy," Norm said.

Roy stopped and kept his distance. "Hi, Norm. What's up?"

"I want to talk to you for a minute but I didn't want it to be too public."

"This already is public. There are surveillance cameras everywhere."

"That doesn't matter. I just wanted to tell you a few things and ask you a few questions."

Roy moved closer. Norm looked seriously upset. That would make sense. His cousin had just died in a shootout.

"How about we sit in my car," Norm said. "It's still running and the heat's on so we won't freeze."

Roy climbed in on the passenger side and felt the jolt of the blasting heat. Norm took off his hat, roughed up his curly blond hair, and stared at Roy, his watery blue eyes slightly closed, his wide face in a frown. He said, "First off, I want to tell you how sorry I am that Ethan's gone. A while back, my wife, ex-wife now, and I used to hang out with his parents sometimes."

"Yeah, Ethan told me that. And I'm sorry about René. Man, that whole thing. It was bad."

"It sure was. Look, I know you told the police you didn't see Ethan or Walter Lazrove leave, but maybe you saw something else."

"No," Roy said, "I was knocked right out." He turned his head and pulled his hair away from his skull. "The stitches are still in there."

Norm stayed silent for a moment, then, "I should have been there. It wouldn't have happened if I'd been there. But the snow was so bad. And you didn't see anything else?"

It was getting annoying. Norm wasn't a cop and had no business bugging him like this. It reminded him of being around Skeet, except he was no longer in prison and didn't have to put up with it. "The only thing I saw was when I came in. A pile of something white on the table. I didn't know you were into the hard stuff."

Norm caught Roy's arm in a powerful grip. "What the hell are you talking about? You did not see what you think you saw. That was a pot deal, just like yours. A big one, but still the same thing."

"Let go of me," Roy whispered.

"Yeah, yeah, sure." Norm let go and lowered his voice. "And I suppose you told the investigators about what you think you saw?"

"No, I didn't. You happy now? I have to go." He opened the door, then stopped. "Maybe I should tell them what I think I saw, make a deal so I don't go to jail for stealing a car." He mumbled, "The dumbest thing ever."

Norm grabbed his arm again and pulled him close, tight, threatening. "No, Roy, the dumbest thing ever is for you to do anything that changes the story as it now stands. You have no idea who you're dealing with here. Understand?"

Norm let go, calmed down, and let out a sigh. Roy opened the car door and Norm said, "Wait a moment, Roy, please. Just hear me out for another minute."

Roy closed the door. Norm continued, "I'm obviously upset about this whole thing. It's made me crazy. So, yes, okay, René had gotten into a lot of bad stuff, doing things I didn't even know about. And those guys, Lazrove and that other one that died, they showed up unannounced, at least to me. And those two are just the front men. There's a whole lot of really bad dudes out there that, if you start saying shit they don't like, would not hesitate to take you and anybody else around you right off the planet. Seriously. So, what I'm going to do is what I believe you should be doing. Keep your mouth shut, your head down, and do whatever you have to do to not get any bad attention."

Roy put his hand back on the door handle. "Are we done now?"

"There's one more thing. I heard about your duffle bag sitting outside the warehouse in the snow. It had a lot of fingerprints on it. Ethan's, yours, and possibly Lazrove's. Why would anybody throw away a duffle bag with six-thousand dollars in it?"

"No idea," Roy said and hopped out of the car.

As Roy drove away, he'd thought how glad he was that he hadn't mentioned the mysterious car imprint in the snow next to René's car that night, and the rapidly disappearing tire tracks that led away. And he'd played dumb about the duffle bag. He'd considered his options. He could just go for it. Tell all. But white powder meant heroin, coke, meth. It could be almost anything. It definitely was not nearly legal weed that the authorities cared less and less about. The more he had thought about it, Norm was right, he'd be an idiot to say anything to try to get a deal, to get his charges dropped. And he'd have to plead not guilty, probably stand trial, and then what?

Two days later, he pled guilty to the charges against him, and two weeks after that, he entered the prison where he stayed for the next sixteen months.

63

Chapter 14

Betsy drove all the way into town so she could shop at the big Stop and Shop grocery store. She had two hundred dollars in cash in her pocket, figuring she wouldn't spend it all. Or maybe she would. She didn't care either way. The only thing she was certain of was she was not going to use her EBT card, and she was not going to buy on-sale generic mac-and-cheese for eighty-nine cents a box. Or pass by the good bread, and instead, pay a dollar-fifty for a gooey bright white loaf that tasted like paper. Or carefully add up every item to make sure she hadn't run over her budget.

Check-out was fun for a change. She appreciated each item she took out of the cart and put on the conveyor and didn't flinch with unease as the register number grew larger. And she didn't suffer the embarrassment of being a young, seemingly fit and capable buyer who was using an EBT debit card. Buying food that way wasn't supposed to be obvious, but the cashiers always knew. She passed on the beer, knowing she'd never be able to pull that off in a Stop and Shop, and she didn't want it anyway.

She drove home with four full bags of groceries in the back seat, blasting the radio and thumping her fingers on the steering wheel in time with the music. She laughed, sang along, and even let out a whoop. When she arrived home, she took a few of the bags out of the car and sauntered toward the trailer. She could see the blue flicker of the TV through the windows and caught a glimpse of the back of Pepe's head and shoulders. She stopped for a moment, took a few contented breaths of the clean night air, and looked up at the dazzling starlit sky. Feeling charged, she walked up the steps and opened the door.

A strong hand grabbed her arm, dragged her through the doorway, and threw her on the floor. The two bags of groceries broke apart and cans and boxes flew everywhere. She lay on her back, stunned, her glasses half off her face. She straightened them and looked up. A man in a long black coat stood over her and pointed a gun in her face. He had jet black, slightly greasy hair and a thin black mustache that matched his thin-lipped frown.

"What…"

"Shut up. Don't talk. Stand up very slowly."

She twisted around. Pepe was slouched in his chair, his eyes closed and his head back. She scrambled to him. "Pepe!"

The man caught her arm again and flung her on her back. "Do exactly what I say, Missy, or you and the old man will die. The old man is okay for now. See?"

Pepe groaned, his eyes opened, and he managed a weak smile.

The man continued, "Now, get up very slowly and sit on the couch with your hands in your lap. We're going to have a nice little chat." He waved his gun toward the couch.

She crawled to the couch and pulled herself onto it. She looked at the gun, at the man, and said, "You're Lazrove."

"No shit."

"I thought you were in for life. You break out or something?"

His frown shifted to a grin. "My lawyer broke me out. God bless him. I'm a free man."

"With a gun in my face." Betsy jumped up and yelled, "Get out of my house."

Lazrove swung the gun away from her and pushed it against Pepe's head. "Uh, uh, uh. Sit back down, Missy."

She sat and he backed away. He stood in front of her and said without emotion, "You obviously think you're fearless, not afraid of anything, but you're not, really. Now listen carefully to what I'm about to tell you. This is what will happen if you don't cooperate. I will first shoot you in the stomach and you will not die right away, just hurt in ways you can't begin to imagine. Then I will disconnect the old man's oxygen and let you watch him slowly die. And then I will shoot you in the head. Sounds like a party, doesn't it?"

Betsy slumped down, dropped her gaze. "I'll do whatever," she whispered.

"Okay then. I have only one question you need to answer. Where is my money?"

"I, I don't know."

"You don't know? Where's your idiot brother?"

She raised her voice. "Please. He's dead. Why are you doing this?"

Lazrove calmly sat down next to her. Betsy backed away, scrunched against the arm of the couch, as far away from him as she could get.

"Why am I doing this?" he said. "I'll tell you why I'm doing this. There are two things your brother did to me, both of which screwed my life up good. First of all, he ran off with every cent I had, wiped me right out. I had to borrow a whole lot of money just to pay my goddamn lawyers. And borrowed money needs to be paid back, especially because the person I borrowed it from is even nastier than I am. The other thing that little shit brother of yours did is put a bullet in my leg. So now I'm a damn broken cripple."

"What? My brother shot you?"

"Worst shot I ever saw. He shoots like a blind man. I thought you hicks knew all about guns."

Betsy slowly nodded. "He thought he killed you. That's why he took off."

Lazrove snarled, "He took off because he had my money."

He stood, walked over to Pepe, gave him a smack on the back of his head, and turned off the oxygen. Pepe wheezed and groaned. "And you're gonna tell me right now where he is."

Betsy didn't answer. Lazrove gave Pepe another smack and said, "He's not looking too good. You better hurry up and tell me."

Pepe caught Betsy's eye and gave a slight nod toward the table. Betsy returned the nod. "All right, all right. I'll do the best I can. Just get away from him. I'll tell you everything I can think of."

Lazrove looked away from Pepe for a second. Pepe pushed the red button on the box on the table.

Betsy continued, "I found a hat of his in a cave. He must've gone there.

But I swear I haven't seen or talked to him since he left. You've got to believe me."

The phone on the table next to Pepe rang,.

"Answer it," Lazrove commanded. "And don't do anything stupid."

Betsy picked up the phone. "Hello...No...Yes...Yes...Please..."

She hung it up and Lazrove said, "Who was it?"

"Uh, somebody keeps having pizzas sent here. A stupid prank. So, they always call to check."

"Whatever. You're going to take me to the cave."

"Now?"

"Yes, now."

"But it's nighttime. It's dark out."

"What difference does that make? It's a cave."

Betsy glared at him, then stood up and yelled, "My brother's dead. He's not out there."

Lazrove shoved her back on the couch. "Listen to me, Missy. He's not dead. No one dies when they just picked up three-and-a-half million dollars.

Betsy gasped. Lazrove tilted his head, his face tight, curious, then broke into another big grin. "You didn't know it was that much, did you? Your darling brother's been holding out on you. Guess he must be or you wouldn't be living in this trailer-trash dump. C'mon. It's time for you and me to go for a ride."

He caught her arm and led her to the door. Pepe began to choke. He tried to turn his oxygen back on but wasn't strong enough.

Betsy pulled against Lazrove's tight grip. "Just fix his tank," she begged. "I'll do whatever you want."

Lazrove adjusted Pepe's oxygen. "What the hell. I must be getting soft."

"I have to go to the bathroom before we go," Betsy said.

"No way."

"It'll be less trouble later on if I go now. You can wait outside the door."

"Just hurry up." He turned off Pepe's oxygen again.

The sliding doors to all the bedrooms were open, one yanked off its runners, and every room was torn apart, drawers ripped open, clothes everywhere, a bed leaning against a wall. Betsy slammed the bathroom door behind her. A half-minute later she ran back and turned Pepe's oxygen back on. Lazrove allowed her to do that, then took hold of her arm and dragged her out the door. He pressed his gun into her side and forced her across the driveway. A large black SUV hid back in the woods. She hadn't noticed it when she'd first come home.

They reached the woods and Lazrove stopped. "What's that sound?"

She heard it, too. He dragged her into the woods and, a moment later, an ambulance, its lights flashing and siren blaring, turned into the driveway.

Lazrove slammed her into a tree. "I ought to blow you away."

"I didn't do anything."

"You tell them I'm here and you know what will happen." He hobbled off through the trees and underbrush.

Betsy ran to the ambulance, screaming, "Please hurry. He's inside."

Two Emergency Medical Technicians got out of the ambulance. One asked, "Is this the home of Gerald Bennet?"

"Yes. We call him Pepe."

Betsy ran back inside and the two EMTs followed, carrying a stretcher. Pepe was slumped over, barely breathing. "Pepe? Pepe, please be okay." She put her arms around him to hold him up.

The EMTs carefully worked Pepe into the correct position, then laid him on the stretcher and covered him with a blanket. One of the EMTs gently moved Betsy aside and took Pepe's vitals. He groaned and his expression turned to panic.

"It's okay, Mr. Bennet. We just have to check you out."

The EMTs looked at each other, nodded, and one of them said to Betsy, "We need to take him to the ER. He may be having a stroke. Betsy nodded in agreement. They loaded Pepe into the back of the ambulance and Betsy rode with him, holding his hand, telling him he would be okay, moving aside when one of the EMTs continued to check his vital signs. She wasn't sure about the stroke but was relieved to get Pepe out of there to somewhere safe. She'd never been in an ambulance before, and when they arrived at the hospital in Plattsburgh, she realized she'd never been there, either. At least, not that she could remember. The EMTs lifted Pepe out of the ambulance and rushed him into the Emergency room. Betsy had to wait outside.

Chapter 15

An hour later, Betsy sat in a chair in a hospital room, trying to calm herself, trying to sit still, not get up every five minutes and pace around. The hospital thankfully was having a slow night. The medical staff had rushed Pepe through the ER, giving him several tests, and pre-diagnosing him with a possible minor stroke. The ER doctor had advised that he be kept at least overnight for observation and Betsy readily agreed. Pepe was sleeping now, hooked back up to his precious oxygen, and a few machines with wires connected to various parts of his body. The machines made soft beeps that blended with the voices and footsteps of hospital staff in the hallway. She would stay the night there, sit up wide awake in the chair, not leave his side, even though he looked so peaceful now. Even though the hospital seemed like a safe place.

When they'd first arrived, she'd tried to call her mom several times but got no answer. Either her phone was dead, which was not unusual, or she was up to something Betsy couldn't bear to think about. Not now. After her third try, she was glad her mom hadn't picked up because she was sure she would have lost it, she would have yelled and screamed, and that was the last thing Pepe needed to hear right then.

However, she didn't want to be alone. She needed somebody, needed to tell somebody what had happened earlier, what was happening now. She left the room, asked the nurse at the nurse's station where she could find a private place to have a phone conversation and was directed to an alcove down the hall. She called Roy and he didn't answer. She tried again, thinking she'd leave a voicemail, and this time he picked up.

She quickly explained what had happened, leaving out many of the more horrific details, and asked him, begged him to first try to track down her mom, hopefully at Marcotte's, but he should try two other bars she named, and bring her with him.

"Of course, yes," he assured her. "Just hang in there. I'll be there soon."

"Roy, listen. Don't go to my house. It's too dangerous."

"Text me her number," he said.

Betsy couldn't sit still, couldn't stay in the chair. How could anybody do that in a time like this? After an awful wait, Roy walked in with Louise. He'd gotten through to her as Bud was driving her home and he'd turned around and driven her to the hospital. Roy had met her at the entrance, and they came in together. Louise ran over to Pepe, took his hand, and whispered something in his ear. She gave Betsy a long, tight hug. She smelled like an herbal bath wash she sometimes used, no booze stench, and actually looked sober for a change.

"I'm so sorry, Betsy. My phone died, and I was charging it. Roy's call was the first one that came in. God, Betsy, I'm so sorry."

"It's okay, Ma. But I can't stay now so you need to be the one in charge here. They said they'd bring in a cot. As long as no other patient is placed in the room, you can stay here. We'll pick you up tomorrow afternoon or something. Just don't leave."

"I won't. I won't leave."

"You have to promise me."

"I won't leave. Now go on. You can go."

***

They got in Roy's car and sat quietly for a few minutes. The temperature was dropping, the wind was blowing, and a light, nearly freezing rain misted the windshield. Roy turned the car on and the heater up full but kept the shifter in park. He would give her some space. Do whatever Betsy wanted.

Finally, she said, "I don't know what to do. This is such a mess."

"You could call the police." It was a terrible idea but he had to say it.

"I know. I thought about that. But what would happen then? They would come here, question Pepe. Upset him more than he already is. And it's not like he can give a good explanation of what happened. If they caught Lazrove, it would be his word against mine."

Her answer was a relief. "You can't stay out there tonight," he insisted. "You're going to have to stay at my house."

"Will your mom care?"

"Not if I tell her what happened."

"Then she'll call the police," Betsy said.

Oh damn. She's right.

Betsy said, "This is just ridiculous. Drive me home. He won't be there waiting. He would never think I'd dare to come back there. And, if he does come back, I'll be in the camper."

"No, that's a bad idea."

"I have a plan, Roy. Don't worry. I have a plan."

He let out a sigh. Just like her brother. Of course, she had a plan. If he wasn't so scared, he would have thought it was funny.

They left the hospital and headed out of town. Roy drove much slower than usual, because of the potential for black ice, he said, but also because, the closer they got to the trailer, the more his anxiety tried to spiral out of control.

A few hundred yards from her driveway she said, "Slow down a lot and turn your lights out."

"Huh?" He slowed but left his lights on.

"Don't worry. There's a pull-off here. It's wide. You won't hit anything. Now, right now, turn here."

He flipped the lights off and pulled into a pitch-black, muddy, rutted space. The car jerked and bounced violently and she said, "Turn the car off and we're gonna sit here until our eyes adjust to the dark."

They got out and stood next to the car. The rain had stopped and the moist air had dried up, leaving a crisp and clear sky. The moon hadn't yet made an appearance but the stars offered enough light to make out the silhouettes of the trees. They started up a small trail, and in a few minutes, broke into the field where the pond was, where Roy had first seen Betsy a few days earlier. She kept to the edge, shaded by the trees from the minimal starlight, and he stayed close behind her.

When they reached the trail leading to the trailer, Betsy stopped and whispered, "Lazrove is a city guy. He wouldn't go into any woods like this without a big flashlight. So, if you see light, we run into the woods. But, most likely, if Lazrove is waiting here, he'll be sitting in his very obvious vehicle."

When they neared the opening behind the trailer, Betsy gently took Roy's hand and led him off the path, into the thicker woods. They circled far around the trailer, with slow and careful steps to minimize the noise from their feet breaking sticks and scraping rocks. The near-total darkness left only faint outlines of where they could safely walk. They passed Ethan's car and continued through the woods on the other side of the driveway until they could see the small pull-off where Lazrove had parked his SUV earlier. They stood silently behind a thick clump of trees until they were positive the space was empty.

"Listen," Betsy whispered.

"What?" Roy stopped and pulled himself tight against a tree.

"Hear the owl? It's so beautiful. The other night I heard coyotes and an owl at the same time. It was quite a concert."

Roy relaxed and let out a big breath, relieved that the anxiety was draining out of him. "So, what do we do now?"

"I'm going into the camper to get some sleep."

It was not even close to the response he expected. "And what should I do?"

"You can go home if you want. Just walk down the driveway, take a left, and your car is about a three-minute walk."

"Oh, well, okay. I guess goodnight."

She let out a long breath. "Look, Roy. You can stay here if you want but it will be cold and we're gonna be close and I just want to sleep, nothing else."

He stood still for a moment, then said with dripping sarcasm, "Wow. Yeah. No kidding. I mean, we've just been wandering around in the pitch-black woods, trying to avoid some whacko who wants to kill us and all I can think about is sex." He lost the sarcasm and switched to anger. "I'm kind of scared, you know. For both of us. I thought we should stay together. Aren't you scared? Or maybe you're not afraid of anything. Man, Ethan was right when he said you're not like anybody else out there."

"What are you talking about?"

He didn't answer. He grabbed her hand, hurried to the camper, opened the door, and climbed in. She followed, and fumbling in the dark, first spread out a thick opened sleeping bag on the mattress and four large blankets on top of it. Then she crawled in and told him to do the same. He got under the blankets, moved as far away from her as he could, and turned on his side so his back was to her.

After a few minutes of silence, Betsy asked, "What was that about Ethan saying I'm not like anybody else?" He didn't answer so she poked him in the back, trying to lighten the mood.

"All right, okay. I'll tell you." He rolled over, now facing her. "I made some comment about how you were really pretty and he said"—he did his best Ethan imitation— *"you're not her type, man."* So, I called him an asshole and he admitted he was and then he talked about you living in this thing. He said you probably weren't anybody's type because you were kind of weird."

Betsy quietly laughed. "Good Ethan imitation. He sure was a pain in the ass sometimes. And that protective thing. I was so done with it." They were silent again, then, "You really think I'm pretty?"

Roy moved a little closer. "Well let's put it this way. If you weren't so damn strange, you'd probably have crowds banging down your door trying to get you to go out with them."

That got a full laugh from her, but too loud. She put her hand over her mouth, then changed the conversation. "You asked me if I'm afraid of anything and, yeah, of course I am. Everybody's afraid of something. For me, well, I've been so scared of somebody finding Ethan's dead body out there. But now, I'm every bit as afraid, maybe even more, of finding out he's alive with all the money somewhere and it's more important to him than just coming home. That would really hurt."

"I know. I understand," Roy said.

"But I guess we have to keep looking. And I have to confess something. I was going to go somewhere by myself tomorrow but I see now that it would be really selfish and also dangerous."

"Huh? Where?"

"I think you went there once with us," Betsy said. "We went down into a little room and there were those two holes, and one was filled with water."

"Yeah, I remember. That was like four years ago. But we didn't go in anything."

"Ethan and I went back a few times and never told anybody. We found other parts to it. There's another hole way back behind the other ones. You can go down in pretty far and there's one hole way back that stays dry for some reason."

"Why didn't you tell anybody? It coulda been where…"

She cut him off, raised her voice, pushed away. "I didn't want to know, okay? I kept telling myself it was too dangerous to go in. And it is. You have to use ropes. But the thing is, if he's in there, he's definitely dead. So, if you want to go with me, come along. But you better be ready for that."

Roy turned on his back and thought of sleep. Within a minute, the cold seeped through the blankets and he turned on his stomach and huddled his arms under his chest. He wanted to push closer to Betsy's warmth but didn't dare. A few minutes later, he felt her shoulder next to his.

"I can't sleep," she said. "Too much stuff rumbling around in my head."

"Yeah, me too."

"Are you up for a question?" she asked.

"I guess so."

"I've been wondering about this for a long time. I knew you guys were selling weed but I never knew where you got it from. So, how did you ever get connected to René Dupuis?"

"Ethan arranged it. He always did that part. He and Norm LaMarche arranged the whole thing."

She sat up and yelled, "Norm LaMarche? What the hell. You guys were doing drug deals with Norm LaMarche?" She punched her fist into the blankets and grumbled, "I can't believe you were dealing with that shithead."

Roy waited a moment, then said quietly, "I only met him for a minute one other time. Ethan said he was a good guy and you all used to hang out with him.

"Yeah. It was something he and I never agreed on. He didn't see some of the sick crap I saw or refused to see it or something. Maybe he just didn't want to believe it. But, as far as I'm concerned, he's the reason my parents split and my dad took off. He's also the reason my mom became such a fricken drunk."

"Wow. What'd he do?"

"I don't want to talk about it. Hell with him. I'm going to sleep."

Betsy rolled over on her side, her back to Roy, and curled tightly into a fetal position. After a few more minutes, she said, "What if they're all in this together?"

"Who?"

She sat up. "Lazrove, Norm LaMarche, even Skeet."

Roy tried to pull the blankets tighter to him. "You acted like you kind of like Skeet. Thought he was funny."

"Yeah, and there was a time I thought Norm LaMarche was kind of funny, too. Roy, let me tell you, if those guys are all working together, using us, we are so screwed."

She laid back down and didn't move or make a sound for the next few hours. Roy again did his best to contort into a position that would keep the cold from sucking away what little body heat he had left. He also revisited, once again, the disappearing tire tracks leading away from the AmCan warehouse on that awful night. And then, his meeting a few weeks later with Norm LaMarche outside the mini mart. It was all so confusing. And scary, really scary. Even so, he wasn't going to share any of that part with Betsy. At least, not yet.

Chapter 16

The morning rays streamed through the tiny camper window and danced on Betsy's face. She slid from the bed, picked out a few clothing changes, and carefully climbed out without interrupting Roy's quiet snore. As she walked toward the trailer, a few bits of wind-blown garbage blew down the edge of the driveway and she hurried over to pick them up. At the side of the trailer, the garbage can lay on its side and trash was everywhere. Lazrove must have done it. She furiously scooped up non-recyclables and anything related to compost that she didn't want to throw into the woods.

She was religious about the compost. Whatever qualified as actual food for the animals, she always lugged far away from the trailer and into the woods, because over the last few years, the black bears had become a little too friendly for her comfort. She loved them from a distance but wasn't wild about walking in the dark from the trailer to the camper and running into a grumpy protective Mama and her cub picking through the leftovers, looking for a late-night snack.

She picked up a few envelopes her mom must have mistakenly thrown in the wrong bin, carried them into the trailer, and set them on the kitchen table. One of them caught her eye, a small size manila envelope with bubble wrap inside. It had no return address but the postmark said it was mailed from New York City. She didn't give it much thought, thinking it was something from a relative. She knew her mom still had an uncle who lived in New Jersey and who she kept in touch with, and she knew New Jersey bordered the city. But beyond that, it had always seemed like such a foreign place because they never visited and she'd only met him a few times when she was much younger.

The trailer was still a disaster and she wanted to clean it up. But it was already past eight and she needed to get moving, get her day going because, with so little sleep, she'd be dead tired by the afternoon. She hurried down the hall to Ethan's room, still holding the envelope. The room was already a mess before Lazrove had gotten to it, and it looked like the worst thing he'd done was pull more clothes and a pile of papers out of the small closet and throw them on one of the piles that was already there. She dropped the envelope on top of a few of the papers and began to load her backpack with the helmets, lights, and ropes.

The trailer door squeaked open, then lightly closed and a voice said, "You in here?"

"Back here, Roy."

Betsy met him at the hallway entrance, dragging the full backpack behind her. She dug out two water bottles and handed them to him. "Would you fill them with cold water? I'm gonna take a quick shower."

"This is awful in here. Shouldn't we put it back together?"

Betsy shook her head. She kicked a couch cushion back into the living room and went into the bathroom. She took her shower, pulled her clothes on, and went to the kitchen where the smell of hot coffee greeted her. "You're the man, Roy." She poured a cup. "Thanks for this."

"Hey, you know what?" he stumbled.

"What?"

"Well, I could really use a shower, too, but I don't want to go all the way home."

"So, do it. It's no problem."

"Yeah, but clean clothes."

She hesitated, knowing what he meant. She said with a measured tone, "All right. Yes. We're going to just do this. Come with me and I'll pick them out."

They went into the back bedroom and Betsy scavenged through the mess and found all the right clothes, all things Ethan used to wear. One of them was a torn and stained coat he only used for going into caves. She handed it to Roy.

"Are you sure?" His voice had a slight tremor.

"Yes. Really. It's okay."

She hurried out of the room.

***

Roy's phone pinged with a text message. It was Skeet telling him to call.

Roy texted back: Am in Betsy's trailer. She will hear us.

Skeet texted: So what?

Roy: Lazrove came last night. Freaked her out.

Skeet: She okay?

Roy: Pissed off. Wants to kill him.

Skeet: Going to another cave I saw on a forum. Near where we were before. You coming?

Roy: Staying here with her.

Skeet: Do not do anything stupid! Remember?

Roy didn't answer. He climbed into the shower, forced himself under the barely lukewarm water, and started to shake. This was awful, all of it. He wanted to get out of the shower, put on his dirty clothes, and go home to his mother's house, the hell with everybody else. He imagined spending the day sitting in his bedroom, playing with all the strange stuff still laid out on his table. But it wasn't going to happen. He wouldn't leave. He couldn't.

He finished the shower, dried off on a hand towel—the larger towels were in a pile on the floor—and put on his dirty boxers and t-shirt.

He looked in the mirror over the sink and didn't like what he saw. When he was in prison, he had never bothered with the scratchy, stained, metal mirrors in the shower room. He never cared what he looked like then and never wished to linger where somebody else might take an unwanted interest in him. He looked now and this guy staring back at him was a mess—tired, and skinny, way too skinny. He'd lost so much weight—he had always been thin but this was ridiculous. His dark eyes appeared like sunken circles and his nose and cheeks were sharp and angular. He vowed to start eating more and lift weights or something. And cut his hair and trim his beard. Or just shave the damn thing off.

He squirted a line of toothpaste on his finger, brushed his teeth, and hurried into the kitchen. Betsy had made a bowl of oatmeal and raisins for each of them, and also put together a few peanut butter sandwiches to bring along on the adventure. It was a nice gesture and he forced himself to appreciate it, or at least act as if he did.

He offered to drive her car, and surprisingly, she agreed. She looked out the passenger-side window, absorbing the scenery, and he stared straight ahead, silent, focusing solely on the road, trying to block out any negative thoughts. After a while, Betsy said, "You okay over there? Or are you too tired to talk?"

"Yeah, just tired." A moment later he said, "So, not a lot of folks know about this other cave, right? Like it's not on that website with all the New York caves?"

"I don't think so. I haven't looked at that site in, well, since Ethan left. The only ones it used to show around here were the one we were at yesterday and the big one just down the road from here. You know, on Perkins Hill road."

Maybe that was what Skeet was talking about, the Perkins Hill cave. For a few minutes, he felt better but as they got closer to their destination, his brain, once again, raced all over the place. Should he tell Betsy about Skeet or not? If Skeet was up to no good, then they were heading into a nightmare. But, if he told Betsy, then what? She'd go ballistic and something even worse could happen. He slowed down when they approached the parking lot where they had parked the day before. Two pickups that were not Skeet's were already there, and a group of men wearing orange vests and holding rifles stood talking.

"Deer season's not until tomorrow," Betsy grumbled.

"So, tell 'em that."

She pressed the button to lower the window.

Roy yelled, "No. Don't."

"I was just kidding."

Roy drove past the parking lot, and in a few hundred yards, pulled onto a small rough patch of grass and tried to angle the car behind some trees. They hopped out and Betsy took out two plastic orange vests from under the back seat. They put them on and headed into the woods.

A slight wind had blown all night and encouraged enough leaves to fall off the trees, so that, in some parts of the woods they passed through, the vests made them easy to spot. *Simple targets if somebody wants to take us out.* But Betsy charged along noisily. Roy couldn't take it any longer. He was going to insist they both stop and take the vests off. And he would share Skeet's conversation, tell her everything. Before he could speak, they broke into a barely visible overgrown path.

Betsy turned left and Roy followed tight behind. "If we'd gone the other way, we would've ended up in the parking lot," she said.

The path was thick with brush and downed branches that caught their clothes and swiped at their backpacks. A few times, they lost it and had to stop and re-orient themselves. They came to a steeper section, forcing them to scramble up large granite boulders that scratched at their hands. Betsy buzzed right along and Roy struggled to keep up.

She stopped suddenly and turned around. "Wait. Hold on."

"What's wrong?"

"I don't know. Something's not right again. I don't know. This keeps happening."

Roy moved off the trail and crouched behind a rock. She dropped the backpack and huddled next to him. He whispered, "You think somebody's watching us?"

"Maybe that's it. It keeps happening. Like I can sense things out there. Does that ever happen to you?"

"Yeah, I guess so," he said. He remembered the night in the warehouse when Ethan went in first. He'd seen Lazrove's black SUV parked in the lot and knew something bad was about to happen. "Actually yes, I know what you mean."

"We're like animals, you know? We can sense danger."

Roy looked at her, crouched down like a rabbit ready to run, or more accurately, like a wolf ready to catch that rabbit for its next meal. Her animal instincts were on full display. He doubted his own, in comparison, were even close to hers.

She peeked around the boulder. "We're just about at the opening of the cave."

She took off the orange vest and Roy did the same. She crawled on her stomach through the brush and piles of leaves, dragging the backpack alongside her, and he followed close behind. In a minute, she stopped, and still lying on her stomach, began pulling equipment out of the pack.

She turned over, laid on her back, and looked up at the sky. "Let's just rest a second before we go in."

Roy sat up and looked around. "I don't understand. Where's the cave?"

She pointed behind her. "In there." The sunlight caused the peaks and juts of the rocks to glitter and the indents to appear as uniform dark shadows, making the opening look like nothing more than a small crease in the granite. A thick tangle of vines added to the disguise.

Roy yanked back the vines, swept away clumps of wet leaves and dirt, and shone his flashlight through the opening.

"That's like the size of a manhole."

Betsy went into prep mode and handed him a hardhat and put one on herself.

"Flashlights?" Roy asked.

"I'm bringing the backpack down in with me."

"You got extra batteries?"

"I have everything. And it's all coming with us. It's all good. Don't worry."

They crawled through the opening and slid on their stomachs on a slight incline for about twenty feet until they entered a space about ten feet across. Betsy stood, took off her pack, and propped it against the wall. She took out two flashlights, handed one to Roy, and switched hers on. The room smelled of moss and dampness but was free of graffiti or any leftovers from human visitors.

The flashlights revealed two other openings on the back wall. Roy directed his light into one and poked his head in. A nearly vertical chute connected to the opening and dropped about ten feet to a pool of water of unknown depth.

"The other one is the one we want," Betsy said.

"Want for what?" He flashed his light into the other opening and pointed it downward. This one was not as steep and appeared to have a sharp turn about ten feet down. But no water. "We're not going in there, are we?"

She touched his arm. "I was hoping you'd go first because, well, you know."

She tied a rope around a boulder and tossed an end down into the opening. She stood to the side and shone the light inside. He squeezed tight on the rope in case he slipped on the wet rocks, and slowly inched down backward.

He made it halfway down and she said in a shaky voice, "I'm sorry, Roy."

"It's okay."

He reached the bottom, disappeared through the turn, and entered another chamber, this one so small he couldn't stand up. He ran his flashlight along the floor and walls, leaned into the tunnel, and shouted, "There's something down here."

"What? What is it?"

"It's nothing bad."

A minute later, Betsy entered the chamber and Roy showed her some writing scratched into the dirt on the floor. She started laughing.

"It's my name. I did it a few years ago. I can't believe it's still there."

"Not much to see here," Roy said. "Let's get out."

"Wait," she said. "Look what's here."

She crouched down, moved a small rock, and picked up a twenty-dollar bill. "Ethan left this. He figured if somebody else ever came in here, they could never resist taking a twenty and he'd know we weren't the only ones who knew about this place."

Her light caught another rock and another bill under it, this one a five. She scooped it up and stuffed it in her pocket.

"Did Ethan put that one there, too?" Roy asked.

She didn't answer.

***

They climbed out of the cave, using the rope as an assist, and sprawled out on a patch of dry ground with their backs against a boulder. The sun broke through large patches of puffy white clouds and beat down with a comforting warmth. Betsy pulled the water bottles and sandwiches out of the backpack and surprised Roy with candy bars for dessert. He finally relaxed, positive now that Skeet didn't know anything about where they were.

When they finished eating, neither of them made a move to leave. She pushed next to him, and another surprise, leaned her head on his shoulder and breathed a happy sigh. A flock of honking geese on their way to their winter retreat crossed the sky in a V formation. She asked, "Where do you think they're going?"

"I don't know. Maybe it's a sign that we should consider going somewhere, too."

"You mean if we find the money?"

"Yeah, I guess."

"If we do find the money and Ethan is still out there, what would you do with yours?"

He thought a moment and said, "How about this? We would buy Trombley Auto and I would be the head mechanic. Then Ethan could go around and set up shops in other towns, like Saranac Lake, Lake Placid, maybe even in Vermont."

"And what would I do?" Betsy asked.

"You'd be the one to scare the crap out of anyone who didn't pay their bill."

She laughed at that.

Roy's thoughts shifted again slightly. "I was wondering, if hardly anybody knows about this cave, how did you and Ethan find out about it?"

She sat up and shook her head. "Wow, I can't believe I forgot. I think Norm LaMarche told Ethan about it. Ethan might have even come here with him and never told me."

She began stuffing the climbing tools into the backpack. The mood was broken.

Roy caught a small movement back in the trees, probably a deer or a group of deer. He started to get up, then switched directions and leaped on top of Betsy, pulling her flat onto the ground. She yelled, "What the..." but was interrupted by a gunshot and a crack in the stone behind them.

Roy pointed to a string of bushes in the undergrowth about twenty feet away. "We can crawl over there and then run," he whispered.

"Did you see who it was?"

"Only a rifle sticking out behind a tree."

They abandoned the backpack and squirmed across the low dirt, trying to keep out of the shooter's vision. It worked until the last five feet when another shot blasted over their heads and pinged off the rocks again. They entered the thick woods and ran hard in what they hoped was the direction of their car. In a few minutes, they burst onto the trail and nearly slammed into somebody. It was Skeet Burke.

He backed away a few feet. He was decked out in hunter's orange blaze clothing and held a rifle in his hand, a .30-06. Concern clouded his face. "Who was shooting up there?"

Betsy looked from Roy to Skeet, shook her head slowly, then spit out, "Why the hell are you here?"

Roy said as calmly as he could manage, "Somebody shot at us. I couldn't see who. We have to get out of here."

"It's got to be Lazrove," Skeet said. "Right, get out of here. I'll circle around and see if I can catch him."

"What?" Betsy yelled. "What's going on with you two?"

She turned and ran down the trail. Roy hesitated, then took off after her. He frantically tried to catch up but the distance between them grew increasingly wider until she was only an occasional flash of clothing through the trees or a flick in the underbrush. He was about to give up when she stopped abruptly and charged back toward him until her angry face was inches from his.

"He knew we were here," she hissed. "And he knew all about Lazrove,"

Roy faced her and glared back. "We're lucky he did."

"How stupid are you?"

She took off again, and this time, he didn't try to keep up. He still had her car keys in his pocket. He followed the path to where it ended in the parking lot. The same two pickups that were there earlier were still parked, and now, next to them, were Skeet's pickup and a new smaller SUV that looked out of place. Possibly a rental?

He skirted around the edge of the lot and ran down the road and into the woods to where Betsy's car was. She was leaning against the car, and when she saw him, barked, "Gimme the keys."

She unlocked only the driver's side, climbed in, and put the key in the ignition. Would she have the nerve to drive away without him? Probably. She turned the key and the engine tried to start but wouldn't turn over all the way. It sounded like the spark plugs weren't working again. Or somebody pulled the wires off? How would they have opened the hood without unlatching it from the inside? And the car was locked.

Betsy continued to crank the starter motor and Roy yelled to her to stop. He checked the keyhole of the passenger side and saw scratches all around it. Somebody had broken in and the door was still unlocked. Even on an old car, that wasn't an easy trick to pull off unless whoever did it had some real professional, or criminal skills. He opened the door and climbed in.

"Get out of my car," she said.

"Just be quiet and pop the damn hood."

As he suspected, the spark plug wires were pulled from the plugs. He re-connected them and hopped back in. She turned the key again and began to slowly back out. She was almost to the road when Roy told her to stop.

She kept going. "I'm perfectly capable of backing onto the road without getting us killed."

"No, no, it's not that. I want to get out."

Now she did stop. "Why?"

"Something else is going on here. It's not what you think. You should go and I'll get a ride back with Skeet."

"Are you out of your fricken mind?"

He tried to speak with a calm, measured tone. "Before, you said that sometimes you just know things. Well, now it's my turn. I think I know what's happening, who shot at us. Just go home, Betsy. I'll be okay."

He hopped out of the car and ran back into the woods. Skeet was the one who'd shot at them with his rifle, he was almost sure of it. The way those bullets hit, they had to be from a hunting rifle, and Skeet's .30-06 was certainly that. Also, if it was Skeet, and he'd wanted to hit them, he could have done it easily. But he didn't. Why? The only thing Roy could come up with was that Skeet was putting on a show for Lazrove. Lazrove might have also had a rifle, but Roy doubted it. He had to sneak up on Lazrove and get a look to make sure.

As he neared the cave entrance, he left the trail, and in a crouch with slow steps, circled through the woods and around the clearing. He stopped, listened, and heard voices: angry conversation and swearing. He stayed low and found a hidden spot on the edge of the clearing where he could get a closer look.

Chapter 17

Walter Lazrove, yelling, gesturing wildly, stood about six feet from Skeet Burke. Unlike Skeet and the other hunters with their orange vests, Lazrove had dressed in a matching camo hat, coat, and pants. He held a pistol in his hand, waving it around like it was a magic wand and he was trying to cast a spell over Skeet.

"You could have just shot 'em," he yelled, "killed 'em and been done with it."

Skeet said calmly, "I tried but I missed."

"That's just pathetic. I thought you country boys were all hunters. That was as bad as that Ethan kid who shot me in the leg." Skeet shook his head slowly. Lazrove continued, "So now what do you plan to do?"

"How about for starters I ask you a few questions?"

"Huh? Lazrove backed away and brought his gun up."

Skeet managed a smile. "Oh, come on. It's no big deal." He pointed to a boulder. "Sit here with me. I only want you to fill me in on a few things. Like what you did with Louise Racine the other night?"

Skeet sat down and Lazrove stared at him.

Skeet put on his biggest eager grin. "So, tell me already. I want to hear the story."

Lazrove sat next to him. "I went into that bar you told me about, Marcotte's, and I figured out which one was her. It was pretty easy because she was the drunkest one in the whole place. She started to leave so I walked out with her. I tried to get her to talk, you know, converse, but she was too shit-faced. Jesus, she tried to get in my car but started puking. Some of it got on the door. Then some guy pulled in and she got in his car and they took off."

Skeet laughed, then said, "Probably Bud."

"Her boyfriend, I guess."

Skeet lifted his arm in front of Lazrove, pointed, and said, "What's that over there." Lazrove looked away and Skeet yanked the pistol out of his hand, leaped up, and tossed it across the field. He backed away about ten feet and pointed his rifle at Lazrove's face.

"What are you doing?"

Skeet yelled, "Shut up." Then, calmly, "You move and you're dead. You talk before I tell you to and you're dead. So, listen carefully to what I say. Now, first of all, I know you think you're the big city smart guy and I'm just some dumb hick from the sticks. Fine, I don't give a shit. Never did. But I knew right from the start down in Sing Sing that you were playing me. I figured you thought you'd eventually get released, and all the bullshit about me finding the money and splitting it and helping out your family was just that. Bullshit. But you came to me first, because you knew I was from up here. I didn't come to you. And you knew a whole lot about me. Why was that? Tell me who filled you in."

Lazrove slowly reached his hand around behind his back like he was scratching an itch. Skeet rushed forward and pressed the rifle barrel against his forehead.

"Go ahead," he said. "Scratch away."

Lazrove put his hands in his lap and Skeet backed up again. He continued, "And then, you call me this morning, I tell you where to meet, we park our cars, and you head off down the right trail. Now, how did you know where the right trail was? Who told you? I knew because I'd been here before. But you knew because you called somebody else after you called me."

"Hey, hey, c'mon. Calm down. Please."

"And so you tell me to take out those two kids? Why would I do that? Maybe the guy, Roy, is not much help but that girl knows where her brother is. She just hasn't figured it out yet."

Skeet backed further away until he was next to Lazrove's gun on the ground. He picked it up and put it in his vest pocket. "You can go now, Lazrove."

"What, and you're gonna keep my gun?"

"Just stand there and I'll give it to you."

Skeet rested the rifle against his thigh, pulled a handkerchief out of his pocket, carefully wiped the pistol, and wrapped it in the handkerchief. All while keeping an eye on Lazrove.

He shifted his gaze up and said, "Hey, Lazrove. What's that behind you?"

As Lazrove turned, Skeet lobbed the gun over Lazrove's head into the cave opening. The handkerchief fell onto the ground outside the opening and the gun disappeared. Lazrove scurried to the entrance, started to climb in, realized he couldn't, and spun around to run away. Skeet fired one shot and Lazrove slumped halfway in. Skeet ran over and tried to lift his feet, to push him the rest of the way in. The body was stuck on something and Skeet pulled it back out, climbed in himself, and yanked it back over the top of him. It wasn't good enough, long term. But he'd come back when he had the time and would drag the body way down in there, weight it with rocks, and push it into that water hole where it would stay forever. A minute later, he re-emerged, brushed himself off, and took off on the trail, back to his pickup.

***

Roy laid flat on his stomach behind a pile of downed trees, and through a slit between two logs, watched the whole encounter. He could only make out the words when they were loud but he followed the general script. Excitement tore through him because he was right, Skeet was the one who had fired the shots at them. And Skeet had purposely missed. He stood tall and strong, controlling the situation, not backing down from that scumbag, Lazrove. Skeet was rough, moody, weird, and a real asshole. But he was their asshole, on their side. Maybe he would send Lazrove packing, scare him enough that he'd leave them alone.

When Skeet threw Lazrove's gun into the cave, then calmly, methodically fired a bullet into his head, Roy's hopeful fantasies shattered into a thousand pieces. He watched in horror as Skeet wrestled with Lazrove's body. When he briefly disappeared into the cave, Roy ran down the trail faster than he'd ever moved in his life. He tripped on roots and rocks, slammed into trees, lost the trail, and still kept going. He unexpectedly burst into the parking lot and ran into Skeet's pickup.

Betsy had left. No surprise there. He needed to find somewhere to hide until Skeet came back for his pickup and left. Then what? He would have to walk back to where he'd left his car the night before near Betsy's trailer, and even if he didn't get lost, which he probably would, it was fifteen or twenty miles away.

He made up his mind and started back into the woods when he heard a voice, Skeet's voice—funny, happy—say, "Hey Roy? What are you still doing here?"

Roy collected himself, calmed down as much as he could. He had to be convincing. "Betsy was all pissed off so I told her to leave without me. Can I grab a ride with you? My car's at her place."

Skeet stopped and looked Roy up and down with the prison stare the COs gave to the inmates. Roy stood up straight and forced a smile. "Did you find Lazrove?"

"I did not. I'm betting city-boy is going to spend his first night in the woods tonight. It ought to be fun, right?"

Chapter 18

By the time Betsy arrived back at the trailer, the daylight had already begun to fade. She stormed inside, rushed up and down the hallway, and checked all the bedrooms.

"Anybody in here?" she screamed. "Cause if you are, I'm gonna rip your heart out."

It felt good to yell, to threaten. She found a bag of pretzels, sat on a kitchen chair, and munched down a few handfuls. For a few minutes, the food took the edge off her anger—until it hit her that Pepe was still in the hospital, and her mom might still be there with him. She called her mom's phone a few times, got no answer, and tried to psych herself up to go into town and make sure everything was okay. She decided she'd wait a little longer, and instead, she put all her attention into cleaning up the results of Lazrove's visit.

She re-attached the sliding door, straightened up the living room, and moved on to her mom's room, picking up clothes that were thrown all over the bed, the floor, and into the hallway. She started by folding anything that was going in the dresser drawers and then worked on what needed to be hung in the closet. A cardboard box filled with photo albums had been pulled off a wooden shelf at the top of the closet and sat at an angle on the closet floor. Fortunately, the box had survived the fall and was still in good enough shape to be put back. She hoisted the box above her head and onto the shelf but couldn't push it back far enough to slide the closet door shut. Something was in the way and she wasn't tall enough to see what it was.

She got a chair from the living room, hopped up on it, and reached her arm to the back of the shelf. A piece of the paneling stuck out about three inches. She felt something behind it and pulled it out—another manila envelope. This one had no writing, canceled stamp, or postmark, and bulged out with something inside it. She jumped off the chair, opened the envelope, and shook its contents onto the bed. A mix of crisp unused hundred-dollar bills and used twenties dropped out in a large loose pile, a whole lot more than what she'd found the day before.

She furiously counted it, first the hundreds—sixty—then the twenties—fifty. A total of seven thousand dollars.

"Oh my God."

The trailer door opened and she heard her mom's voice. "Betsy? Betsy? Are you here?"

She stuffed the money back in the envelope and kicked it under the bed. "I'm in here, Ma."

Footsteps thumped into the kitchen, then through the living room and down the hall. "Betsy, what happened here? Who did this?"

Betsy moved close to Louise, smelled her, examined her face. Drunk again. "Walter Lazrove paid us a visit, Ma. I guess Pepe didn't tell you."

"What?" Louise crumbled onto the bed and started crying. "Oh no. Oh no."

"Did you know he was going to get out? Is that why you're always reading those damn newspapers and all that stuff online from around New York City?" She put her hands on Louise's shoulders, shook her, and made her sit up and look at her. She pulled the envelope from under the bed and dumped the money in another pile next to her.

"Where did you get all that?" Louise slurred.

"No, Ma. The question is, where did *you* get all that?"

Louise's slurring got worse. She could barely speak. "Uncle Frank sent it to me."

"Uncle Frank didn't send this. Where's the envelope it came in?"

"I don't know. I, I, I, threw it out."

"What was the postmark?"

"I, I..." Louise slid back down on the bed, rolled on her side, and closed her eyes.

Betsy pulled her upright again. "Goddamn it, Ma! Do you have any idea how insane this all is? There's like seven-thousand dollars there and... Don't you understand? Ethan sent it to you." Betsy's voice dropped to a whisper. "It's just crazy."

Louise forced herself off the bed, stepped to the door, and pushed it shut. She stood over Betsy and carefully took both her hands. The fuzziness, the drunkenness faded back a little. She said gently, "No honey, it's not crazy. It's not crazy at all."

Betsy looked up, wide-eyed, tense. "Ma, what? What's happening to you?"

Louise continued, still slurring, but with a hint of focus, like she was attempting to take control. "Betsy, honey, listen to me carefully. Lazrove was never supposed to get out of jail. And Skeet Burke? And you and Roy? All of you looking for Ethan and this money? That's got to stop. It's way out of control."

"Ma, are you even drunk? You're acting so different."

"Oh, I'm very drunk, believe me. I'm sorry, Betsy, I'm so sorry." Her face quickly turned wet.

She sat next to Betsy on the bed, put her arm around her, and pulled her close. She tried to talk but choked on her words. She managed to say, "You've got to leave here for a while. It's way too dangerous."

"Where am I supposed to go?"

Louise pulled herself together enough to manage a full string of coherent sentences. "I'm going to give you a lot of money and you're going to go to Uncle Frank's camp down in the Catskills. Remember when we went there? Nobody else ever goes. No one will be there. And you will call me when you get there and then, every two days, you will check in."

Louise found a pencil and a scrap of paper. Her hand shook as she scribbled down the address of the cabin. "Put this in your phone."

"And Ethan? Will he be there?"

"No. No he won't." Her voice sounded firmer than ever, in authority. "And you have to promise me you will stop trying to find him, do you understand? He's hiding and he's safe and this is all going to end. I promise you."

Betsy sat silent, in a daze, while her mom squeezed her close. She thought she would lie on the bed, fall asleep, and wake up many days later. She would get up early and make a big breakfast for her sober mom, her returned brother, and her healthy grandfather. They would laugh and maybe even sing and Betsy would say some kind of prayer of thanks before they all started to eat. And then she would get in her car that always worked, always started, and drive to a job that made enough money for them all to live on.

Louise closed her eyes, began to fade out, and pulled herself back. "What about Roy? Would he go with you?"

"He couldn't because of his parole stuff. And, at this point, I don't trust him at all. Ma, I don't trust anything. I don't understand anything. Are you even an alcoholic?"

"Oh yes, honey. I'm sure I am."

Louise scooped up the cash, and after giving Betsy two thousand dollars, stuffed the rest back in the envelope. She hopped onto the chair and pushed the envelope behind the loose paneling. Betsy watched, amazed. Her mother was still raging drunk. She couldn't walk in a straight line and nearly slipped off the chair. But she functioned. She could actually do things.

She told Betsy that Bud would be by shortly to take her back to the hospital and then to his place where she would stay for a few days. Also, Pepe was going to stay in the hospital for at least a few more days for further tests and observation.

"And it would be better if you pack up and leave tonight. Drive until you can't go any further, maybe just to Glens Falls, and sleep in a motel. And don't use any of the hundreds around here on your way out."

"Ma, this is so weird." Betsy's voice shook. "It's like you're almost sober. Like when I was younger."

"I'm so, so not sober...such a mess." Her voice trailed off into a mumble. Then, much brighter. "But I will be, I promise."

"Does Bud know what's going on?"

"Oh God, no. That's why I hang around with him.

"He won't be drunk now, will he? Like driving?"

"No, no. We always avoid that. Or try to."

"Ma, is Uncle Frank even alive anymore?"

"No dear, he's not."

"So, who owns the cabin I'm supposed to go to?"

"I think we do but I'm not sure."

The moment Louise stepped into the shower, Betsy took the slip of paper and pencil and went searching for numbers. Louise had thrown her purse on the couch and Betsy dug through it, found her phone, opened her contacts, and scrolled down the list. She quickly came to the letter E and found entries for Elwood, Edgar, and Emory, all with no last name. Any or all of them could belong to a cheap burner phone Ethan might have bought at a Walmart somewhere. She wrote down the numbers, figuring she would enter them later in her own phone, and put Louise's phone back in her purse. She'd promised her mom she wouldn't try to find Ethan but she hadn't said she wouldn't try to call him.

After Louise left, Betsy made a pot of strong coffee, poured a cup to drink right then to wake herself up, and the rest into a thermos for later. As she sipped from the cup, careful not to burn her mouth, she reflected on how strange it was that there was no big moment when she learned Ethan was still alive. Finding all the money and her mom's reaction to it was the clincher, yet she had already gradually switched to believing it was true. But where was he and why was he still gone? A wave of rage, directed at her mom, surged through her. She should have forced her, maybe even physically, to tell her everything, especially the why of it all. But the rage faded into a deep well of sadness as the full depth of her mom's own fear and misery encompassed her. Most of it made no sense. Except for the one part that was so upsetting it made her want to throw up. All this time, her incoherent pathetic drunk of a mom, had been desperately trying to protect her kids.

As soon as Betsy finished the coffee, another thought flooded her now caffeine revved brain. What if Louise was only fixated on the money? Just like Skeet or Roy and possibly even Ethan, what if she didn't care about anything else? She quickly let that one go and put it into perspective. Louise would never be that bad. Of course, she wanted the money—for herself and her kids and Pepe. Like everybody else out there, she wanted a better life, and with the awful one she currently had, nobody could blame her for that.

The money. A new connection burrowed into her thoughts. What she had found in her mom's closet wall was in a small manila envelope just like the one that she'd found outside in the trash mess. Except that the one she'd found outside had a stamp and a postmark on it. She ran down the hall and fumbled around until she found the envelope on the top of some papers. She read the postmark—New York City, 10031. It didn't necessarily mean anything because Ethan could be living anywhere down there—New Jersey, Connecticut—and just happened to send the letter from the city. The whole idea of the city was hard for Betsy to grasp because she had never been there, or even near it. The closest she had ever gotten was the few times they all went to the cabin where she was now headed. And she was pretty sure that it was much closer to Albany than New York City. The sad truth was she had never really been anywhere.

She absently leafed through the pile of papers, and when she realized what they were, she zoomed in with full attention. Although Ethan understood how to use phone maps, a compass, or the sophisticated GPS that was still somewhere in the room, he also collected printed maps, and many of the papers in the pile were either originals or ones he'd photocopied out of books and magazines. They included a number of different Adirondack topographics, a general Catskill map, and a few from Vermont. Further down the pile, Betsy found two detailed street maps of New York City, one of the whole city and one of just Manhattan. She also found two articles, copied from magazines and paper-clipped together. One was titled, *The World Below Penn Station*, and the other, *Cave Living Manhattan Style*. In both articles, Ethan had highlighted with magic marker important words and phrases.

Betsy skimmed the articles and recalled memories of Ethan's blossoming fascination with what he had described as *urban exploration*. It was all about the sneaking into, or even living in, old abandoned buildings, underground tunnels, or any other worlds of human neglect and despair. When she'd found the book on the Catacombs of Paris in the used book store, she'd bought it for Ethan because she figured that, if he talked her into one of those types of adventures, she would rather go there than to some horrible empty blackness in a big city like Buffalo or New York. She wondered if that was where he'd gone. New York City? At this point nothing would surprise her.

She pulled out from under the bed another one of Ethan's backpacks, a smaller one, and put the clipped papers in an outside pocket. She brought the pack out to the camper and filled it with clothes, toiletries, and a pair of back-up glasses. She took the photo of her and Ethan out of the picture frame and fit it in with the clipped-together magazine articles.

Her phone rang. It was Roy. She wanted to know what he had to say but she wished he had texted because she didn't want to hear his voice.

She answered it. "Yeah?"

"Are you okay," he asked.

"Who wants to know? You or Skeet?"

"I'm done with this thing. I'm not doing it anymore."

"Yeah," she said. "Me too. I'm leaving for a while."

"I should come with you."

"No, you should not. And you can't leave anyway because you're on parole."

"Where are you going?"

"Roy, no. Just leave me alone. Do whatever you want but leave me out of it. I don't trust you and I really, really don't trust Skeet Burke."

"Betsy. I have to tell you…"

"Goodbye, Roy."

She hung up. She stopped her frantic packing and sat on the bed, confused. And then, guilty. That was kind of mean. But, so what. She had two thousand dollars in her pocket. Things were changing, maybe for the better. And it was true, she couldn't trust Roy. Not now and most likely not ever.

She finished packing, went back to the trailer, cleaned up more of Lazrove's mess, turned off the lights, and locked the front door. She took a deep breath of the chilled air, climbed into her car, and turned the key. The dashboard lit up with three different warning lights. She turned it off and tried again. The same lights came on and the engine chugged like it was going to stall. She sat for a moment, punched the steering wheel, and let out a yell.

She went back to the trailer and scrounged through a few drawers until she found the keys to Ethan's station wagon. She had only driven it a few times when Ethan was still around, and then that one awful time right after he'd disappeared. Her mom had learned from Norm LaMarche where it was and had driven her—this was before she'd lost her license for a DUI—to the farm road where Ethan had ditched it. She'd driven it back to the trailer, and on her mom's insistence, parked it where it still sat, left for the hopeful day when Ethan would return and reclaim it. Every time Betsy saw it, it was a painful reminder that he was gone, and when she'd asked her mom if they could sell it, she had said absolutely not. Not ever. Her mom had even renewed the registration and insurance, *keeping it ready for Ethan when he returns*, she'd said.

And there it sat, ready to go, ready for her to take it. Betsy unlocked the door, first checked the oil, then started the car, and got back out to check the tires. She would stop by a gas station on the way out of town, gas up, and give the tires a little more air. She got back in the car, drove through some tall grass and weeds, down the rutted driveway, and onto the road.

Not long after, she passed a green metal sign with white letters reading, Plattsburgh 5 miles, and a minute later a red warning light on the car dashboard blinked on and the car's engine shut off. Betsy coasted off the road onto a wide shoulder. She tried restarting the car a few times, gave up, popped the hood and made sure all the wires were attached, and turned the key again. Like before, it didn't start.

When she got out of the car, put on her backpack, and began walking down the road toward Plattsburgh, the alternate plan that had swirled around her for the last few hours, creating conflict with the promise she'd made to her mom, happily resolved itself. Now she no longer had a choice of what to do next. She had to leave but had no car, so she would walk the rest of the way to the bus station on the edge of the city and catch the next bus out of there. And she doubted there would be a bus that would go to a tiny town in the northern Catskills where an old, funky cabin sat deserted. But there would most certainly be many buses to where she really wanted to go.

She would get a night bus to New York City, sleep the whole way there, and be rested for whatever happened next. And she would call Roy first thing in the morning, not tell him where she was, and ask him to get Ethan's car towed. She left the door unlocked and the key on the front seat. She didn't care if somebody tried to steal the car. Good luck with that.

An hour later, she entered the bus station through a large glass door, dropped her backpack on a chair, and shuffled, exhausted, up to a ticket counter. Nobody was behind the counter, and looking around, the station was empty. She rang the bell, waited, and still, nobody came. Eventually, a sleepy man stumbled out of a back room.

"Can I help you?"

"When's the next bus to New York?"

"Not until eight-fifteen in the morning."

"Can I buy a ticket now?"

"Sure, if you want. One way or round trip?"

Betsy pulled a hundred-dollar bill from her pocket and laid it on the counter. "One way."

He processed her ticket and handed it to her with her change. She went over to where her backpack was and sat in a chair next to it. "Uh, Miss," the man said. "It's almost one in the morning. Your bus doesn't leave for, uh, more than seven hours from now."

"That's okay. I can wait."

"Not in here. I'm about to close up."

"Oh, all right," she said. "I'll come back."

The man disappeared again into the back room. Betsy picked up her backpack, opened the glass door, and instead of leaving, hustled over to the door to the women's restroom, gently opened it, and closed it behind her. She went into a stall, hung her backpack on a hook on the stall door, and hopped onto the toilet seat. She stayed that way for the next ten minutes until the restroom light shut off. A few seconds later she heard the front glass door open and close and the deadbolt slide shut.

A single overhead light in the main station room created enough visibility for her to be seen through the front glass door. Another choice was made for her—to spend the night sitting on the restroom floor with her back propped against the tile wall. She examined the floor, determined that it had recently been cleaned, and tried to position herself so that she could find even the slightest bit of comfort. She resigned herself to a rough night, and for the next six hours, drifted in and out of a miserable sleep.

Chapter 19

Skeet ambled out of the woods, happy, laughing, doing his usual goofy antics, and for a moment, Roy wondered if he'd only imagined what had just happened. It was as weird and unsettling as the night in the warehouse, in some ways even more so. On the ride back to Roy's car, Skeet rattled away, telling stories, making jokes, and Roy stayed mostly silent. Skeet had just killed somebody, killed Walter Lazrove, and was acting like it was no big deal.

Skeet slowed down in front of Betsy's driveway. "Where's your car?"

"Keep going just a little more."

The car was still tucked away in the small space. Skeet didn't ask Roy why he had parked there, mostly likely because he already knew the answer.

Roy raced home, pulled in the driveway, and ran into his house. His mother was still out somewhere—it seemed like she was always out somewhere. He went into the kitchen and found on the counter his old iPhone and a sweet note his mother had left saying she had put him on her account again. She'd also left a bowl of rice, beans, and veggies in the refrigerator for him to heat up. The events of the day had killed off any desire for food, but he forced himself to eat half the bowl, and he dumped the rest into the garbage disposal so his mother wouldn't worry or feel bad.

He went up to his room with his iPhone and fussed with it until he had its settings and functions set up. He looked at the old clock on his wall, and even though it said only eight o'clock, he sighed as a wave of exhaustion crept over him. It felt paralytic, yet he knew what would happen if he tried to sleep. His body might lie there without movement but his brain would be on fire.

He lay on the bed and stared at the ceiling. Around ten, he sat up, wide awake, his body a little unfrozen and his thoughts clear. He ran through every detail of the entire day and tried to objectively draw conclusions from each part of it so that he could come up with a plan for going forward. Skeet was obviously unhinged, an absolute psycho. Sure, taking out Walter Lazrove wasn't the worst thing in the world, although, even for him, Roy felt a little bad. But Skeet's jokes and goofiness after killing somebody the way he did? That was way too much to handle. There was no way Roy was going to continue this. He was done, he had to get away.

He felt especially bad about Betsy because he was the one who had gotten her into the whole thing. If he'd really thought about it, he would have known that Ethan was certainly dead and the money would never be found. So, why had he egged her on? She had every right to be furious with him. He decided to call her, explain the whole situation, and ask her to take off with him for a while.

She answered the phone and didn't give him a chance to talk, hanging up before he could tell her anything about Skeet. At first, he didn't know what to do, but then something shifted and the whole situation came into focus. It all made sense. He had a mission now, a clear and overriding responsibility. No matter how any of this played out, he was determined, committed, to protect Betsy from Skeet Burke. His newfound courage and the relief that accompanied it calmed his spirit and quickly put him into a deep sleep.

***

It wasn't until Skeet dropped Roy at his car and drove another five miles—alone, silent— that he grasped what he had done less than an hour earlier. He'd killed somebody. For the first time in his own life, he had ended somebody else's. Even when he was a marine for four years, joining just out of high school, he'd never done it, never had to. He had begun his service a few years after the Gulf War started and ended it before the Afghan conflict, missing out on action that likely would have resulted in him shooting it up in battle, being forced to pull the trigger on somebody. He'd finally done it, and the further he drove, the less it bothered him. If ever somebody deserved to die, it was Walter Lazrove. He was as heartless, cruel, and manipulative as they come, and Skeet, having worked in the prison system for twenty-two years, had seen the worst of the worst.

From his first conversation, Skeet had known Lazrove was playing him. He'd also determined that, no matter what Lazrove said, the game involved more than just him. A much smarter player had always been hovering in the background. At first, he'd mostly watched and listened, trying to separate the facts from the fiction, and didn't care about naming names he wouldn't recognize anyway.

But one morning, he'd walked by Lazrove's cell and Lazrove invited him in, saying he had something he needed to share. Skeet stood close enough so Lazrove could whisper in his ear. He told him there was talk going around of a new drug pipeline from the outside and into the prison. Maybe Skeet wanted to know about it. Skeet turned and walked out without a response, and for the rest of that day, he had become increasingly unsettled by the conversation. He'd heard only a few quick sentences but they were disturbingly familiar, exactly like a proposal he'd received years earlier from somebody else.

When he had left work, he went home and spent an hour researching everything he could find about what had happened at the CanAm warehouse. Although he'd grown up in northern New York State and initially worked in one of the area prisons, he didn't know René Dupuis, the warehouse owner who was shot, and he wanted to find out how Lazrove knew him. Without asking Lazrove. There had to be somebody else from up there, some other connection Skeet possibly did know.

He got nowhere until he googled the name, René Dupuis, and clicked on the images tab. He skimmed through a few rows until a black-and-white photograph from a Quebec newspaper grabbed him. Two men in black suits stood at a pulpit, one speaking and the other standing close by like his turn was next. The bottom of a stained-glass window showing part of a robe and the bare feet of somebody, probably Christ, hovered in the background. Skeet didn't recognize the one speaking but the other man looked vaguely familiar. The caption below identified the speaker as René Dupuis, at his father's funeral, and as Skeet's memory awakened, he'd realized that the other man was Norm LaMarche, somebody with whom he'd had a long and troubled history.

Skeet didn't care much about inmates cooking up moonshine or having access to the occasional upper or downer. But big-time drug movement? No way. It was people like Lazrove and Norm LaMarche who were responsible for the hell-mess his daughter had lived in for so long. She'd had enough trouble as a kid, depressed all the time, not eating, and wasting away to nearly nothing. And then, along came the opioids, and after that, the heroin showed up. Everything about Lazrove's short string of words pissed him off and he had decided right then that he would raise his alert level ten steps higher whenever he had dealings with him in the future.

But Skeet was desperate. He had already raided his pension and other savings, trying to get his daughter into the places she needed to go to get help. She had just gone back to another rehab facility for two to six months, and this time he'd had to re-mortgage his house to cover the bill.

And now his wife—or ex-wife— with cancer? He needed those millions and nothing was going to stop him from getting it. Scumbags like Lazrove were a stain on the earth and Skeet wasn't going to waste time with guilt about killing him. Norm LaMarche was another story. Skeet couldn't stand the guy, but if Norm led him to the money, even if he ended up having to split it, then Skeet would have to keep a lid on his temper and go along with whatever Norm wanted to do.

***

A loud obnoxious ring-tone blasted in Roy's ear, waking him from his escape from the real world. In a daze, he clicked off the ringer, but then had to look because it might be Betsy. It wasn't her, it was Skeet, already calling at six-thirty. Way too early. He rolled out of bed, used the bathroom, and went into the kitchen to eat something. His mom had already left for work and he took his time making coffee, eating cereal, and munching down a granola bar.

Skeet called again and Roy slumped into a chair and answered.

"Meet me at the diner at eight-thirty, I'll buy," Skeet said.

"I already ate."

"So, eat more. Be there." Skeet hung up.

Roy left the house at seven-thirty and drove to Betsy's trailer, hoping if he talked to her in person, he could convince her to take off with him. When he got there, her car was in the driveway but Ethan's car was gone. He knocked on the trailer door and tried to open it, but it was locked. He walked around the trailer, looking for a way to get in. He examined all the windows and they were all locked tight. He pulled a tree stump from the wood pile over to an unused door with no stairs to it that would open into the back bedroom, Ethan's room. He stepped onto the stump and tried the door knob. Also locked.

The camper door had no working lock and he yanked it open and climbed in. The daylight filtering through the one small window revealed a difference from two nights ago. There was less clutter, only a few items still hung on the clothesline, and the picture of Betsy and Ethan was gone, pulled from the frame laying on the bed.

Betsy had already left. She had packed her things and taken off. Roy ran to his car and sped toward town. She might not have gone that way, she could have taken any route, gone anywhere, but the road toward Plattsburgh seemed like a logical first choice. About five miles from the city limits, he whizzed by a car parked on the shoulder on the side of the road, caught a fast glimpse, and immediately pulled into a driveway, turned around, and went back to investigate. As he thought, it was Ethan's car.

He looked in the window, spotted the keys on the driver's seat, and tried the door. It opened and he climbed in, put the key in the ignition, and gave it a crank. The engine chugged a little but wouldn't turn over. Probably a bad fuel pump or clogged injectors. He wished he had given the car a thorough checkup when he'd had the chance a few days before. But, as far as he could tell then, nobody had been driving it.

He didn't have time to bother with it. He either had to find Betsy in the next fifteen minutes and talk her into letting him take her wherever it was she was going, or say to hell with it and to hell with her. But he couldn't leave the car sitting there on the side of the road. He had one more option.

He gave her a call.

The phone rang eight times before she picked up. "What do you want, Roy?"

"Where are you?"

"Escaping."

"I'm at Ethan's car here on the side of the road. What's happened to it?"

"Yeah, about that. Do you think you could get it towed somewhere? I'll tell my mom to pay you back."

"Sure, but what are you riding in right now? I hear road noise."

She took a moment to answer. "I hitchhiked."

"You shouldn't be doing that. It's not safe. Tell me where you are."

"I know the people. It's not your problem so don't worry about it."

A muffled voice, sounding like it came over a loudspeaker, said something in the background. It sounded like the daily orders broadcast throughout a prison. Loudspeaker. Road noise. Whoever Betsy was with was playing something strange on their sound system. Maybe it was a podcast or an audiobook. Or maybe she wasn't even in a car. But she had to be because the road noise was so distinct. And then it hit him. She was on a bus.

"I have to go now," she said and hung up.

Roy googled the Plattsburgh Greyhound bus station for a phone number and got through on his first try. "Could you tell me what time the last bus left?"

"You mean the one to New York?"

"Uh, yeah."

"It left right on time. At 8:15 this morning."

Roy needed to clarify. "Was there one that left last night?"

"No. Not last night."

Roy sat for a moment, putting the pieces together. Betsy was most likely on a bus to New York City. That made some kind of sense because he remembered Louise was originally from there so relatives could be involved. But Betsy had money to buy a bus ticket and to have her brother's broken-down car towed somewhere for repairs. Where did that come from? And, unless these relatives she was on her way to stay with were going to pay her way for the next month, two months, or more, she had to have the cash to support herself. Another piece to the puzzle danced around at the edges of his memory. Something Ethan had talked about a few times. Something Roy had nodded along to, acted interested in, but actually didn't care much about.

Urban exploration. It was the buzzword Ethan had used a few times, the new type of adventure he'd tried to get Roy excited about. He talked about making a trip to Buffalo and exploring old grain elevators, or going to Rochester and sneaking into an abandoned car parts factory. And something more. Roy remembered a specific article Ethan had shown him, had read aloud to him. Something about old subway tunnels and underground encampments, all located in New York City. And Betsy was now on her way there. All of which might mean that Ethan was still alive—or at least Betsy believed he was.

Roy ran to his car and took off. He understood why Betsy had ditched him and he didn't blame her. However, somehow, he needed to get Skeet to leave them both alone. First of all, he had to distract Skeet long enough so Betsy could hide herself wherever it was she was going, so Skeet would never be able to find her.

As he drove to the diner, he did his best to psych himself up to act the exact way necessary to fool Skeet. By the time he parked his car, he had put on the full façade. He strolled into the diner, waved to the waitress, and when he plopped down in a booth across from Skeet, cracked a big smile. "Morning. Nice day."

"What are you all cheered up about?" Skeet snarled.

"Well, I guess these days, whenever I wake up and realize I'm not still behind bars it puts me in a good mood."

Skeet smiled back. "Oh yeah. I hear you. So, what's your girlfriend up to today? Trying to make some more plans without me?"

Roy's smile switched to a frown. "She's not my girlfriend and I have no idea what she's up to."

Skeet didn't answer, just stared. Roy backed into his seat and tried not to squirm. Finally, Skeet said, "I don't trust her at all and you shouldn't either. She's trying to do an end-run around us."

Roy stood up. "I have to go to the bathroom." He hurried across the diner and through the door to the Men's room.

***

A phone rang. Skeet checked his pocket but it wasn't his. He leaned over the table and the phone was there, dancing on Roy's empty seat. He picked it up and answered it. It was a spam call so he shut it off, but then leafed through the list of recent calls and spotted the two Roy had made to Betsy in the last twelve hours. He figured he had nothing to lose and pressed the call button and let it ring.

Right before it went to voicemail, Betsy answered. "Did you figure out the car, yet? Maybe you could have it towed to Trombley Auto. They could fix it."

The road noise in the background piqued Skeet's interest but the giveaway was the hint of a nearby female voice speaking with a thick New York City accent. It was all so familiar—the city woman who came by bus way upstate to visit her husband or boyfriend in prison, and was now on her way back home. By bus. That was the key. Skeet didn't answer. He hung up.

Roy came back and sat down. He picked up his phone, looked it over, and said, "What are you doing? You just called her. You can't do that."

Skeet sneered, "Really? I can't do that? I just did that. She's on a bus, isn't she? Most likely going to the big city. But you already knew, didn't you?"

A waitress came over and asked them if they wanted coffee. Skeet relaxed, softened his face, and said, "If you could just give us another minute, we'll be ready to order."

Roy leaned over the table, shakily stared at Skeet, and hissed. "You know what? Fuck you. I'm done with this. I'm not doing this anymore."

"Oh, fuck me? Really? Mr. Parolee? Mr. ex-con? You're not done with anything until I say you're done."

Roy put his hands on the table and pushed himself closer to Skeet's face. He whispered, "I saw you kill Walter Lazrove. I saw you shoot him and drag his dead body into the cave."

Skeet stared straight ahead a moment, then also leaned forward, his mouth forming a small grin. "Interesting. I thought you might have shown up for that. Now, think about this, Roy. Think long and hard about this. You saw me kill Walter Lazrove. And here I am, sitting with you, having a nice quiet conversation like nothing happened."

Roy backed away, flopped on his seat.

"Now, this is what's going to happen. You're going to get in your car and drive like hell to your house, and pack a few things for a short vacation. Then, I'm going to pick you up in," he looked at his watch, "a half-hour from right now. And don't worry, I'll get you back for your parole appointment next week."

They both headed to the door and Skeet said to the waitress, "Sorry, we can't stay. We didn't plan our day too well and have to go."

They walked out into the cold morning air and Roy said, "Oh no, it's Louise and Bud.

As the two walked by, Skeet said, "You two look like you had a good night."

Louise looked straight ahead. "We sure did."

Bud had parked his car next to Skeet's pickup. Skeet opened his door, then spun around and looked in Bud's car. A small purse sat on the front passenger seat. It had to belong to Louise. He crouched down, out of sight, and tried the door. It was unlocked and he opened it just enough to get his arm in and take the purse. He tossed the purse into his pickup, pushed it under the driver seat, and drove off.

***

The first thing Louise noticed when she opened the door to Bud's car was that her purse was gone. She looked under the front seat, in the back on the seat and floor, and under the car.

"You sure you didn't leave it at the hospital?" Bud asked.

"I'm positive. I know I left it on the seat."

She got on her hands and knees and looked again under the car. She stood and put her hands on the car roof.

"Skeet took it," she said.

"Oh c'mon, Louise. Why would Skeet take your purse?"

"I know he took it."

"Was your phone in it?"

She reached in her coat pocket and pulled out the phone.

"Call him," Bud said.

"You got his number? Because I certainly don't."

"I'll get it later. Somebody at the bar must have it."

***

Roy followed Skeet out and hopped in his own car. He was preoccupied with what to do next and didn't see Skeet stealing Louise's purse. For most of the trip home, he drove way over the speed limit and almost hoped he would get caught so he'd have an excuse not to be there when Skeet came to pick him up. But a growing part of him knew he had no choice. When Betsy walked off the bus in New York City, Skeet would be waiting for her. And Roy was determined to show her that he wasn't a spineless wimp, that he would do whatever it took to see that she didn't get hurt.

He ran up the stairs to his bedroom, dragged a backpack out of his closet, and stuffed it full of clothes. He ran out to the stairs, stopped, and considered another possibility. He went back to his closet, stood on his toes, reached to the back of a high shelf, and pulled out a small cardboard box he had long ago stuffed underneath some old sweaters. He worked the box around the clothes to the bottom of the backpack and zipped it closed.

He hurried back down the stairs and opened the front door just as Skeet pulled up.

Chapter 20

The bus slid out of the parking lot, passed through a few traffic lights, and merged onto the interstate, the Adirondack Northway, two lanes heading south. Betsy was too exhausted to be nervous, and the sleep she wanted so desperately hovered nearby, taunting her. She stared out the window at the passing scenery, watching the flat fields outside Plattsburgh quickly change to the early ruggedness of the mountains. When she saw the sign, *Entering the Adirondack Park*, she finally slipped away.

But not for long. First Roy called and then called again and hung up. She couldn't imagine what was going on with him, and at that point, no longer cared. She fell back asleep and drifted until the bus made its first stop, already almost two hours from Plattsburgh. She woke, refreshed, relieved, and hopeful. She was on her way to find her brother, she had a big wad of money in her pocket, and she'd ditched Roy Collins and Skeet Burke. Her mom and Pepe? She tried not to think about them.

A short time later, the bus pulled into the Albany station for a half-hour lunch break. She dug her wallet out of her pack, went inside, and bought a pre-made sub sandwich, salad, and a soda from the cafeteria cooler. She paid with a hundred-dollar-bill, received back eighty-eight dollars and some change, and sat at a table near the window. She looked around at the other people and tried to imagine who they were, where they'd come from, and where they were going. She picked at her sandwich and wondered if Ethan had taken a bus, maybe this same bus, when he took off to the city.

Unless she was wrong about all of it. Unless he'd never gone to the city, this trip was a huge mistake, and he'd gone somewhere else. Or, what if he did go and he was no longer there? She took the paper with the numbers she had copied from her mother's phone out of her pocket, stared at them a moment, and entered them into her own phone. She couldn't bring herself to call any of them. Not yet. She would wait until she was actually in the city. She crumpled the paper and set it on the counter. She didn't need it as long as she had her phone. She touched the pocket of her coat and made sure it was there. She put her wallet back in her pack.

The bus left the station, twisted through the city streets, and quickly re-entered the city-bound interstate. The long sleep and coffee forced her into wide-awake mode. She continued to stare out the window and became increasingly nervous about the downstate shift to the more densely populated scenery. She longed for a book or magazine—anything to read, anything to focus on. She settled on a detailed reflection of the last few days, on the people involved, and everything that had led up to where she was now headed.

Norm LaMarche scared her more than anyone potentially involved in the whole stupid drama. Way more than Skeet or even Lazrove who had pointed a gun at her. Throughout her entire life, he kept showing up, always in ways that brought varying levels of disturbance and uncertainty. She knew her mom had met him in college and was his on-and-off girlfriend. Her mom had been a theater major, which was how she had met Norm, how they first got together. In the beginning, they had starred opposite each other in a play and then continued as a couple. When they both graduated, her mom had followed Norm back to northern New York. She must have been so different back then. Betsy had seen many earlier photographs of her when she was young and she always looked so happy, usually with a wide grin and big dancing eyes.

As far as Betsy knew, her dad, Doug Racine, had been one of Norm's closest friends growing up, and shortly after moving upstate, Louise ditched Norm—or maybe Norm ditched Louise—and she took up with Doug. Eventually, she got pregnant with Ethan and married Doug a few months later. Within a year, Norm had also married a local girl, and the four worked out their differences and became friends.

Norm never had kids, and as time went on, looked to Ethan to fill that space. Betsy recalled being about eight years old, Ethan would have been nine or ten, and one day Norm came by with two fishing poles—not three, just two—for him and Ethan. She had asked if she could go with them and he'd said no, she wasn't invited. He turned her around, gave her a little push, and told her to go play with her dolls. When she started to cry, he told her to stop being a baby. Nobody else was around to hear the exchange, Ethan in his room, and their mom packing a bag and getting him ready for his adventure, and she'd never told anybody about it. And her father? From the pieces of the past she could put together, she had come to believe that he'd already put in motion a plan to abandon the family.

The snowboarding came next. At Christmas, Norm showed up with two presents, a snowboard and boots for Ethan and Barbie and Ken dolls for Betsy. Every few weeks for the rest of the winter and the one after, Norm would take Ethan over to Whiteface Mountain and the two would go wild on the steep slopes. At first, Ethan would come back and want to tell Betsy and his mom all about his fabulous day, but after returning one time and finding Barbie and Ken on his bed, their bodies disfigured and their heads cut off, he got the message and no longer included his sister in those conversations. Whiteface Mountain. The furthest north high Adirondack peak, somewhat separated from the other high peaks and always the most visible. She loved the mountains as much as she loved nearly anything else in the world. But not that one. Whenever she saw it, she either turned away or blanked it out, trying to forget the memories.

Two years later, Norm split with his wife and started to hang around the Racine house, mostly with Ethan. Betsy was still too young to understand the dynamics of the situation, but it seemed like, the more Norm hung around, the more her dad was gone. Then one night, she'd overheard one of her parents' initial parting conversations, and she began to understand.

"He's not even my kid," Doug had said. "So why should I care?"

Louise stifled a sob. "You've got to stop saying that. You don't know. And Norm doesn't know, either. And there's absolutely no doubt about Betsy."

"Of course there's doubt. Those two kids look so much alike. And, you know, they do both look kind of like Norm."

"Doug. You need to stop this. You need to stop this now. Norm LaMarche is a creepy man who's just trying to get you to leave. That's it. And, if you think I still have any interest in him, you are dead wrong. I'd just as soon kill him as look at him. He's deranged."

The next day, Betsy looked up *deranged* on their computer. She agreed with her mother on that one. From that day on, *deranged* was the word she always associated with Norm LaMarche.

The family friction became bad enough that Norm stopped coming around. About a year later, it all changed when Betsy's dad finally left and moved across the country. At first, Norm would respectfully knock on the door and wait to be let in, giving Betsy enough time to hide in her room. But it didn't last long. One day, while Ethan and her mom had gone out shopping, Betsy came out of her room, went into the kitchen, and there was Norm, sitting at the table, eating a sandwich. Betsy ran back to her room and slammed the door. When her mom and Ethan came home, Betsy crept back out of her room and listened from the hallway to the conversation. Her mom had asked Norm to leave, said she was busy, that she had too much to do.

Ethan, happy, excited to see Norm, said, "Hey, Norm, you want to take me to the movies? The new Star Trek just came out."

He said with a smug tone meant for her mom. "Sure. Good idea."

And they raced out the door.

Betsy charged into the room and pushed right up to her stunned mom. "Why, Ma? Why'd you let him go?"

Her voice cracked. "I don't know, Betsy. I don't know what to do here."

They ate a thrown-together dinner and turned on the TV. At one point, her mom went into another room and came back a minute later with a glass of something golden brown.

"What are you drinking, Ma?"

"Just a little whiskey."

By the time Ethan and Norm came back, her mom had had two more glasses. She greeted them at the door, stumbling and slurring. Ethan pushed by her, frowned, and looked her up and down. "Ma. What's wrong with you?"

Norm moved close and sniffed near her face. "Are you drunk, Louise?"

She gave him a wobbly smile.

"You know I hate that. I don't like drunk people."

"Oh come on, Norm. I just had a little bit."

He'd backed out the door, and as he hurried to his car, her mom mumbled, "What a jerk. He snorts coke and smokes pot, and he can't handle a little alcohol."

From then on, whenever there was a chance Norm would come around, her mom had always gotten drunk. As time went on, even if she hadn't seen Norm in weeks, months, or years, she still had to swill down the whiskey every night, and sometimes in the day, in case he might show up. Ethan didn't remember, or want to remember, the details of that day, and the few times Betsy had mentioned it over the years, he'd tried to change the subject or act like she'd imagined or exaggerated it. But Betsy knew what she'd seen, knew how it had all started. It was something she would never forget.

***

Betsy briefly dozed off again. When she woke, she looked out the bus window and bolted upright in her seat. A large black pickup sped by in the passing lane. Skeet's pickup? It couldn't be, it wasn't possible. She caught a glimpse of the back of somebody's head in the passenger seat with straight black hair, just like Roy's. She checked out the license plate but it didn't tell her anything and there were no identifying bumper stickers. As the pickup pulled away, she made out a small outline of a sticker on the lower left of the rear window. It was too far away to determine what it was.

Her nerves jumped all over the place. She told herself to calm down. She played a few games on her phone and made sure it was still plugged into the charger and the cord was secure in the seat connection. She told herself over and over that everything was going to be okay. In another few hours, she would call Ethan, he'd come find her, and the whole awful nightmare would have a happy ending.

Chapter 21

Roy opened the back door to Skeet's truck and tossed his pack onto the seat. This time, no threatening guns stood there for all to see, although one or two pistols had to be hiding somewhere. For the first half-hour, Skeet kept silent, focused on his eighty- to ninety-mile-an-hour driving. Roy didn't care since only a few other vehicles shared the road, and the radio played at a nice volume, picking up a station out of Vermont. When they reached the mountains, Skeet slowed a little and shattered Roy's peace.

"I'm going to try to catch that bus when it stops in Albany," Skeet said. "They do a half-hour stop so it's possible."

Roy ran some numbers in his head. "Isn't the bus station downtown? You'd have to average about eight-five and then not hit any traffic in Albany."

"Wow, another numbers man. Impressive. That's right about what I was thinking."

Skeet sped back up to ninety.

"You're gonna get a ticket," Roy said. "Then what?"

"It's worth the risk."

For the next half hour, Roy listened as Skeet rambled on about what it was like to be a prison guard, how he actually cared about the prisoners, how he wished the best for them. He even told a few stories to make his point, and if the image of a grisly bullet slamming into a man's head hadn't been dancing around Roy's brain, he might have believed that Skeet Burke was a good guy. Bizarre, unbalanced, but not evil.

Roy finally reached his limit. He had to get Skeet to shut up so he brought up the first topic that came into his head. "Hey Skeet. What do you know about Norm LaMarche?"

Skeet slowed the truck way down, seemed to stifle a flood of anger, and put on his joking persona. Roy caught it all and regretted what he'd just asked.

Skeet cracked a full-face smile. "I guess the question is, what do you know about Norm LaMarche?"

"Uh, well, he was the one who set up the weed deal at the warehouse."

"So, you know him?" Skeet asked. "He's your good buddy?"

"No, not at all. I only met him once for about five minutes. Ethan knew him from way back, I guess."

Skeet sped up again, popped the cruise on at eighty-five, and launched into a quick history of his connection with Norm LaMarche. No more careful grilling, no more trying to pry info out of Roy. He was merely telling another story.

Skeet and Norm went to different high schools and got to know each other through sports and parties. Norm was always an arrogant asshole, thought he was better than everyone else, but somehow, he always had a lot of friends.

"And then he went to college," Skeet said, "and came back with your friends' mother. With Louise. She was a real beauty, that one. She'd walk into a room and all the heads would turn. And funny, too. Charming, sweet, and funny. Quite a combo. Now she's such a mess. When she walks in a room now, all you see is a pathetic drunk."

He rattled on a little longer about how he used to see Norm and Ethan out together sometimes, at the mall or the movies, like Ethan was his kid. But never Betsy.

"Yeah," Roy said, "because Betsy hates him. She told me Norm was the reason her parents split up. When she found out he was Ethan's contact at CanAm…"

Skeet hit the brakes and slowed way down. "Whoooooh. So you were asking her about him. Not the opposite."

"What difference does that make? Norm wasn't there that night and I wanted to know why."

Skeet cranked the steering wheel, raced into a rest area, and slammed on the brakes. He looked at Roy with that prison guard stare. "Why do you care so much, Roy? Why are you asking people about Norm?"

"Jesus, Skeet. I don't know."

"You're still hiding something from me, aren't you? I know you are. So tell me or you will face the consequences."

"Consequences," Roy mumbled.

Skeet continued his brutal stare, then changed his tone, softened. "Look, I know you're not any scummy Walter Lazrove type, you might even be a nice kid. But I'm going to get that money and you can either help me in any way you can and we can share it when we get it or you can decide you don't want to help and you can get out right now, right here."

"I thought you needed my help."

"I do. Especially with your young friend, Betsy. But you have to tell me everything you know about Norm LaMarche."

Roy looked out the front window and recounted the day Norm had followed him to the FastTrac convenience store and convinced him to plead guilty to car theft. "If it hadn't been for that, I would have pled not-guilty and probably gotten off. Never gone to prison. But he told me there were a whole lot of scary guys out there who wouldn't like me talking at a trial."

Skeet bobbed his head up and down and laughed. "Yesserree, a whole lot of scary guys. Norm and one dead Walter Lazrove. I'm shaking." He held his hand out and made it shake. "See?" Then he moved inches from Roy's face and yelled, "Now, tell me the rest. Tell me where Norm was when his cousin got killed."

Roy looked down at the floor of the truck. He wanted the conversation to stop. But Skeet would never give up at this point. "When I woke up, regained consciousness, I ran outside. I found René's car and the keys under the seat and left."

"And what else?"

"There was a car outline in the snow and tire tracks leading away from it."

Skeet slapped the steering wheel and nodded vigorously. "Yes!" He floored the truck back onto the highway, got it up to one-hundred and held it for a while. He laughed maniacally and said, "Good old Norm. Good old Norm." Then, a moment later. "We can't beat the bus to Albany. We're going all the way to the big city."

Skeet didn't seem to notice the high speed and launched into another lecture. "Now, this is one of the main reasons we need to stick together on this adventure we're on. I need help with the brother and sister and you're going to need help figuring out what to do with your share of the cash. You can't just stick it in the bank, you know. It's a complicated process to launder it and I've got a good plan worked out on how to do that. Like you, I'm a numbers man but I have a ton more experience. I've been doing this for years."

Roy hoped, prayed that a state trooper would pull them over. About sixty miles north of New York City, it finally happened.

Skeet hit the brakes and slowed way down to seventy and Roy looked around, trying to see what the reason was. Up ahead, a barely visible outline of a small car came into focus in the center divider. Roy was impressed— even when Skeet gabbed away, he was still paying attention. They passed the trooper's car, the blue and red lights flashed on, and it pulled out behind them.

Skeet kept driving until the trooper car was directly behind him. He said, "He'll see my Corrections Officer sticker." He pulled onto the shoulder as far as he could, put the truck in park, and took his license and registration out of his shirt pocket. He'd already had it ready. As the state trooper approached the truck, Skeet lowered his window.

"Good day, officer," Skeet said.

The trooper leaned down, looked in the window, and checked out Roy. "License and registration, please."

Skeet handed the cards to the trooper and stared ahead, calm and silent.

"You a Corrections Officer?"

"Yes sir. I'm a sergeant, currently upstate at Altona Prison."

"So, what's the rush?"

"I'm trying to make it to a wedding on time. A family friend. My daughter's already there and we're supposed to meet her, uh, in the next hour. Just one of those things."

The trooper looked at Roy. "Who are you?"

"My name is Roy Collins. I'm friends with the groom."

The trooper walked to his car and came back a few minutes later. He said pleasantly, "Ok, Sergeant Burke, this is what's going to happen. I'm going to give you a warning. But your plates will be in the system, so if you get pulled over again further down the road, you will get a ticket. This is different down here. A lot more cars on the road than where you're from. You have to be careful."

"Thank you, Officer," Skeet said.

"Enjoy the wedding."

Skeet pulled back onto the highway, clicked the cruise on, and said, "You know what, Roy? I did something stupid and careless that might cause some real trouble."

"You mean the guns you have hidden in here?"

"No. I didn't bring guns on this trip." He reached under his seat and pulled out Louise's purse. "But I did bring this." He tossed the purse onto Roy's lap. "Check it out."

Roy opened it and looked inside. "Whose is this?"

"Find her phone, look for numbers, and check her wallet."

Roy opened the wallet and read the driver's license. "My God. How'd you get this?"

"I got it out of Bud's car."

"Skeet, man, you're too much."

Skeet flashed a curious look but Roy put on a big smile. He dumped the contents on his lap: a comb, brush, lipstick, lottery ticket, condom packet, and the wallet.

"Where's the phone? We need her phone," Skeet said.

"There isn't one."

"Well, go through her wallet. Maybe there's an address or something in there."

Roy rummaged through the wallet and found a small scrap of paper with two phone numbers scribbled on it. "Two phone numbers. One of 'em could be Ethan's."

"Maybe. Or Bud's or some bar."

Skeet pulled into the left lane to pass a bus. He was halfway past it and said, "Oh no. Roy, turn your face away from that bus."

"Huh?" He turned for a second to the bus, then looked at Skeet. "What if she's on it and sees us?"

"It doesn't matter." Skeet passed the bus and saw in his mirror the destination rectangle above the front window that said New York City. "We're going to beat it and that's what's important."

"Should I try calling these numbers?" Roy asked.

"Wait until we're in the city. I'll catch Betsy and try to talk some sense into her. And, if one of those numbers is her brother's, you can try to set up a meeting. But keep your phone in the charger. When we get there, we need our phones fully charged."

Roy punched the numbers into his phone contacts and named them both Ethan. He dropped the slip of paper into the console next to him

Skeet negotiated the maze into the city, made a few lefts and rights in Manhattan, and pulled into a parking garage near the Port Authority bus station. He drove up a few floors to find a space, they both hopped out, and he said. "We need to split up. And take your pack, just in case."

"In case of what? Where are you going? I don't know my way around here."

"Just try to set something up. I'll call you when I get Betsy back on board."

"What are you gonna do to her?"

"Nothing. Just talk to her. Anyway, why do you care?"

Skeet ran a few hundred feet, then charged through a door marked Exit. Roy hurried after him, opened the door, and yelled, "Skeet. Where the hell are you?" He had disappeared.

Roy took out his phone and tried the first number. It rang a few times, then stopped. He was about to call the second number when he got a text that said: Who is this?

Roy texted back: It's Roy. Ethan?

Return text: What's the make, model, and date of my old car?

Roy punched it in.

Ethan texted: Wow! Where r u?

Roy texted: In the city. Can we talk?

Ethan texted: Not now. Can we meet?

Roy texted: Yes. I'm by the Port Authority bus station.

Ethan texted: Go to a playground near you. Jared Jones Park. Use your phone. Go in a little way and find a bench. Sit down. Be there in a half hour. You alone?

Roy texted: Yes.

Ethan texted: Sorry but if you're with anybody else it's not going to happen.

Roy texted: I'm alone. Really.

Roy rushed down a stairway and opened a door to the street. The assault of the crowds and noise overwhelmed him. He leaned against a building for a moment, took a few breaths, and got himself ready for his walk. He opened the maps app on his phone but it didn't work, probably because it hadn't been updated in years. He thought he'd taken care of all the phone stuff but must have been too tired or something to do it right. And he had no idea where he was or how to get to Jared Jones Park.

He spotted a policeman standing next to a Dunkin Donuts entrance and hurried over to him. The cop saw Roy coming, stood fiercely in front of him, and yelled, "Stop right there."

Roy backed away and said, "Sorry, officer. I'm lost."

"Where are you from?"

"Upstate New York. Near Canada. I'm supposed to meet a friend at Jared Jones Park."

"What for? You buying drugs?"

"No sir. He's just a friend from up there. I'm visiting."

"Jared Jones Park. Two blocks south," he pointed south, "then four blocks west."

Roy took off, crossing busy streets and weaving in and out of the crowded sidewalks, until he came to the park. It was small, half a block in size, with a playground, a basketball half-court, and a few benches. Other than two women and a few kids carousing at the playground, it was quiet and nearly empty. Roy sat on a bench facing away from the street. At first, he squirmed and fidgeted, and every half-minute, turned around and looked back at the park entrance. A slight wind blew through and added an icy chill to his unease, forcing him to huddle down into his coat.

He heard somebody coming up behind him, but before he could turn around, a body slammed down tight against him and he felt something small and hard, pressed against his side. "Huh?"

Norm LaMarche pushed next to him and the solid object digging into his side was the barrel of a gun. "Don't move and don't make a sound."

Chapter 22

Betsy read the sign, *Welcome to New Jersey*, and wondered what was going on. Why New Jersey? She checked out the map on her phone and saw that this was the correct way. Or, from what she saw on the map, one of many, possibly hundreds, of correct ways.

The traffic slowed way down and came to a halt, and a minute later, the bus driver announced that there had been an accident up ahead and he expected as much as a half-hour delay to their arrival time. Groans and complaints floated around from some of the nearby passengers. At first, Betsy was relieved that she had a little more time before she would have to leave the safety of the bus and deal with whatever came next. Annoyance followed because part of her just wanted to get it over with.

The traffic started again, bringing the bus through new levels of development, confusion, and chaos, and then slowed back down as the highway eased onto a long circular turn giving Betsy her first glimpse of the city. For the next minute, the view came and went until the foreground trees and buildings finally gave way to the glint and shimmer of the Hudson River and a full-size panorama of the city skyline behind it. It was both terrifying and beautiful and she desperately hoped that, within the next hour, she would be talking to Ethan, hugging Ethan, safe with Ethan.

The highway curved around in a sinking spiral and disappeared into the Lincoln Tunnel. Betsy watched for a minute, then laid back in her seat and closed her eyes. It was too much, all of it. When the bus finally docked and the mumbled announcements came on, she waited until the other passengers had picked up their belongings and hustled off before making her move. In a daze, she lugged her pack in front of her, plopped down the bus's stairs, onto the platform, and entered into a new form of insanity.

Port Authority was jammed with every kind of human sight and sound she could imagine. She needed to find somewhere quiet so she could figure out the phone numbers she took from her mom. A sign above an escalator said *Exit*, and she stepped on the stairs and rode them down. The next floor, the main floor, was much different from the one she'd been on, more like a giant shopping mall, like one she had been to once in Syracuse. She didn't like it but figured she could handle it.

She wished she had brought Ethan's maps of New York City with her because her phone app was so unreliable. *A dumb mistake, I can't afford any more of those.* She went into a bookstore, asked for a map of the city, and was directed to a rack at the back of the store. She bought a map of Manhattan that folded small enough to fit in her pocket and another larger one of the entire metropolitan area. She examined the smaller map and saw that Central Park was not far from where she was. Surely in that giant park, she could find somewhere quiet, somewhere to settle down for a while, make a phone call, maybe even meet Ethan there. She continued down the length of the first floor, put her pack firmly on her back, and walked through the gigantic doorway onto 8th Avenue.

The intensity of the urban street chaos nearly sent her back inside. So many people, so much noise. She pulled out her little map, walked a block, and realized she was going in the wrong direction. She turned around and raced the other way, weaving in and out of the hordes as best she could.

She had to stop, she couldn't continue. She turned onto a side street, leaned against a building, and tried to calm down. She looked back the way she'd come, to the packed 8th avenue, and watched the distant flow rushing past—taxis, trucks, buses, long limousines, police cars, and ambulances with their sirens screaming. A racket overhead grew louder as it echoed down to the street, the noise bouncing off the buildings. More noise came from above her as a fleet of large helicopters flew overhead. A group of four people, maybe her mom's age, walked by, dressed in suits, fur coats, and fancy hats, two of them holding leashes with little dogs on the other end. They barely noticed her as they passed, deep in their own conversation. She told herself to stop being such a wimp, that she was tough, adaptable, and she'd get used to it all soon enough. Nobody else seemed to mind the cacophony so why should she?

She was about to go back to 8th Avenue when she spotted near the corner, the top of a black vehicle peeking out over an SUV in front of it. It couldn't be Skeet's pickup, no way, but just in case, she turned the other direction toward 9th Avenue. She walked by another black pickup, parked and empty across the street, and this time ignored it, telling herself to stop being so stupid.

***

As Skeet drove the last few miles in New Jersey, then into the Lincoln Tunnel and to the parking lot near the Port Authority bus station, it became apparent that his plan for what to do next was, at best, shaky, and more likely, doomed to fail. He had been in way too much of a rush when he'd left that morning and now, for what was coming next, Roy could easily be a fly in the ointment, a stick in the spokes. He did the right thing and ditched Roy, believing he could easily find him later.

He ran the short distance to the bus station, found the arrival gate for the bus from Plattsburgh, and was overjoyed that it was going to be a half-hour late, arriving in another forty minutes. He went back to the parking lot, drove his pickup onto the streets, circled around until he found a parking spot on a relatively quiet side street a few blocks to the north of the station, and made it back to the arrival gate minutes before the bus pulled in.

His thought was: Betsy will leave the station, get out on the street, freak a bit because she's never been in a big city—and New York is the biggest—and go to Central Park. Hopefully. He wanted her to be overwhelmed, exhausted, desperate, looking for that white knight to rescue her, to help her out of the mess she'd gotten herself in. She got off the bus, the last one off, looked around like she was brand new to a war zone, and hesitantly made her way out of the station. Perfect. She stopped at a bookstore and came out holding what might be a map. He didn't like that.

But she did head north toward the park, and from what he could tell from her body language, she was behaving exactly as he wished. When she turned onto the street his pickup was parked on, he panicked. She would see it, know it was his, and take off so fast he'd never find her. He should have left it in the parking garage. But what were the chances she'd pick that street to turn down? Another dumb mistake. He'd reached his limit. He waited a few moments, peeked around the corner, saw her hurrying away, and ran after her.

***

A noise behind Betsy caught her attention, she turned to look, and a thick black stick swung around and hammered her on the side of her head. She crumpled in a heap on the sidewalk, still conscious, but too stunned to get up. Powerful arms scooped her up like a rag doll, the pack still on her back, and tossed her on the back-seat floor of the black pickup across the street. The pickup pulled out, sped a few blocks, then turned a corner.

She tried to sit but couldn't find the strength. Her head throbbed, her body felt disconnected, and she didn't understand where she was or what had just happened. She pulled her arm from underneath her and touched the rapidly growing bump on her head. She rubbed her eyes, realized her glasses were gone and started to panic.

"Where are my glasses? Where am I?"

"You still alive back there?"

It was Skeet Burke. She wasn't surprised.

"They fell off and broke. Now, don't you dare move back there.

She rolled over on her side and closed her eyes.

The pickup stopped at a light and Skeet turned around and looked down at her. "Hey, I didn't hit you that hard. Wake the hell up."

She stayed quiet and kept her eyes closed. A driver in a car behind them honked a horn a few times.

"Dammit," Skeet muttered.

He twisted further around and leaned toward her. When he was about a foot away, her fist flew up and caught him in the jaw, knocking him back. She opened the rear door, grabbed her backpack, and almost made it out, but he got a grip on her coat and hauled her back in. She went limp for a moment, didn't resist, then swung her pack at his head. The pack's zipper had opened and half of the contents fell out. But he let go, and with a chorus of car horns and angry city voices now serenading in the background, she made it through the car door and back onto the city street. She ran the wrong way down a one-way street while Skeet screamed after her to stop. But he couldn't abandon his truck in the middle of the road so he gave up and drove off.

He would be patrolling the area looking for her and she had to find somewhere to hide. She also had to figure out where she was. And, she had to check her pack and see what had fallen out of it. She came to a small fenced park with the front gates open and ran down a short path until she came to a clump of bushes to hide behind. She could still hear the noise on the streets—the rumble of the vehicles, the horns, the loud voices. But the few birds chattering in the branches and the pigeons scurrying around the blacktop sidewalks calmed her down a touch. She scanned the area around her to make sure she was at least mostly alone, emptied her pack on the ground, and took an inventory.

She scooped up the hazy rectangle of her backup glasses case, let out a sigh of relief, clicked open the case, and put on the glasses inside it.

"Oh my God. What are these?" She pulled the glasses off her face, shook her head, and choked back tears. She had so many cases containing old frames and prescriptions and she'd taken, not only the wrong one, but one of the worst ones. They weren't even hers. They were an old pair of Ethan's from when he was maybe ten or eleven, before his vision had gotten so much worse.

She put the glasses back on. They sort of fit—Ethan's head was always much bigger than hers, the same size at ten or eleven as hers was now—and she gained some clarity with her distance vision. However, anything close up appeared as a blurry mess. Which meant she wouldn't be able to read the maps on her phone. Her phone. She scrambled frantically, looking for an outline, feeling through the small pile of clothes. Until she remembered it was thankfully still in her coat. She pulled it out but was afraid to touch it, afraid it would lock up or she would hit some wrong button and would be too blind to even attempt to fix it.

She hovered on her hands and knees, staring at the fuzzy pile of clothes, and wondered what she should do next. A wave of exhaustion began to edge out her adrenaline-fueled focus. Her head throbbed, her vision fogged even more, and now her brain wanted to follow down the same path. She sprawled out on top of her clothes, pressing them flat on the frigid ground, and lay there motionless for a minute. Until another thought came roaring in. Where was her wallet?

She frantically pawed through the clothes, dug around in her pack, opened all the zipped pockets, but found no wallet. She now had no driver's license, and no money. Except for the eighty-eight dollars and change she'd received back from the hundred she'd broken in the Albany bus station. She shoved her hand in her pocket to make sure it was still there.

A voice behind her said, "Excuse me, miss. You can't sleep here."

Betsy jumped up, spun around, and stood face to face with a New York City police officer. She had heard somewhere that New York cops were strict and scary. However, this one was a woman so maybe she'd be nicer.

"Oh, sorry, Officer, I was just leaving."

The officer pointed to Betsy's clothes and pack. "Is this all you have?" Betsy nodded. "Where do you usually stay?"

"Uh, in the old subway tunnels."

"How old are you?"

"I'm eighteen, Ma'am."

The officer moved closer and looked at the now large bump on Betsy's head. "I'm going to need to see some ID."

Betsy stood up straight, regained her composure, looked directly at the officer, and said, "Ma'am, I'm sorry. I just said something that's not true. The fact is, I'm not from here and I don't sleep in the subway tunnels and I just got robbed. I really am eighteen and I'm looking for my brother who likely really is homeless. I just got off a bus and was walking, trying to get my bearings, and the creep who held me up slammed me in the head with something and stole my wallet with two-thousand dollars in it. Now, I still have another eighty-two dollars in my pocket and I have my phone so I can try to call my brother. If he doesn't answer, I can call my uncle in Staten Island. And, if I do find the creep who robbed me then I'll probably get arrested because I'll beat the…"

The officer's radio crackled and a voice said something about a domestic dispute and officers in the area needed. The officer said, "Okay, okay. I have to go. But, if you get stuck tonight," she reached in her vest pocket and pulled out a small brochure, "here's a list of women's shelters you can sleep in. Make sure you get there early because they fill up." She turned to walk away and said, "And don't go looking for whoever robbed you. That's how you end up dead around here."

Betsy shoved her clothes into her pack and hurried back onto the street. She still didn't know where she was and the map wasn't going to help. She had the paper with the numbers from her mom's phone if she could figure out a way to read them. She would go to Penn Station, go underground. She still had the photo with Ethan and she'd show it to people. Maybe somebody would recognize him.

She tapped on the window of a parked taxi, the driver rolled down the window, and she asked, "How much to get to Penn Station?"

"Could be twenty-five bucks, could be fifty. Depends on the traffic."

Betsy couldn't do it. She would take the subway or walk if she had to. As she approached a corner, she made out the name of the street she was on—Riverside Drive. She pulled out the map, unfolded it, and squinted at it with no luck. The blur would not go away. The street sign for the right-hand turn said W. 95th St. and, looking left, was a glimpse of water through the leafless trees. From her brief look at the map, she was sure that Penn Station was down in the lower-numbered streets. That would mean she was going in the wrong direction. She turned around but didn't like the way Riverside Drive looked. It was too curvy. She crossed the street and started down West 95th Street.

When she reached the first corner, she asked a couple walking by where the nearest subway entrance was to get to Penn Station. "Keep going one more block to Broadway and look to your left. You'll see the entrance." Broadway. She'd heard of it. Everybody had heard of it. She still didn't know where she was in relation to anyplace else but it sounded nice and was a good distraction. Maybe she would find Ethan, he would give her a pair of his glasses, and they could go to a Broadway show together. It was not something she'd ever thought about doing, but her mom sometimes talked about the shows she'd seen growing up, on and off Broadway.

A few steps from the corner, a strong hand grabbed Betsy's arm and flung her around. Her reaction was a firm kick which missed Skeet's most vulnerable spot but knocked him away from her. She ran across Broadway's southbound lane, dodging cars, and down the stairs to the subway station. She looked around frantically, trying to make sense of the ticket machines. A line of ten or so people blocked the kiosk where she could ask a question from a live person. She needed to hide. But where?

As Skeet appeared, charging toward her, Betsy screamed full volume, "Don't let him get me. He's trying to kidnap me. He wants to rape me."

Skeet stood a few feet away from her. Everyone in the station stared at the two of them.

"Please, somebody help me," Betsy said.

Two large men slid between Skeet and Betsy, facing Skeet.

A woman gently took Betsy's hand and said, "I'm going to swipe you through the turn-style. Where are you going?"

Betsy leaned toward the woman and whispered, "Penn Station."

"Perfect. Take a 2, or 3 train going south and you'll get there."

Betsy went through the turn-style, down a flight of steps, through a short tunnel, and into a long white-tiled room, packed with people. Skeet could still figure out a way to get to her, probably would, so she had to get on the next train. But it still could be all wrong.

She asked a man next to her, "Is this the right train to Penn Station?"

"Should be the next one coming in."

The train screamed into the station, the doors opened, and Betsy rushed in and grabbed a hand strap near the door so she could see out the window. The train lurched and bucked, and when it came to the next station, stopped so quickly she almost lost her balance. She didn't know how many stops there were before Penn Station and hoped she hadn't missed it. But, in a few minutes, she heard the loud-speaker announcement and saw the artistic sign on the station wall, large enough to read. She hurried off the train and aimlessly followed the crowds, hoping something would soon make sense.

She veered off from the tunnel to another smaller passageway that became increasingly populated with poorly clothed, ragged looking men and women, and a few children, leaning against the walls or sitting on the ground. In a strange way, the scenario was familiar—just another cave, except this one was filled with dwellers.

Two older women sat huddled together on a small mat, their ratty coats pulled tight around them. A large bag of potato chips was wedged between them and one of them stuffed handfuls in her mouth. The other one had her eyes closed and was making snorting and snoring sounds. Betsy stopped for a moment and stared.

The wide-awake woman held out the bag and said, "You want some, girly?"

"No, no thank you. Uh, are you usually here? Is this where you hang out?"

"What are you? Some kind of reporter writing a story about us? It's been done, dear. Done to death."

Betsy crouched down in front of her. "No, I'm looking for my brother."

"Yeah, you don't look like a reporter." The woman sat up and moved close enough that Betsy could smell the alcohol on her breath. She put her hand on Betsy's jaw and gently turned her head.

"Oh, honey, what happened to you? That's a nasty bump there."

Betsy opened one of the pockets on her pack, took out the photo of Ethan, and showed it to the woman. "Have you ever seen him around here?"

The woman nudged the sleeper next to her. "Wake up, Connie. You need to see something."

Connie opened her eyes and looked at the photo. "Never seen him."

"Me either."

For the next hour, Betsy roamed the station, asking the same question to anyone who would answer. Nobody recognized Ethan. Until one man who was lying flat on his back in one of the dirtiest hallways, laughing and talking to himself, said, "Oh yeah, I saw him yesterday." He sat up and grabbed

Betsy's arm. "I ate him for lunch and today you'll be my meal." Betsy pulled away and ran off, to the sound of his hysterical laughter echoing throughout the tunnel.

This was going nowhere, a truly stupid waste of time. Betsy had to figure out how to read the phone numbers on the slip of paper in her pocket. She didn't want to ask somebody for help but she had no choice. She had another idea, to buy a good magnifying glass. It just might work. She found an information kiosk, waited in line, asked the attendant where she might find one, and he suggested a nearby office supply store. He gave her directions and she hurried out of the station.

Back on the street. She turned and looked back to where she'd just come from. Madison Square Garden, with its enormous well-lit façade and two-story advertisements for something happening then or some later date, towered over her. At least if she got lost, she could always find her way back there. The sky above the Garden let her know that daylight had left the city and nighttime had taken over. She had to act quickly because, if nothing else worked, she had to find a place to stay for the night.

A few minutes later, she left the office supply store with a new magnifying glass and walked until she found an empty bench under a street light on a quieter street where she could try it out. First, she tried the Manhattan map so that, if she got through to Ethan, she could at least tell him where she was. It almost worked. The lines of the streets were clear on the map, and if she tried hard, squinted just right, she could make out from the signs the actual street names. She knew she was on 34th Street near 10th Avenue and as she looked at the map, she tried to imagine walking from one point to the other. If she kept out of the southern end, the streets mostly ran in a sensible grid and didn't seem intimidating. She took the other map out of her pack, the one displaying the entire city, and studied it. Queens, Brooklyn, the Bronx—they were all so big and complicated and she hoped she didn't have to venture into any of them.

The phone numbers came next. She found the numbers in her phone contacts, the three with the different names beginning in E, and tried the first one. The phone rang a few times without an answer and no voicemail broke in after the ringing stopped. She was about to try the next number when her phone pinged with a text.

Even with the magnifying glass, she could barely read it. She squinted and struggled to find a hint of better focus until she was almost certain she knew what it said: who called this number?

She responded: Betsy. I'm in the city. Is this Ethan?

The reply was: You need to prove it's you. What is our father's middle name?

Betsy texted: Two names. Jackson Palmer.

Ethan texted: Betsy!!! It's Ethan. Where are you? I'll come get you.

She gave him the exact directions and he told her he'd be there in twenty minutes or so: Don't leave. Just wait. I'll be there.

Betsy scanned the environment around her, right, left, and behind, for any potential danger. Up and down the street, the area appeared to be well-lit, with a lot of pedestrians on the nearby sidewalk. Maybe Skeet could find her but she doubted it. And Ethan was on his way. She sat motionless, stunned, as the full implication of what was about to happen sunk in. Then she cried, laughed, and even turned a few pedestrians' heads when she let out a whoop.

After about twenty minutes, a hand reached from behind her and pushed a cloth over her face. When she woke an hour later, she was in a much different, hellish place.

Chapter 23

When Norm LaMarche pushed a gun into Roy's side and commanded him to follow instructions or end up dead, Roy's prison experiences once again imparted a certain wisdom he had learned to follow to stay safe. And now, in this situation, to stay alive. He needed to act scared, which wasn't a problem because he was, in fact, terrified. He would also do exactly what Norm said so that Norm would always feel like he was in charge. Again, no problem because, at that moment, Roy was not about to argue with or in any way challenge this man holding a gun.

They walked down the street tight together, almost like a couple. They were about the same height but Norm was more than fifty pounds heavier. He draped his left arm around Roy and reached his right arm inside his partially unzipped coat to keep the gun pushed into Roy's chest. Awkward but effective.

A few people approached and passed by them with no reaction, not even a casual glance. Within half a block, they came to a white SUV and Norm said, "It's unlocked. Get in the passenger seat, reach under the seat, and show me what's there."

"Huh?"

"Do it."

Roy did as he was told and pulled out a pair of handcuffs with a long chain connecting them.

"Use your right hand to click one on your left wrist, then slide the other one through this door handle."

Norm pointed to a special handle that was attached at both ends. Again,

Roy did as he was told.

"Now, I'm going to close the door a bit and you're going to grab the other cuff with your left hand and click it onto your right wrist."

Roy hesitated and Norm slammed the gun into his throat and said, "Is this what you want?"

Roy obeyed.

Norm got in the driver's side and said, "Turn your head. Look out your window."

Roy turned his gaze and a tight eye shade came down over his head, covering his eyes and erasing his vision. The vehicle drove endlessly, turning corners over and over. After what seemed like forever, the vehicle moved up a slight incline, and with a few forward/reverse moves, stopped in what was probably a parking space.

Norm pulled off the eye shade, revealing a small deserted paved lot behind a brick building. He got out of the vehicle, opened the passenger door, and used a key to unlock one of the cuffs. He backed up a few steps and pointed the gun at Roy.

"OK, now get out of the car, walk over to that metal staircase and go up it. I'll be right behind you, ready to shoot."

"What about my backpack?"

Norm picked it up. They climbed the steps to a small deck with one door leading inside. Norm said, "It's open so go right in and sit on the couch." He threw the backpack on the floor.

A faint glow through a window cast just enough light for Roy to find the couch. He sat and didn't speak. Norm sat next to him.

"Do you know why you're here?" Norm asked.

"You think I know where Ethan is. You want the money."

"So where is it? Where's the money?"

At first, Roy didn't answer, then said, "You know what? I can give you an honest answer. I have no idea where the money is or Ethan is and I don't think anybody else knows, either. This is all so stupid, everybody thinking he's here in the city. He could be anywhere in the world, hanging out on a beach or something. Or dead may..."

"Shut up! You answer my questions and nothing else. Now, who's with you? Is Betsy down here somewhere?"

"I don't know where Betsy is. Honest answer."

"Then why are you here, you little turd? Why would you come here?"

Norm stood and pointed the gun at Roy's forehead. Roy said, "okay, okay, I came with Skeet Burke. For some reason, he thought Betsy took a bus down here."

Norm smiled, calmed down. "Good old Skeet. Who woulda thought? He always comes through in the end. I guess I should give him a call."

Roy's head spun. He wanted to puke. Betsy was right—if Skeet and Norm were in this together, they were both totally screwed. At least Lazrove was out of the picture.

"And how's Walter doing?" Norm asked.

"Walter?"

"Lazrove, you idiot. I heard he paid Betsy and Pepe a little visit the other night. But no word from him after that. Maybe he fell into one of the caves."

Roy squeezed his cuffed hands together to stop them from shaking.

Norm moved closer to Roy. "So, this is what you're going to do next. I know your phone is still in your pocket and the reason I didn't take it is because you're going to calm down, put on a cool, calm, and collected voice, and call little Miss Betsy. You're going to convince her that you're all alone, not with Skeet, and you want to meet. Then I'll go get her and bring her here. Now, if you don't do that, you refuse for some stupid reason, then I'll just shoot you in the head. But…but, if all goes well and we find the money, which I happen to believe Betsy now knows exactly where it is, then I'll give you each a nice fat gift, say fifty thousand each. Now, you might ask, why am I not offering to split it? And I'll tell you why. Because it's my money. It's always been my money. The drugs that burned in the fire were mine, all three-and-a-half million dollars of them paid for, and I intend to get that back.

Roy slipped up, "What about René?"

"What about René? He tried to rip me off, rip Walter off. He got what he…Hey. I told you not to talk. I should kill you right now."

"Sorry, sorry, I'll do it. I'll call her." But he didn't think she would answer. He didn't know if that was a good or a bad thing. Likely both. He took out his phone and was about to punch in Betsy's number when Norm's phone rang.

Norm didn't answer. Instead, he waited a few minutes and fired off a text. He pointed the gun at Roy. "Get up. Turn to your left. Walk down that hall, and into the first room on your left. I'm right behind you."

Roy entered the pitch-black hallway and felt along the wall for a door.

"Now left," Norm said. He switched on a light revealing a small windowless room with a head-height shelf that ran along one wall. Below the shelf was a bar to hang clothes on. Other than one plain wooden chair in a corner by the shelf, the room was empty. The walls were painted an off-white and the old wooden floor had a faint shine as if it had recently been mopped.

"Put your phone on the floor," Norm said. He motioned to the chair. "Now sit down and hold out your hands."

Roy sat, not understanding what Norm was going to do. When he realized what was coming, he shrunk back and put his hands down. "No, please don't do this. Just close the door. Lock it."

Norm flipped his gun around and smacked Roy in the face with the handle, knocking him nearly unconscious. He unlocked one of the cuffs, wrapped the chain around one of the metal clothing bars, pulled on the chain until one of Roy's nearly limp arms stretched high above his head, and re-fastened the other cuff. The chain between the cuffs was just long enough so Roy could still sit in the chair, but now he had both hands raised up like a devotee praising his savior. Except nobody was being saved this time around. The door closed and a lock clicked. Through a blurry haze, Roy heard it all. At least the light was still on.

Roy's consciousness returned, accompanied by overwhelming fear. He stood and pulled so hard on the cuffs that he created a bleeding bruise on one of his wrists. He tried to sit back down but the chair was low enough that his shoulders felt like they were about to exit from their sockets. He had to regain his composure, he couldn't freak out, not now. He had to escape.

But, even if he could get away, where was he? He listened for noise and heard almost nothing, no road noise, no voices. Yet there was a rumbling, more of a vibration than a sound, that pulsed through the floor. And the smell. It was an industrial version of the oily garage bay smells he remembered from his days as an auto mechanic, more like that of old abandoned machinery than the new lubricants he had poured into modern vehicles.

His phone, lying on the other side of the room, far out of reach, rang a number of times, then went to voicemail. It was Skeet, most likely.

He stuck the fingers of his left hand straight out, pushed them together and his thumb underneath, and tried to pull his hand through the cuff. He almost succeeded but his hand was a little too big. He tried the other hand with the same result. Next, he hung on the metal bar, hoping his weight would break the wood holding the bar. Again, with no result other than excruciating pain in his wrists. The holes in the wood were drilled all the way through so he tried pulling the bar out from one end. At first it didn't budge, but after a minute, he was able to slip it out so that now it was only held up on one end. If he leaned on it, maybe he could force it out.

A door opened, something crashed on the floor, somebody groaned, and Norm yelled for them to shut up. Feet clumped, something dragged, and the groaning continued. Roy managed to push the metal bar back into the end so that it no longer hung down and he was still attached to it. The door's lock clicked, the door opened, and a body was pushed inside. Betsy fell to the floor and rolled on her side, facing away from him. Zip-ties held her hands together behind her back.

Norm said, "Just who you wanted to see. Right, Roy?"

He slammed the door and locked it again.

Chapter 24

Her head throbbed, her body shook, and she tasted the remnants of a vomiting episode she didn't remember. Her first coherent thought was the hope that she had puked all over Norm's car. Was it Norm or Skeet? It could have been either. No, no it was Norm. She recognized his voice telling her to shut up. And then again, something about Roy. What did that mean? She opened her eyes and saw a blurry blank wall, closed them again, and resumed her drifting.

A voice, Roy Collins's voice, whispered, "Betsy, Betsy. Are you okay?" She was dreaming. Had to be. Something nudged her back. She flipped over and saw Roy hanging above her, his face full of concern. He shushed her.

He kept his voice quiet. "I can get out of this but not yet because he'll hear. He must have drugged you. It'll wear off."

"How do you know it'll wear off? I feel like absolute shit. And I'm boiling. Why am I so hot?"

"You've got that heavy parka on. I'm hot, too. Betsy, listen to me. We can get out of this. We wait a bit and then we take him down. I have a plan."

She moaned. "Oh God, no. Really?"

She turned over, her back facing him again, and closed her eyes one more time, hoping, pleading to whoever was out there in the universe, that when she opened them again, she'd be somewhere else.

A phone rang in the distance, and a few minutes later, a door opened and closed. She twisted herself back and forth until she reached a wall. She pushed against the wall and worked herself into a crooked but standing position.

"Where are we?" she slurred.

"I don't know."

***

Roy again pulled the end of the bar out of the wooden support, slipped the chain down to the end, and broke the bar out of the hole on the other end. He jumped back as the bar crashed to the floor, freeing the chain that still held his hands together. He scrambled to his phone and texted Skeet, telling him where he was—locked in a room somewhere. He explained how he'd gotten there, thinking he was texting with Ethan when in reality, it was Norm LaMarche. Skeet didn't return the text.

Roy gently put his hands on Betsy's shoulders and turned her around so she faced the wall. He bent down and examined the zip-ties. "I can get these off you."

She slid back to the floor and laid down again on her side, her face pressed against the baseboard.

"At least it's somewhat clean in here," Roy said.

"How are you gonna get my hands free?"

"I have to find something sharp."

"Oh, yeah. Wait, wait. Let me think. Yes. I have a tiny Swiss Army knife in my pocket."

"You have to be kidding."

"It's in my front right pocket. Just get it out and cut the damn ties."

Roy knelt down and leaned across Betsy. He positioned the long chain connecting his handcuffs on her thigh, leaned on her with one elbow, and pushed a hand into her pocket.

She lifted her head and looked at her thigh. "What the hell's that thing on me?"

"My hands are chained together."

"This can't really be happening."

Roy got the knife out and opened it. "Be still now. I don't want to cut you."

"I don't care. Just get these things off of me."

The zip-ties fell off and Betsy tried to stand on her own. She plopped back down in a seated position, her back against the wall. "Not ready. Need a few more minutes."

Roy didn't have a few more minutes. He ran at the door, wooden but old and solid, and slammed his shoulder into it. Because the door swung inward, it didn't budge. He tried it a few more times with no luck. He picked up the metal bar and swung it into the wall next to the door. The old drywall cracked and fell away, and after a few more blows, revealed two upright studs. He moved a little to the left and whacked a series of holes in an oval through the wall. The entire time, the chain connecting his cuffs bounced and clanked and added to the racket.

Betsy managed to stand up. "You better be done before Mr. Asshole comes back or he'll probably just shoot us both."

"I know, I know."

Sweat poured off Roy's forehead. Wearing the canvas farmer's coat all that time was like being inside an oven. He turned sideways and kicked the wall a few times, blasting a large hole through the side of the room and all the way through the outside wall in the hallway. He pounded the edges of the hole a few more times with the pole and squeezed through the opening. He looked back through at Betsy, sitting cross-legged on the floor, eyes closed, still in a daze.

"Betsy, look here. Can you make it through this?"

She shook her head. "I don't think so."

He tried to figure out how the door was locked, gave up, and charged at it. This time, because it swung inward, he broke the lock and crashed it open. He took her hand and tried to pull her upright.

She got part way up and pushed his hand away. "Yeah, yeah, I can do it myself."

She stood, shook herself off like a dog that had just come out of the water, and walked out of the room. "Where's my pack?"

"Oh shit." Roy rushed around her, into the outer room, and found his backpack on the floor next to the couch. Betsy's pack was behind it.

He handed it to her and she said, "Lotta good it'll do me. No glasses, no wallet, no money, just a few clothes I can't change into 'cause I smell bad and…oh my God. I gotta pee so bad."

She ran down the hall and Roy followed her. "Yeah, me too."

They found a tiny bathroom, dark and dirty, took turns using it, and hurried back to the front room.

Roy noticed the large bump on her head. "Did Norm do that to you?"

"No, Roy, he did not. And he's not the one who broke my glasses. That was your good buddy Skeet."

He said urgently, "All right, we have to get out of here right now, can you do that?"

"What about your handcuffs?"

"Doesn't matter. I'll figure it out later."

She put her hand on his arm. "Thanks for getting me out. Really. I appreciate it. You probably saved my life."

"We're not done yet. We need to hurry."

Before Betsy put on her backpack, she checked the outer pocket. Her maps and the photo of her and Ethan were still there, but any of the information she'd had about living underground in the city was gone. She sighed and put on the pack. Roy picked up his own pack, but because of the handcuffs, couldn't get it on his back.

Headlights briefly lit the parking lot below. They switched off but the engine still hummed as the vehicle parked. Betsy and Roy backed into the hall as footsteps clomped up the back steps.

Roy picked up the metal bar and raced to the side of the doorway. As the door opened, he lifted the bar above his head and swung down hard. A groaning body fell to the floor. In a second, Betsy jumped on, punching it in the face. Then she stood and kicked it in the stomach.

Roy held her arms and tried to pull her back. "Wait, stop. He's got the key to these cuff things in his pocket. We have to figure out a way to tie him up."

She looked around the room. "How about this? Help me here." They dragged Norm's heavy body over to the couch. "Now, we pick the couch up and lay it down on top of him."

They positioned Norm facedown, lifted an end of the heavy, smelly couch, and dragged it so that, when they laid it back down, it rested solidly on his back.

"Now, let's get outta here."

Roy hesitated, shook the handcuffs. "He's got the key to these things in his pocket."

"Which pocket? You want to go digging in there?"

"No, we don't have time."

Roy had his hand on the doorknob when the door slammed back into him, knocking him and Betsy onto the floor.

Chapter 25

After Betsy escaped in the Broadway subway station, Skeet frantically drove around Manhattan, up and down the avenues, across the streets, his frustration level epically ramping up. When he'd swung by his house that morning to grab his things, he'd taken two expensive devices he had bought a year ago so he could keep tabs on his daughter when she did one of her drug-fueled disappearing acts. He'd forgotten that one of them never worked correctly, even though they were both top-of-the-line quality. It was one more example of how plans made on the fly can fall apart so easily—the one that didn't work was the one he'd shoved into one of the pockets of Roy's backpack.

Now Roy had disappeared, wasn't answering his phone. It was probably his plan all along and he never should have trusted him. He also never should have done a few other things, like whacking Betsy on the head. It was definitely not his finest moment. But God she was a wiry one. He had to admit, he kind of admired her. *Ah well. So it goes. She's tough enough that a whack on the head isn't the end of the world for someone like her.*

He turned onto a side street and slid the pickup into an empty parking space where he could rest a minute and try to figure out his next move. And straighten up the vehicle a little bit. A few of Betsy's things, mostly clothes, were still scattered on the rear seat and the floor, and he pushed them into a pile. He felt something square and solid, fished through the pile, and pulled out her wallet. Now that was interesting. He opened the wallet and a wad of hundred-dollar bills stared back at him. Even more interesting. He counted eighteen one-hundred-dollar bills, not a lot to somebody like him, but a sizable chunk for Betsy or her mother. Now, where did it come from? Roy might have given it to her but he doubted it. He'd find out when he caught up with him. If he caught up with him.

He sat back in the driver's seat but still didn't leave. Another piece of the puzzle stared back at him—the slip of paper from Louise's purse with the phone numbers sat there in the middle console. He had nothing to lose, he had to try a number. He punched in the top one, a phone rang, and there was no answer or voicemail. A minute later, he got a text: Who's calling this number?

He texted back: This is Skeet Burke. From Clinton County. If this is Ethan Racine, you probably remember me. I came down to the city with Roy Collins and he disappeared on me. Maybe he found you.

If Betsy was with him, or Roy, too, no way was he going to answer back. The whole damn thing would already be over.

A text came back: Roy is with me. We're trying to find Betsy. But I have to make sure you're who you say you are. Tell me where you went to high school.

Skeet texted back the information and another text returned giving a location where they would meet in an hour. Everything about the exchange reeked of some type of setup. He called Roy's phone, listened to it ring and flip to voicemail, and then hung up. What a perfect switch of events. The idea that action might be about to happen excited him, got his blood pumping, his adrenaline surging. He hunted up one of his hidden weapons, made sure it was locked and loaded and started driving. Whatever he was about to get into, he had no doubt he would be able to control the situation, to have the upper hand.

Anything was possible and he was going to play all the angles. He googled locations for a specific type of store and was delighted that one was on the way to where this so-called meeting was about to take place. He still had Betsy's wallet, and if a scenario unfolded where he could politely give it back to her, he wanted to add a small item to its contents that might prove useful later on. He wasn't sure how well that small item would work because it was somewhat new technology. But it would add to the fun. And, if he was in a position to give her back her wallet, she might also want her mom's purse, also with something he would put in it.

A half-hour later, Skeet, now on foot, raced through the entrance to a small park on the Upper West side of Manhattan. Clumps of bushes lined the edges of the park, thick enough even without their warm-weather greenery to still create a perfect hiding spot for him. The park had two entrances and he placed himself so he could see them both. If somebody he recognized showed up, he had the option to duck down further and not be spotted.

The wait was long. Another half-hour passed and nobody showed, at least nobody he knew. Ten minutes later, a man ran into the park, did a fast scan, then hurried to the other gate and stood, leaning against the fence. Skeet moved so that his full body wouldn't be visible but he could still get a quick glimpse through a hole in the bushes. The man wore a ski hat, a heavy coat, and a scarf pulled over much of his face, making an easy identification impossible. Still, it had to be the person who had texted.

The man waited another fifteen minutes, then hurried across the park and left through the same gate he had come in. Skeet followed, happy the man had turned right, the opposite direction of where his truck was parked. The man unlocked a white SUV and climbed in, but didn't leave. Skeet repositioned himself so that, when the SUV moved, he could be in his pickup and following in a few seconds. A minute later, the game was on.

Skeet's pickup was large and possibly easy to spot and maybe that didn't matter. Maybe that's what the guy wanted. But following a big white SUV was downright easy. And fun. They drove across Manhattan, crossed the East River into Queens, and kept going until they reached a dark and partially deserted industrial neighborhood. The SUV passed an old brick building, likely once serving as housing for factory workers but now seemingly empty, and turned into a driveway at the far end of the building.

Skeet yanked the steering wheel, pulled over in front of the building, snuck around to the far end and down the driveway, and peeked around the back corner into a small parking lot. The man went up an outside staircase to a small deck and charged through a door.

Skeet ran through the dark along the back of the parking lot until he came to the SUV. It had New York license plates but no identifying plate holder or bumper stickers. He refrained from trying the door, not wanting to set off an alarm.

His phone, safe in his coat, pinged with a text but he ignored it. It was likely from Roy, and if so, he suspected he would be seeing him shortly.

He waited another five minutes in case the man came back out, then crept up the stairs. Next to the door was a cracked and cloudy window letting out a few wisps of light. Skeet crouched low and peered through a corner into a small room which at first appeared to be empty. As his vision adjusted, he saw something that made no sense—a couch slightly raised up at an angle, and a human head and shoulder sticking out from under it toward the door. When he heard voices, Roy's and Betsy's, hushed but frenzied, like they were pumped up and ready for action, he knew who the head belonged to.

Time to go in. He rammed the door open, aware that he knocked over an obstacle on the other side. He stepped in, towering over the two figures on the floor, and said, "Time to get up, kids."

Chapter 26

Betsy scrambled backward, stood up, and edged toward the hallway. Skeet pointed a gun at her but didn't look, focused instead on the couch with Norm squashed under it.

Skeet said in a monotone, "Don't do it, Betsy. We're all here now and we're going to figure this out."

He crouched down by the couch and pushed at Norm's protruding shoulder. "Now this," his tone switched to excitement, animation, "this is absolutely amazing." He turned, looked at Roy and Betsy, and at the metal bar on the floor. "You did this? I'm impressed." Then to Roy, "Nice bracelets you got on."

Betsy edged toward the door. Skeet waved the gun at her. "Betsy, now c'mon. You know you can't leave now. We're all here together, finally, and we need to sit down and figure this thing out. So, the first thing you're going to do is you and Roy are going to get that couch off psycho-man there and hoist him onto it, preferably with him sitting up."

Roy nodded and Betsy gave in. Moving the couch was the easy part. With a lot of struggling, they dragged Norm onto the couch, and flopped him into a corner, his head slumping nearly into his lap. A thick line of blood ran through his hair and traveled down his face, ending finally in his lap.

"We need some chairs," Skeet said. "At least two. Anything down that hall? You two go first."

When they left the room, Skeet took Louise's small purse out of his coat, stuffed it far into Betsy's pack, and followed them.

Light from the first room poured out of the opened door and the hole in the wall. Betsy and Roy hurried past and Skeet stood in the doorway, examining it.

"So Norm zip-ties the girl and hangs the guy from the clothes hanger bar. And they both bust out. Like out of a bad…" he turned and they were gone, "Hey, where'd you go?"

Two other doors stood open, one to a dark room, the bathroom, and the other allowing another dim light to flood the hallway. Betsy's voice grumbled from the lit room. "There's only one way out unless you jump out a window so don't freak out." She walked out with a chair and Roy got the one out of the room they'd been locked in. They set the chairs by the couch. Norm groaned, opened his eyes, tried to sit up, then slumped backward with his head resting on the back of the couch. His mouth was now visible, swollen and red from when Betsy punched him.

Skeet arranged the chairs so that he faced the couch about ten feet back. Roy sat at the opposite end of the couch from Norm and Betsy sat on a chair between Roy and Skeet.

For a moment, Skeet stayed quiet, not even a mumble, his gun lying in his lap, then said, "Okay, this is what we're going to do. We're going to go over everything we've figured out so far. And we're too far enough away from each other to slit anybody's throat."

"Except you have a gun," Betsy said.

"Which I don't plan on using unless somebody forces me to. Listen, both of you, I may be a rough guy if I don't get my way but I'm not completely deranged like this character here." He pointed to Norm. "It's kind of like badasses in a movie. Some are pure evil, like Hannibal Lecter or Voldemort. That's who's sitting there on the couch right there. Take your pick Hannibal or Voldemort. Now me, I'm more of a tough guy like Stallone or maybe even Schwarzenegger."

Norm's eyes fluttered and he shook a little. He groaned one more time, opened his eyes, and worked his gaze from one nightmarish person to another. He settled on Skeet and forced a smile. "Skeet. Good to see you." He waved his arm toward Roy and Betsy. "You want some help with these two?"

"No, Norman, I want some answers. And I can see that you're dying to stand and get past me and out the door. Give it a try if you want. Give us some entertainment."

"I'm not going anywhere so just calm down."

"Real nice place you got here," Skeet said. "Can you tell me what's going on downstairs? Why there's a rumble coming up through the floor but no light from any of the windows. What are you making down there? Meth? Crack?"

Norm ignored him. "These two here." He pointed again at Roy and Betsy. "They're a real problem."

"And why is that, Norman? I'll tell you what. Throw Roy the key to those cuffs. I'll give you five seconds and, if you don't do it, I'm going to put a bullet in your head. One...two..."

"All right. Just let me find the damn thing."

He searched his pockets, found the key, and tossed it next to Roy. Roy put it in his own pocket. He didn't dare interrupt, draw attention to himself right then by unlocking the cuffs.

Betsy was another story. She glared at Norm and said, "Yeah, Norm. Why is it that we're a real problem? Is it because you don't need us to find the money? You never did need us?"

Norm grumbled, "Shut up right now. Nobody cares what you have to say."

Skeet stood, walked over to Norm, towered over him, and poked his shoe in Norm's shin. "Not true, Norm. not true at all. I'm very interested in what she has to say." He backed up to his chair and sat down again.

Betsy continued, "As I see it, Norm, there are three possibilities of what could have happened. Maybe your beloved Walter Lazrove isn't as dumb as he makes out to be. I mean, why the hell would he come up to the frigid Adirondacks and think he could find the money when nobody else could? Maybe he's been playing you guys and took the very heavy bag out of Ethan's car and stashed it somewhere himself, just waiting until he got out. And then did this stupid trip up north to fake you out. To try to fake me out."

She looked at Skeet and then Norm. Skeet looked like he was fighting a world of panic and Norm looked like he was hiding a world of glee. "Or how about this idea? Ethan lugged that damn bag through the woods, and walked all night, which, knowing him better than any of you, is a good possibility. He's like nearly super-human in that way. And then he made a call the next day for help. But Norm, when you picked him up, where was it, in Saranac Lake maybe? Was he lugging a big heavy sack of cash?"

"Hey, why don't you just shut up," Norm growled.

Skeet yelled this time. "Norm, no interrupting."

Skeet nodded to Betsy and she continued, "You did pick him up, didn't you? How else would he have gotten down here? The police checked the flights, the buses. And, when you picked Ethan up, he didn't have the bag, did he? You didn't even know about the money then. Thought it had burned up in the fire. Well, here's an idea for you. Maybe Ethan hid it and came back for it later and took it somewhere. So now it could be anywhere in this entire city, maybe even under your bed. Or maybe he brought it up to Uncle Frank's cabin in the Catskills. Remember that place?"

Norm gave a nervous laugh and said, "No way. Didn't happen."

"Why not, Norm?" Betsy asked.

"Because I killed the little shit."

"Yeah, and guess what. I killed Walter Lazrove so now we're even."

"Betsy, stop," Roy said.

She ignored him and continued, "And I know my brother is still alive because…"

"Betsy, you really do need to shut up now," Skeet said.

Roy fidgeted, Skeet put on a stone-faced expression.

Norm looked at each of them. "What the hell's going on here? What did you do to Lazrove?"

Betsy's thoughts flashed on Skeet and the gunshots at the cave. It felt like a year ago. She couldn't believe Skeet would have killed Lazrove but she'd love it if Norm believed it.

She sneered at him. "Well Norm, guess what. If that sick asshole, Lazrove, is in fact dead and you really want your money back, you better hope Ethan's the one who hid it somewhere. Just imagine the possibilities of where it could be."

Norm slumped back in his chair, defeated. He put his head in his hands. Then he sat up and looked at each of them, one by one. He said, "You really fucked this up, you know that? All three of you. And you're all going to pay."

Skeet stood, paced back and forth, began to turn, and in less than a second, Norm reached behind him, took hold of a heavy glass ashtray stuck behind the cushion he was sitting on, and hurled it at Skeet. It hit him hard in the forehead and knocked him backwards to his knees. The gun flew out of his hand onto the floor. Norm lunged for it but Roy was there first and kicked it to the far side of the room.

Norm ran to the door, opened it and stepped through, then leaned his head back in and said, "Hey Skeet. Remember that time in the playoff game when I hit you in the head with a pitch and took you out of the game? I did it on purpose."

Norm's footsteps echoed down the metal stairs, his car door opened and slammed, the engine started, and as he drove away, the sounds faded back to the silence of the room.

Betsy said, "Well, that's one more creep gone. Two out of three down."

Skeet's gun lay about ten feet from him but only five feet from Betsy. Roy looked at her but she didn't move, just stared at the door. Skeet scrambled across the floor, picked up the gun, and forced himself up and into his chair.

Betsy said, "How's your head feel, Skeet? Maybe we should give Roy a few whacks so he can join the club. Oh, I forgot, Roy. I noticed your swollen mouth before. Must've been from Norm. I guess you're already in the club."

Betsy stood, picked up her backpack, and calmly walked to the door.

Skeet turned in his chair. "Stop."

Betsy faced him. "No, I'm not going to stop. And here's why. I don't give a crap about this money. I never really did. The thing is, none of us have any idea where it is, including the asshole that just left here so why bother looking? And, if I understood correctly, the one who probably did know something is dead. Money, money, money. That's all any of you care about. Even you, Roy? Well, I'm done with it so I'm going to walk out that door, into the freezing night and do the only thing left I do care about which is to try to find my brother. If he's still alive. And I'm not going to let any more big, burly disgusting old men try to stop me. If you feel the need to shoot me in the back of the head, go for it. That's another way to end this nightmare."

Skeet stared at her, actually cracked a smile. He reached into a coat pocket and pulled out her wallet. "See this? I'm going to give this to you before you go. But you have to answer one question for me."

Betsy looked, wide-eyed, at her wallet. "Sure."

"This Uncle Frank's cabin you mentioned. Norm went there?"

"Yeah, once when we all used to hang out. Probably ten or twelve years ago."

"And you're sure your brother's not there?"

"The place burned down about five years later."

"Would Norm know that?"

"We didn't even know about that until a few years ago. It was my Uncle Frank's thing. And he doesn't have anything to do with us. Some cousin or something told my mom."

Skeet held the wallet up. "It's got money in it. You sure you want it?"

He tossed it to her. She caught it and stuffed it in her pocket.

"I'm coming with you," Roy said.

Betsy answered, "No, Roy, you're not," and walked out the door.

***

Roy fished the key from his pocket and quickly undid the cuffs. "Now what do we do?"

"Follow her, of course."

Chapter 27

Betsy bumped down the metal stairs and forced herself to run through the small parking lot, empty now except for a few dumpsters. When had she last slept? It was on the bus, the first part of her trip, just that morning, although it seemed like a lifetime ago. She took out her phone and it still had a charge but the exact amount was a blur. It didn't matter. The phone was old and needed a new battery, and if it wasn't dead yet, it would be soon. The time displayed itself in numbers large enough that she could actually read them. Ten: forty—and still the same day when she'd gotten off the bus in Port Authority and arrived in the city. She shut the phone off, hoping to save what little charge might be left until she needed it.

At the end of the lot, she turned onto the driveway, and when that ended, turned again onto a dark street, deserted except for Skeet's pickup. She imagined using a large rock or brick and smashing in all the pickup's windows, but even if she could find one, she'd never have the energy to do it. The street cut through a neighborhood of rusting steel and brick warehouses that appeared to be abandoned and in various states of disrepair. The weather had changed dramatically since the afternoon. The wind howled around the buildings and a freezing drizzle stung her face. A few of the clouds split and a large moon peeked through and cast eerie shadowed outlines of all the structures. She raced down the street, digging into her pack for her hat and gloves as she ran. Graffiti covered most of the buildings' walls, some with only scrawled names or words but a few with wild, colorful murals. For a moment, she wished it was daylight and she had her good glasses back so she could make out more than just the rough blur.

Skeet and Roy would follow her, because what other options did they have? She needed to hide somewhere, small, tight, and unexpected. Roy probably knew her well enough to spot where that would be and maybe Skeet would, too. Or perhaps they would think she was so determined that she would hustle right out of there, she would find a cab or hitch-hike or steal a car, and go back to the subways, stalk the underground folks, show the picture of Ethan until someone gave her an answer.

None of it was going to happen. Not then. She had reached the end. Like a fawn abandoned by its mother, her only goal, was to find a safe space to curl up in and hide. The space would likely be frigid and icy, but the wind wouldn't find her, and the wolves might not, either.

The roof on one metal building had caved in and the loading dock doors were smashed open. The concrete steps next to the dock were pulled apart so Betsy hoisted herself up onto the dock and the building's concrete floor. She could only catch occasional glimpses of the moon's glow through the cracked roof, and like a blind person, which she nearly was, she moved slowly with her arms in front of her.

At first, she had a clear path and sped up a little. She continued to pick up speed until she slammed her knee into an old oily machine. She stood surrounded by other tables and equipment and had to negotiate an obstacle course to keep moving.

She reached a far wall and went through an unlocked door. This room had a window that let in the outside night glow, illuminating the remains of an office: a tipped over filing cabinet, a few office chairs with the material torn apart, and two still standing metal desks. She twisted a crank to open the window, vigorously jerking it back and forth to loosen it. With a small cracking noise, it opened far enough so she could squeeze out of it if she had to. She crouched down, felt around one of the desks, and pulled out a blanket—ripped, damp, and smelly, but good enough. She wrapped the blanket around her, crawled under the desk, and twisted into a tight fetal position.

Her thoughts raced a minute. *I can't see, my phone's probably dead, I have no idea where I am, my head hurts, my entire body hurts, I'll never find Ethan, I...* And she fell into a long and restless sleep.

She dreamed she was in the cave, the one Ethan had slept in when he took the dare, the one where they had found his wet sleeping bag. And he was in the cave with her, poking her with his foot, waking her up.

A voice said, "Hey, you alive under there?"

The foot was inches from Betsy's hand. It was blurry but well-lit with some kind of glow. Specs of sand on the concrete floor glittered all around like jewels. It took her a moment to understand that daylight had come and she had finally slept.

Now there were two feet and then, two more. A face stared at her. It wasn't Skeet and it wasn't Roy. She'd never seen this one before—young, crusty green eyes, dirty mud smear, a missing tooth.

She sat up and bumped her head on the desk bottom. She yelled, "Backup!"

The face scrambled backward and Betsy crawled out and was on her feet in a second. She kept a hand in her coat, like she had a gun or a knife, and made a fist with the other hand. "Get outta here or I'll kill you both."

They backed into the doorway. They looked alike, same eyes, skinny lips and nose, probably brothers. One wore a green parka and the other one a dark blue parka. She took her hand out of her pocket, and with it, the little Swiss Army knife she'd forgotten was there. She opened it and waved it at them.

The green parka cracked a hint of a smile and said, "You got any money?"

"Do I look like I have any money? Huh?" She waved the knife. "Do I? How about you give me your money." She took a step forward.

The dark blue parka said, "Let's go. She's nuts."

The green parka said, "Listen, you don't need that knife. If you need some money, I can give you some."

"Huh? What are you talking about?"

"Are you a junkie? Heroin? Meth?"

"No." Betsy shook her head, wondering if she was still dreaming. She said in a near whisper, "Do I look like I am?" Neither of them answered. "Well, you can think whatever you want. I don't need your help or your money. I'm only looking for my brother and some assholes are doing everything they can to stop me. Now get out of my way." She picked up her pack and pushed her way through the door.

She was a few feet past them when one of them asked, "Who's your brother?"

Betsy stopped, turned around, and walked slowly toward them. She set her pack on a nearby table, rummaged through the pockets, and took out the photo.

The two guys looked at it, looked at each other, didn't speak. Finally, the blue parka said, "You're Ethan's sister. I should have known. You look just like him."

Betsy slowly sunk down to the hard, concrete floor, sat cross-legged, and put her face in her hands. She tried to hold it back but the sobs had a mind of their own. The two guys sat down on either side of her.

The blue parka said, "We know how it is. We're brothers and we got separated for a while." He put his hand on her knee. "My name is Jimmy and my brother here is Johnny. We live in one of the other buildings with a few others. Ethan stayed here for a bit."

Betsy fought to stop crying so she could speak. "Where is he now? Can I see him?"

Johnny said, "We don't know. He hasn't come around for a long time. Like a year or something. He was with us for a few weeks and then some trouble started and he took off."

"What kind of trouble? What did he do?"

"He didn't do anything. Some guy was after him, he'd caught him and had him tied up, or something really bad. Ethan got away and we found him and hid him. But the guy figured out that Ethan was here because it's pretty close to where he was tied up. The guy kept bugging us, threatening us. A complete nutcase."

"Norm LaMarche," Betsy mumbled.

"Oh God, yeah. Sorry."

The panic pounded through her like a raging beast. She hopped up, paced around. "So Ethan left, just took off?"

The brothers got up, stood close, concerned. Johnny said, "Yeah, we never saw him again."

Betsy's head swirled. She thought she was going to tip over and she put her hands on a table to keep upright. "Oh no, oh no, oh no. I was sure Ethan was down here somewhere and I just told Norm LaMarche that he was somewhere else, somewhere he very well could be right now. Or else he's dead already."

"Hey, hey," Jimmy said. "There are other scenarios here. There always are. Can you call him?"

"I didn't have the right number. I have to go. I have to figure this out. Thank you"

She hugged them, ran to the other end of the building, jumped off the loading dock, and ran back to the street. What now, what now? She raced down the street with no idea where she was going other than that it was away from Norm's prison. She should call Roy or Skeet. Tell them she'd lied about the cabin, that it was still there, that Ethan might be in it with the money and they needed to go immediately. But, if that was true, why did her mom insist that Ethan wouldn't be there? Unless she didn't know he was there. Damn, damn. It was probably too late anyway. Norm had probably gone up, all the way to Catskills, and done something terrible. He might even be back looking for her again. She wanted to smash all of them, maybe even Roy.

She would call her mom and insist on getting Ethan's number, the correct number. She tried to turn her phone on and wasn't surprised that it was dead. She added the phone to the list of things she wanted to smash.

She walked in one direction for the next ten minutes, stopping every hundred yards or so to scan for a vehicle following her or parked suspiciously on the side of the street. The grunge and rust of the abandoned buildings ended abruptly and transitioned to endless rows of small wooden houses or stretches of brick buildings with five or ten front doors. The street, which now had sidewalks on either side, was filling up with people walking, getting into cars, and hurrying to wherever they needed to go to start their day. The cross streets had numbers but the street she was on had a name. She turned onto one of the numbered streets, came to a coffee shop, and went in.

A few people stood in a line in front of the counter and she moved behind them. She ordered a large coffee and two croissants and asked the server, "Can I charge my phone here?"

"Sure, all the tables have charging outlets."

She raced over to a table, dug through her pack, found the charger cord—one tiny bit of good luck—and plugged it in. She'd wait ten minutes and then call her mom. It would be long enough for the phone to be charged. It had to be. But she had to use the bathroom, couldn't wait another minute, and certainly not ten. She also couldn't leave the phone exposed for somebody to steal. The charging outlet was visible above the table so she snaked the cord behind it, down to the floor, and set her phone against the baseboard. She took off her parka, laid it on the table so it covered the outlet, picked up her pack, and rushed to the bathroom.

She used the toilet, then scrounged through the pack for anything to help her clean up. No toothbrush, toothpaste, or deodorant. Only a hairbrush. Her mouth burned from all the crud in it and she smelled worse than ever. She scrubbed her teeth with water and a finger, washed her face and upper body with soap from the dispenser, and dried herself with paper towels. Her final act involved vigorously brushing the knots and snarls out of her hair. She even pulled the brush over the bruise, ignoring the pain. She thought of braiding it but didn't want to waste the time. She rushed out of the bathroom.

A blurry figure sat at her table. Betsy knew it was normal behavior in coffee shops, especially when they were crowded. In a big city, it was probably always like that when things got busy. The figure faced her, head up, and even though the details were unclear, she knew it was Roy.

She sat across from him. "Where's Skeet?"

"He's driving around and I'm walking around."

"And now you're going to call him. Tell him I'm here."

"No, Betsy. I'm not."

"Why? Why are you still doing this?"

"Because I don't want him to hurt you again."

"Or you want the money just like everybody else."

"Where did you sleep last night?" The tone in his voice—quiet, gentle, a hint of real concern—triggered something. He could have been faking it, or not, it didn't matter. His hands rested on the table and she reached across, held them, and put her head down.

"I screwed it up, Roy. So bad. I might have killed him. If he's not already gone."

She told him about Jimmy and Johnny and confessed that she'd lied about the cabin burning. She said she wanted to get a car, maybe rent one, and drive up there. Or Roy could talk Skeet into going. She would call Roy right then and leave a message, explaining the whole thing. And then he could play the message back to Skeet.

Roy said, "I don't think Skeet would believe it. He'll say you're just trying to get him to leave."

Betsy sat up, composed herself. "I'm gonna call my mom, or try to anyway. If she's coherent and actually has a real number for Ethan, I'll make her give it to me. If I can't connect with Ethan, then, then...God this is so awful. We'll have to get up there somehow."

"Can you even see at all? Anything?"

"I had this magnifying glass." She dug around in her pockets one more time. "Who knows where it ended up? But I can push numbers into my phone. I'm not that helpless. And, Roy. I hope I don't regret ten minutes from now showing you this, but what the hell." She took out her wallet and held it open so he could see all the bills. "My mom gave it to me. So, what does it all mean? I have no idea. Or, or, yeah, I do have a few ideas but they all make me too sick to take seriously."

Roy touched her hand again across the table. She wished she could see his face more clearly, read the expressions. She only had the tones of his voice to go by.

"Don't go out the front door," he said. "I see a back door. Don't let Skeet see you. Take a taxi or something and get away from here. And please, please check in with me."

Betsy unplugged her phone, picked up her pack, and went out the back door. She entered a tight alley running parallel to the main street, came to another street, and stayed back, still in the alley. She scrolled around her phone, and through the blur, hit what she thought was the button to hear voice mails. She heard her mom's panicked voice and tried to return the call but did something wrong and reached a spam recording. She called her mom's cell. No answer and it went to voicemail. She tried the landline, let it ring ten times, and hung up.

She left the safety of the alley and re-entered the throng. She had no idea where she was but had an idea of what she needed to find. She came to a group waiting at a street corner for the walk sign and asked a man, "Is there a drugstore near here?"

A few minutes later, she stood at a rack of reading glasses, trying on the different ones, hoping to find a pair strong enough to use her phone and read her maps. None had the strength she needed to replace the blur with anything close to a clear image. She left the drugstore, angry, swearing, mumbling, all loud enough for others to hear. When the heads of pedestrians turned her way, she didn't care because she couldn't see their expressions anyway.

She passed a window with a large pair of glasses painted on it. Something Optical. She could almost read the name. Yes, that's what she needed. She went inside, sat in a chair near the window, and waited.

Eventually, a woman walked over. "Can I help you?"

"Yes, I lost my glasses and I'm nearly blind without them. How much would a new pair cost?"

"Uh, we would have to make an appointment for an exam and then go from there. It would take a few weeks until you had them."

Betsy closed her eyes and slumped into the chair. "Do you take old glasses as donations? Maybe you would have something I could use."

"We send all those out to an organization that distributes them to the needy."

Betsy looked up. "Ma'am, when I look at your face right now, all I'm seeing is a blur. I'm not from here, I'm just here in the city until I find my brother. And yesterday, I got held up and the guy busted my glasses and stole my back-ups. Do you think I might be somebody who qualifies as needy?"

The woman led Betsy to a back room, opened a cardboard box, and said, "Please hurry. I don't want the store manager to know. And please don't take anything else."

Betsy tried on about twenty pairs and found one with thick black frames and progressive lenses. The distance was a little blurry but the close-up was good enough to read the map and her phone. And that was what mattered the most.

She still had no idea where she was. She should have asked Roy or those brothers in the abandoned warehouse. She should have asked in the optical store. Now she would have to walk up to somebody and say, "Excuse me. Can you tell me where I am?" If she asked the wrong person, she would sound like she was crazy and probably end up being taken away again to some other awful place.

She could be anywhere—in New Jersey, Connecticut, Long Island. She couldn't read the state names on the license plates but they were mostly yellow or white like in New York State, so maybe she was still in the city. She tried to remember the names of the other New York City boroughs. The Bronx, Brooklyn. What was the big one on the map? Queens. Maybe that was where she was.

One more time, she tried her mom's cell, and this time Louis's hysterical voice answered. "Betsy, where are you?"

"It's okay, Ma. I'm safe."

"But where? Your car's here. And Ethan's car."

"Where's his car right now? Did it get towed?"

"It's at Trombleys but I'm getting it towed back here."

"Why? Have 'em fix it."

"Don't worry about that now. I need to know where you are."

"I'm in Manhattan. I took a bus and stayed at some cheap hotel last night. But Mom, I need Ethan's phone number. The real one. I tried one of the other ones.

"What do you mean? What other ones? Oh my God, Betsy. From my phone?"

"Sorry, Ma. I shouldn't have done that. But I figured out real quick who was on the other end."

"And you're sure you're okay?"

"Ma, yes, but now, please just give me Ethan's real number."

"It's not in my phone."

Betsy moaned. "Oh, no. No, this can't be happening."

"No, it's in my phone but not in the contacts. I have it in the notes. But if I switch out to that I'll probably lose you. But I remember it."

Louise said the number, then gave two slight variations in case she'd remembered incorrectly. Betsy hammered them into her phone.

"I also keep a copy hidden in my purse. But I lost it."

Betsy asked, "How did you lose your purse?"

"Somebody stole it."

Something clicked, something started to make sense. "Mom, are those numbers in your purse the same ones I got from your phone."

"You went in my purse, too?"

"Yeah, and the numbers on the paper were the same ones on your phone."

"Oh, that paper. I thought I'd thrown that one out. No, no, look again at the one I just gave you. It's different. The paper it's on is hidden in a little tear in the inside lining of the purse. But I don't have it now."

"Don't worry, I'll figure it out. I love you, Ma."

Damn it all, Skeet Burke. He stole her mom's purse. It had to be him, probably out of Bud's car or something. So that was how Roy and Skeet ended up with the devil himself, Norm LaMarche. Smacked in the face, whacked on the head, hung from a clothes rack. They deserved everything they got. And now she had some more numbers, one of which might be correct, or considering that they came from the memory of her dear demented drunk of a mother, maybe not.

The street ended at a park and presented choices—go into the park or go right or left on the cross street. Betsy chose the park. She took note of the street names, found a bench in the park, and opened up the large map, hoping to get an exact location before she tried to call Ethan.

The map shocked her. The full size and complexity of the greater city, with the outer boroughs, was overwhelming. She knew she wasn't in relatively simple Manhattan anymore, and these other boroughs had hundreds, maybe thousands of streets. With her new but still terrible glasses, her eyes would never hold up long enough to figure any of it out. Her damn phone. If she could use the GPS, she could pinpoint her location in a second. But what to do now? She could see the map well enough that it would work to just ask somebody in a store, or even a cop, to make an X on the map that showed where she was. That would be a normal thing for somebody to do.

A paved path, partially hidden by a black cast iron fence and bushes, ran parallel to the street. She hurried along, looking for somebody in the park to ask, or if she spotted a store on the street, leaving the park at the next gate. She passed a few men she didn't want to converse with and came upon a couple, a man and a woman, sitting on a bench. She explained her situation, opened the map, and asked them to show her where she was. The woman pointed to a green square in Queens.

"Can you mark it somehow?"

The man took a pen out of his coat and made an X on the spot.

A car door slammed on the other side of the park fence. A large black pickup had just parked across the street and a tall man walked away from it and entered a small restaurant. Betsy's distance vision had no chance of confirming her unease so she couldn't let it go, she had to find out who the man was. Or who it was not. She thanked the couple, refolded the map, and sprinted back to the gate where she'd first entered the park. She kept low and crept along between the cars and the street until she reached the truck. She didn't remember the license plate number, but the plate holder from a Plattsburgh dealer and the small Corrections Officer sticker on the back window gave her all the confirmation she needed.

He was following her, contentedly following her, not even trying to hide it well. But how? How was he doing it? And, where was Roy now? It made no sense. She turned to run and remembered the purse. She looked in the window but didn't see it. It was in there somewhere, it had to be. She tried the door but it was locked. Nobody would leave their car door unlocked in New York City.

She continued on with her power run, zig-zagging through the streets until she came to a small shopping mall. She went inside and walked all around, looking for escape exits in case she needed them. She found a quiet safe space, leaned against a wall, took a few deep breaths, and punched in the first number her mom had given her. It didn't go anywhere.

She tried the next one and a voice answered, "Hello?"

Chapter 28

Roy spent the night in a crappy motel room and barely slept. Hearing Skeet snore away across the room reached the level of, *this is as bad as prison.* In the morning, they sat in the breakfast area with a few other rough-looking folks and forced down white-bread toast, powdered eggs, and watery coffee. Again, as bad as prison.

The night before, when they had first begun following Betsy, Skeet had acted like he was driving around, delivering mail or something. Relaxed, unstressed, laughing, joking. They waited for an hour, down the street from the abandoned warehouses, until Skeet finally said, "Guess she's in for the night."

"How do you know?"

"Where else is she gonna go?"

"She could take off."

"Yeah, well, we'll find her again."

And then, in the morning, Skeet got up and in the shower at six, woke Roy, and made sure they were back on the street by seven. He stayed back in his truck and directed Roy to hide behind some dumpsters and keep an eye on the warehouse with the caved-in roof.

A half-hour later, Skeet texted Roy and told him to check out the other side of the warehouse in case she left that way. Roy hurried back to the street and saw her about a hundred yards in front of him. Without her glasses, she wouldn't be able to see him if she turned around, so he wasn't concerned about being spotted. But this was the second time Skeet seemed to guess or know where she was.

Betsy entered the coffee shop and Roy texted Skeet saying he'd wait outside until she left. He would continue to follow her. Skeet texted back that he was going into a grocery store to buy a few things and to keep his distance but make sure he didn't lose her. It was exactly what Roy wanted to read. He waited a few more minutes, entered the shop, and scanned the room for her. Coffee, pastries, and her parka sat on a table. But no Betsy. He sat down, facing the bathroom, hoping she wouldn't scream at him when she saw him. A few minutes later, she came out the bathroom door and approached the table, this time making no attempt to hide her now familiar look of distress and fear. She didn't scream or even raise her voice. Instead, she nearly melted.

After she left the coffee shop through the back door, he continued to follow her. He kept his distance, as she went first into the drugstore, and then the optical shop, coming out wearing a strange pair of glasses. That changed things. Now that she could see better, he had to be more careful, mix in with the crowds, jump into a doorway if she turned around. She entered the park and he began to cross the street but stopped when he caught glimpses of her through the bushes, walking in the same direction as he was.

When she turned around and ran the other way, he didn't understand why, but he did the same. She ran through the park gate and he ducked into a store before she saw him. She scooted past, in the road, pressed against the parked cars, and stopped at a black pickup. Roy couldn't believe it. Skeet had parked where anybody who cared could easily spot him. And Betsy did. She tried the door to the pickup. Was she looking for something? She had probably talked to Louise and found out about the stolen purse. If that was the case, Skeet was lucky she hadn't smashed the window trying to get in.

Where the hell was Skeet? Roy went down the street, checking out each door and trying to look in windows. The pickup sat directly in front of a restaurant so he had to be in there, probably chowing down on some big breakfast. Roy was about to charge in, confront Skeet, demand he tell him what he was up to, when another idea popped into his head. Skeet had to have placed some sort of tracking device on Betsy. There was no other way he could have followed her so easily. In her backpack? Her wallet. That would be perfect. That would mean that Skeet no longer cared if they lost her for a while. He could always find her again.

Another idea floated in. If Skeet was so sure he could stay on Betsy's trail, then he wouldn't be as likely to smack her again with his billy club or do something else equally sick. That left one other character out there who was, at the moment, a much bigger threat. Roy needed to find out where that character currently was and what he planned on doing next. Because Roy had, once again, developed his own plan.

He punched in one of the magic phone numbers, and as expected, nobody picked up and he received a text a few minutes later.

He texted back: This is Roy. I will call one more time. If u pick up I have info for you. If u do not you'll wish you had.

Roy called again and Norm answered. "What do you want?"

"How's your head feeling today, Norm? Is that sweet Catskill air taking the pain away?"

"I should have killed you when I had the chance. Just like I'm about to kill Ethan."

Roy cringed but kept it out of his voice. "That's an interesting twist. Does he have a twin? Because I'm looking at Ethan right now."

"Put him on the phone."

Roy fought to keep the shake out of his voice. "How about you put him on the phone, Norm? See, that's the thing. Neither of us have any idea where he is, including Betsy. But I do know where the money is. So, the best plan is for us all to get together in a neutral place and discuss what we can do about it. Right now, I'm calling from a small park about a ten-minute drive from your torture chamber and I want to know how soon you can get here."

"You must be kidding."

"Not kidding," Roy said. "You're the first one I called and I'll get the rest of 'em here."

"You answer me one question and maybe I'll show up."

"Sure."

"Is Walter really dead?"

"Yes, he is. I saw him die. Now you have no choice, do you? When can you get here?"

"Twenty minutes."

Guess Norm never went looking for Ethan in the Catskills. He sent a text to Betsy, saying he was positive Norm had stayed in the city last night. She didn't text back. Next, he had to go get Skeet and tell him he had contacted Norm. Skeet would give him his evil stare, call him a few names, and then they would get their asses out of there.

Roy entered the restaurant and a woman at a table stood and said, "Just you today?" The space was small with only four tables in the center and four booths on either side. The lighting was much darker than the street and the smell of breakfast, a good breakfast, distracted him for a moment. His eyes adjusted and he scanned the room, looking for Skeet.

"I'm supposed to meet somebody here. He's still parked out front. A big guy, late-forties, black mustache, wearing a black jacket."

"Yeah, he ordered something and went into the men's room. He's been in there a while."

"I'll go check on him and be right back."

Roy tried the door to the men's room and it was locked. He knocked on it. "Skeet, you in there?"

Skeet opened the door and glared at Roy. "What do you want? What're you doing?"

"We need to get out of here."

"Why?"

"I called Norm. Tricked him into telling me where he is. He never went to that cabin. He's meeting us in the park across the street in like ten minutes."

Skeet barely reacted. He walked around Roy and mumbled, "This is ridiculous."

He sat down in a booth and stared at a large plate filled with a tempting breakfast, and next to the plate, a mug of coffee. Roy rushed to the door, then turned back and sat across from him. Skeet stabbed a few home fries with his fork, put them in his mouth, and absently chewed. With his free hand, he scrolled through texts on his phone.

He pushed the plate across the table to Roy and said, "Here. Eat something."

"We have to go. Really."

Skeet stood, laid a twenty next to the plate, and slowly walked out. Roy followed and they hopped in the pickup. Skeet didn't leave, didn't barrel out of there and blast around a corner. Instead, he continued to check his phone. Roy glanced at his face and turned away, baffled by what else he saw, baffled by this new character. The original macho man, Skeet Burke, looked like he was about to cry. Now, what could that possibly mean?

"We better get going," Roy said.

Roy looked in the rear-view mirror on his side and thought he saw a heavy-set guy a few hundred feet behind them walking away on the sidewalk. Maybe it was already too late.

Chapter 29

Betsy heard the voice say hello. She couldn't bring herself to respond. It sounded like Ethan as she remembered him, but seventeen months was a long time ago.

The voice said again, "Hello?"

"Ethan?"

Hesitant. "Yeah."

"It's Betsy. I'm in the city."

Monotone. "Where?"

"Ethan, is this really you?"

"Yeah."

Betsy began to slip. She clenched her fist, tightened her jaw, and forced her voice through her rising anger. "I'm sitting in a damn shopping mall in Queens somewhere, I haven't slept in days, and I'm going to tell you where it is. Then you're going to get your ass here right away. Do you understand?"

"Are you safe?"

"I'm assuming you're asking if somebody right now has a gun pointed at my head. And the answer is, no, not at the moment. How about you? Anybody there with you?"

His voice shifted, became more familiar. "No, no, I'm alone. But, for safety reasons, I want you to take a taxi or Uber or whatever you can find to the Staten Island Ferry Terminal at the bottom of Manhattan. Ask somebody where you are. It's going to cost like $40 or something. Can you do that? Call me when you get there and I'll meet you outside the terminal."

"Ethan, this better really be you and you better be alone because, if one other person tries to…"

"Betsy, stop. It's me. And I'm alone."

"I'll do what you say but you have a whole lot of explaining to do."

Before leaving the mall, Betsy opened the map and determined what looked like the shortest route between where she was and where she was going. Ten minutes later, she crawled into the back of a taxi and gave the driver her destination. Before she asked about the cost she said, "I'd like to get right on 278 and go over the Brooklyn Bridge, okay? I'm in a rush."

The driver said, "Yeah, whatever."

"So then, how much will it cost?"

The driver set out and she scrunched into her spacious rear seat and let out a few long sighs. She wondered if she could learn how to survive in this place. It was possible. She stared out the window at everything, mesmerized. For the past twenty-four hours she had been running on pure fight or flight energy, and most of the time, couldn't see enough of what was around her to appreciate it. Now, as she approached the bridge and caught quick displays of the towering Manhattan skyline in all its glory, she began to see something she liked. Everything about it was as different as possible from the magnificent forests, cliffs, high snowy peaks, and wild trails she loved so much at the top of the state. However, the more she looked and marveled at what she was seeing now, the more she began to grasp a weird similarity in how it made her feel. The enormous downstate city was the exact opposite of the upstate wilderness and yet, in some ways, for somebody like her, it might actually be only a different version of the same place. For a few moments, she relaxed and took it all in, even wondered if how she felt right then was how her brother felt, wondered if that was the reason he had stayed down there for so long.

She climbed out of the taxi, walked until she saw an easily identifiable landmark, and called Ethan. "I'm in front of a fancy glass terminal with the giant letters, *Staten Island Ferry*. I'll stand underneath the *I*. It stands for insane because that's what this all is right now."

"Give me five minutes and I'll be there."

A chilling breeze wafted through a wide opening between two distant buildings. From where she stood, she couldn't see the water's edge, only the open blue sky above it. But she could smell the salty ocean scents the breeze was carrying with it. In a few minutes, Ethan and her would walk there together. They would hear the waves slapping into the rocks and concrete, and if they could get close enough, put their hands in the water together. She shook a little and wanted to laugh and cry at the same time. And yell and scream and swear, too. She hoped she could keep it together for a while and save that last part for later.

At first, she didn't recognize him. His hair was much longer—snarled and twisted, hanging past his shoulders—and a thick untrimmed beard hid much of his face. His glasses looked like he'd found them in an eighties reject pile—giant silver wires and large tinted lenses. He swam inside a large and dirty wool coat and had on black jeans with holes in the knees. It all might have hidden the fact that he'd lost a lot of weight. But Betsy could tell that he had. She stepped back, scared, sad. He moved forward, stood in front of her, and looked at her with a familiar bright smile and his same wide bright eyes. She nodded and smiled back. This current look was part of his protection, a disguise that allowed him to move around unnoticed.

She hugged him, hung on him, laughed in his ear. "You even smell kind of bad."

Now he was the one who wouldn't let go. "I missed you so much."

She pointed toward the far buildings. "I want to see the water. Can we go over?"

He stepped back, wary, nervous. "We have to get out of here. It's going to take a little while to get to where I stay."

He took her hand and led her into the subway station. She had no idea where they were going and no longer cared. She relaxed a little more, let go, and did whatever her brother told her to do.

They switched subways two times and Ethan said, "About ten more minutes and we'll be at a safe place."

He looked at the side of her head. "What happened there? Are you okay?

"Somebody whacked me."

"Oh God, no. Norm LaMarche, right?"

"No, this one was from Skeet Burke."

"Huh? Skeet Burke the prison guard? That tall guy?"

"Yup. That's the one?"

"Why'd he do that? When?"

She backed away. "You have no idea what's been going on this last week, do you?" He didn't answer. "Why I'm here, who else is here. All the shit that happened at home."

"No."

"When's the last time you talked to Mom?"

"I tried calling her a few times but she didn't answer."

Betsy sat up, looked around the train, glared at her brother, and shook her head. She hissed in his ear, "And that's the best you could do? Try calling her a few times?"

"It's been a rough year," he said. "A really rough year."

She didn't answer because, if she had, she would have screamed and melted right there on the subway. A minute before they got off, she said, "All anybody cares about is the money. All they want is to find the damn money."

They stepped onto a nearly empty station platform. Ethan touched her elbow and said, "The most important thing until we get there is to stay close and don't lose each other. It may be empty or there may be a lot of people."

They rushed to the end of the platform and Ethan turned around and slid off into a small space in the wall. "Follow me," he said.

"What if a train comes?"

"There's actually plenty of space, but if it's too much at first, just face the wall and cover your ears. You get used to it pretty easily."

Betsy said, "Maybe."

She slid down, they took a few steps, and he turned on a small flashlight. She pushed as close to the wet stone and concrete wall as she could, and when a train did roar by, crouched down facing the wall and hid her head. The lights from the train cracked the darkness and the rumble shook the ground.

A minute later, another flashlight approached them, shaking with each step of its holder. A man and a woman passed by and the woman said, "Hey there Ethan. We're out 'til later."

He said, "Have a good night."

After they passed, Betsy said, "That's nice. You've got friends here."

"I've been here a few months. We look out for each other."

They turned into a thin passageway, went another twenty feet, and came to a small metal door a few feet off the floor of the passage. Ethan yanked it open, hoisted himself in, and flipped on a light. Betsy followed.

She stood in a concrete vault the size of a small bedroom. The absence of windows was offset by the bright light of a powerful battery lamp. Pipes and cables ran up one wall and a single bed sat on a small platform. A plastic milk crate filled with books was next to the bed. Shirts and jackets hung neatly from a clothesline strung across the back wall. A mirror was propped up on a small table, and next to the mirror was a large jug of water and boxes of cereal and crackers.

"I guess I influenced your decorating style," Betsy said. "It looks just like the travel trailer."

"You're still in there?"

"Yes I am."

He shook his head. "Why?"

"Don't start. Not yet. I want to enjoy your presence a little longer before I start yelling at you."

"What do we do now?"

She let out a long breath. "I ask you the first question, the big question, and you give me an honest answer. Did you take the money into the woods and hide it?"

"No. I mean, I grabbed three bundles and stuffed 'em into my pack but I left the rest in the bag in the back of the car."

"So, either Lazrove took it or Norm did and is too psycho to remember. Or somebody driving by saw the car and took it"

He changed his tone, added a touch of annoyance. "It sounds like you're in the game, too. Like that's all you care about, finding the cash."

She clenched her fists and glared. "You're damn right I want to find it. And, when I do, I'm going to burn it because it's ruined my life and your life and our mother's life. And even Roy's life."

"Roy. What's Roy up to?"

"That's a whole other story."

"Can you tell me?"

"Ethan, I don't know what to do here. As I'm sure you can see, I'm rapidly getting so pissed at you I can barely breathe."

He sat on the bed and motioned for her to sit next to him. She wouldn't move. "Please, just sit here," he said. "And let's not talk at all for a few minutes. Just sit."

"I don't know if I can." But she did. She sat on the other side of the bed as far away from him as she could get and closed her eyes.

Chapter 30

Skeet drove around aimlessly, looking at his phone whenever he came to a red light. Roy thought he was reading more texts until Skeet showed him the phone and said, "It's too easy. If you know how to read it, you can even tell if they're on a street or in a subway."

"So, you *are* tracking them."

Skeet turned his head and squinted. "What did you think? Of course, I am." He handed the phone to Roy. "Check this out. If the dot moves away from a street and moves at a reasonable speed, it's likely a subway line."

"What exactly are you using here?"

"Right now, a GPS tracker I brought from home. You have one in your pack. I put it there yesterday but it didn't work. Too bad about that. If it had worked, I could have broken up all of the fun Norm was having with you."

Roy shook his head. "I don't even know what to say to that."

Skeet ignored him. "Now, watch this." He switched to another screen on his phone. "This is one of those tags that everybody's so upset about now. You know, because of stalkers using them."

"You mean like you?"

Again, Skeet ignored the comment. "I think this would work great in a crowded area."

Skeet switched the screen back to the GPS tracker. The dot began to move, winding through a maze of side streets. "It's traveling fast now," Roy said.

"Which direction?"

"Uh, sort of southwest."

"But still on the streets?"

"Yup."

"Shrink the map a little, look for a major route. Route 278."

"It looks like they're about to enter it. Yes, heading south."

At a traffic light, Skeet took back the phone. "I'm betting she's in a taxi and going to the south end of Manhattan. That could get a little complicated because parking could be a bitch. But it doesn't really matter."

"What do you mean, it doesn't really matter? Why not?"

Skeet grumbled, "Best thing would be, they meet, they get the money, and they get out of the city. We'll just follow 'em."

"Unless he never had the money."

"Unless, unless, unless. I hate that word. We'll find out soon enough."

They crossed into Manhattan, found parking on the lower east side, and sat, waiting. More prison time with Skeet Burke. He zoned way out, looking at his phone, receiving texts, sending a few back. Roy stared out the window at the cars and pedestrians and felt like he was crawling out of his skin. Skeet's phone rang, he said he needed to take a walk, told Roy not to leave, and raced away.

Skeet came back a while later and said, "They're pretty far uptown. He likes caves and tunnels and the underground stuff. There's a big abandoned tunnel about exactly where they are."

"So, let's go."

Skeet shook his head and got that same sad look he'd had earlier. "I need to go make another call. I'll be right back."

Roy got out of the pickup, walked a few hundred feet up the street, turned around, and went the other direction. He passed a side street and smelled Chinese food. Three Chinese restaurants beckoned down the street. He wanted to go to one and put in a take-out order but didn't dare leave the pickup, especially because Skeet had the key and it was unlocked.

Skeet came back, this time more energized. "They're moving and it looks like a subway. I'm going to follow it a little bit and see what happens. Probably to one of the banks."

"Banks?"

"If he has three million plus then he's got thirty-four or -five bundles of hundreds. Not going to all fit in one safety deposit box. If it were me, I'd have a lot of banks. So, we'll see where they go next."

At least they were moving again. At least Skeet was paying attention again. He even seemed a little bit excited. Roy wasn't sure if that was a good or bad thing.

Chapter 31

Betsy stood and paced around in a three-foot circle. It was all the motion the concrete vault would allow. In the former weird world of Betsy and Ethan, it made some sort of sense that he would choose to live there, at least for a short time. But she couldn't begin to understand why he continued to stay. If he had no money, no hope, no future—kind of like her— wouldn't he be better off in their dumpy trailer in the woods? He was hiding and believed he was protecting himself, protecting his family. But he didn't have the money and Lazrove was likely dead, so, hopefully, he could come home now.

He would want to know everything about her last few weeks, all the details, and she would have to relive them. She wanted him to go first because, eerily, it was beginning to sink in that, although she was the youngest, she was possibly the most rational, logical, sane participant in this whole sick game, and the more information she had, the better her decisions would be.

She came up with an excuse to leave the vault for a few minutes. "What do you use for a toilet here?"

"Go back out to the tracks, go left, and about twenty feet down is a continuous water flow from a pipe. You do what you need to do and the water will wash it away. If you squat in exactly the right spot, you won't even get wet." He handed her the flashlight and some napkins. "Don't forget this stuff."

A few minutes later, she climbed back into the vault. "I admit it was better than I thought it would be. What about showers?"

"I have a YMCA membership and go a few times a week. And once a month I treat myself to a hotel somewhere."

"A hotel. How much cash was in the three bundles you took? Like thirty-thousand dollars?"

"Uh, no. Way, way more. Three thousand hundred-dollar-bills."

"What? My God, Ethan. That's three hundred thousand dollars."

"Norm took some of it. He caught me and, well, it really sucked."

"And you sent some to Mom, right? How much do you have left now?"

"Two of the bundles are in a bank. And, from the third, around forty thousand, I think."

"Ok, Ok, this is so bizarre. We need to go somewhere that's not here, that's clean and nice and safe. I've got eighteen hundred that Mom gave me that you gave her that you got from Lazrove who might have gotten it from Norm for all we know. It's really shitty money so let's go. Can you do that?"

He shook his head and rubbed his hands together. "It's safer here."

"You must know some out-of-the-way place that's safe enough. We need to tell each other everything we can. You know? It'll be a lot easier, well, someplace else. Not here."

He closed his eyes and let out a sigh. "All right. Give me a minute to pack and we'll do it."

A half-hour later they laid sprawled out, each on their own comfortable queen-sized bed, in a shabby motel in Brooklyn. Before they checked in, they had stopped at a nearby Taco Bell, bought enough food for four hungry people, and planned to eat it all. Ethan also bought a six-pack of beer. The TV blasted some game show, and for a brief period, they thought it was party time. But they both knew it wouldn't last. Once they started talking and spilled their stories, it was going to be the opposite of a carefree evening.

Ethan chugged his first beer, went easier on the second, jumped off his bed, and paced around the edges of the room. This was not the person, the fun happy brother, the definition of easy-going, that Betsy used to know. "What do you want to know first?"

"Hey, it's okay. We don't have to do this if you don't want."

He stopped pacing, sat on the edge of the bed, and forced a smile, "Yeah, we really do."

"Well then. First off, I want you to tell me how, seventeen months ago, late at night in a raging snowstorm, you got from way up in northern New York to here."

Chapter 32

Seventeen months earlier, after Ethan ran out of the AmCan warehouse, drove his car through the snowstorm, and then ditched it and took off in the woods on foot, he did not take the duffle bag filled with millions with him. He probably would have but it was way too heavy to lug through the night. He grabbed three large bundles out of the bag—each one ten smaller bundles banded together—stuffed them in his backpack, and put the bag in the back of his car, purposely leaving it unlocked. He had no idea how much money he had just taken.

Fight or flight mode coursed through his body in a way he'd never experienced before. On the one hand, he conveniently bypassed the tragedy that his best friend had just been shot and killed, and instead, with laser focus, fully embraced that he would be next if he didn't act. Like wartime training, his extensive outdoor experience kicked in and he grasped that the snowfall was his ally, not his enemy. At that moment, his only enemy was the shooter in the black coat and fur hat, whose name he did not know yet but would soon learn, was Walter Lazrove.

A number of factors came into play that helped Ethan's success. An earlier Spring melt had gotten rid of much of the deep crusty snow and now he only had to push through a foot or more of fluffy powder. His biggest advantage was that he had recently studied a topographical map of the area, and understood how the roads ran, and how they eventually connected to a power line route and an old railroad bed.

For the next eight hours, he traipsed through fields, more small dirt or paved roads, and eventually, the longest old railroad bed, now used primarily as a snowmobile trail. Whenever he doubted his sense of direction, he used a simple compass to verify his path, and his strong young body and hyped-up fear kept him awake and present. Until his phone rang.

He pulled the phone out of his coat pocket and stared at the lit screen. It was Norm LaMarche. He tore off his glove, pressed to answer, but the one bar that had first shown had disappeared. The time read five-ten in the morning and he'd walked all night. He didn't know where he was going or why he was going or what he should do next. What a mess. He needed help. He sat down in the snow, thoroughly exhausted, desperation closing in around him. And Roy. Roy was dead.

He forced himself up and continued, now at about half his earlier speed. Every ten minutes or so, he checked his phone for a signal. Every step brought him closer to his home and he felt increasingly uncertain about it. It wasn't okay. It was dangerous, for him and for his family. He had to come up with a plan. He checked his phone one more time and saw two bars. He called Norm.

"Where are you?" Norm asked. "Are you all right?"

"Yeah, uh, no. Not really. I walked all night."

"Through the snow? Where are you? Where's your car?"

Ethan rambled at high speed. "I drove off and left my car because some guy was after me. He killed René and Roy and I picked up a gun off the floor and shot him. But I didn't kill him and he found my car. I saw him drive past so I took..."

"Hey, hey. You have to calm down. First off, tell me exactly where you left your car. I'm going to have your mom get it."

"No, please, no. Don't tell her you talked to me. Make up something, like you found the car. Because she'll try to find me or get me to come home and that guy will kill her and Betsy and Pepe."

"Yeah, maybe you're right. Just tell me where you are right now and I'll come get you. I'll call your mom, too. Does she have a spare key?"

"I left it open and the key on the floor of the car."

Ethan directed Norm to a pull-off on a back road that had an artesian spring where people got fresh water in the warmer months. He hid in the woods, pacing, nervous, confused, the cold finally invading, his winter gear no longer a defense. The snow had stopped and the sun was coming up, bright and full, but a strong wind sucked away any hope for a warmer day. After an hour, Norm pulled in, driving a new white SUV. Ethan ran to the passenger door, threw his pack on the floor, and hopped in.

Norm stayed in the pull-off but left the vehicle running. "Do you have any ideas on where you should go?"

"I just don't know. I don't know what to do."

"What about that cabin we went to that time down in the Catskills?"

"I don't know. Wait. No, that's a bad idea because my mom would ask my uncle and he'd check or, I don't know. Those guys from the warehouse. They could find me there."

"Well how about this? We leave right now and I'll take you to my place in New York. I'm not there much these days and you can stay as long as you want. And when you think it's okay, I'll tell your mom where you are."

"Huh? Oh yeah. Thanks.

Norm stared at Ethan. "Hey, you're shaking. It's going to be fine."

Ethan mumbled, "Roy's dead, he's dead. I can't believe it. And, sorry about your cousin, about René. He's dead, too. Right?"

"Yeah."

"You're lucky you weren't there."

"I wish I had been there. Maybe I could've stopped it."

"Did you call my mom?"

"I sent her a text. Told her I'd call later."

They stayed silent for a while. Then Norm said, "I just have to ask you one question. Did you see what started the fire?"

"Huh? What fire?"

"The whole place burned up."

"Oh my God. I didn't know. Oh, that's crazy. I couldn't see much because I broke my glasses. I guess I did smell something burning when I took off."

At first, Norm drove through back roads, some of which were not yet fully plowed. After about an hour, he reached the interstate, set the SUV on cruise at sixty-eight miles per hour, flipped on the radio, and drove as inconspicuously as he could. For the first few hours, he didn't speak, letting Ethan drift in and out of sleep.

As they approached the Albany area, Norm asked, "Did you get out of there with your money?"

"What? No. I dropped it when they shot at me. It must have burned, I guess."

The money. Ethan had forgotten what was in his pack. He made a split decision. Don't mention it. They killed Roy, he had to hide, and he needed the money he lost, so this was payback.

Norm spit out, "Well, I hope Walter got my money out of there."

"Who's Walter?"

"Walter Lazrove. The guy you shot."

Ethan stopped talking and acted like he was asleep again. What Norm said made no sense. If this Walter guy came to Norm's cousin to buy drugs, why was he using Norm's money? And that was a hell of a lot of money in that bag. He knew Norm was pretty well off but this was absurd. And scary. This was big-time drug stuff with guns and killers. Really scary. Also, where was Norm last night? He was supposed to be there.

The money stuffed in Ethan's pack grew in size, and importance. He wished he hadn't taken it. He wished he hadn't taken the wrong duffle bag. He wished he wasn't sitting in a car with Norm LaMarche, driving to who knows where. Maybe Betsy was right about him all these years.

About an hour north of New York City, they stopped at a rest area to use the restroom and get something to eat. Norm started to gas up the SUV and told Ethan to go in, that he'd meet him in a minute. Ethan didn't want to leave his pack in case Norm thought to check it. But he had no excuse to take it and didn't want to do anything to make Norm suspicious.

He compromised. "I need to dig in my pack and find a toothbrush and toothpaste I left in there."

"You really had all that crap in your car?"

"Yeah, I know it's weird but being weird saved me, I guess."

He positioned himself so Norm, still pumping gas, couldn't see what he was doing. The bundles of cash were at the top of the pack. He pushed them around the clothes and other items all the way to the bottom. He also found a plastic bag of toiletries.

He hopped out of the car and showed Norm the bag. "I found it. I wish I could take a shower."

"We'll be at my place soon."

Ethan hurried inside, used the men's room, and ordered a late breakfast at a fast-food stand. He imagined trying to approach somebody close to his age who looked like they were okay about most things and asking them for a ride. He could make up a story about how he was in trouble and maybe somebody would get him out of there. He saw Norm come in and thought the timing could be perfect to get his pack and run. It was a stupid plan. Where would he go even if he got away? He would have to hang in there, get to the city, and then figure out what to do.

The SUV crossed the wide expanse of the Hudson River just north of the city and wound through a complex maze of urban confusion. As they entered the city, Ethan's mental wiring finally worked its way through the haze of the trauma and all of its circuits reconnected. He stared out the window at the city landscape and acknowledged a tug of unease about being in this strange new place. However, what was most unsettling, was his full understanding of how many ways he was now in a bad situation. The biggest problem was the fact that, if this fur hat guy with the gun, Walter somebody, was still loose, and if he was connected with Norm, then he would be calling Norm and telling him who really took the money. Or maybe he already had called.

Norm pulled into a spacious parking lot next to a tall modern building and said, "Let's get out. I'll take you up to my digs."

Norm carried a small suitcase, Ethan took his pack, and they walked over to a side door. Norm punched in a code on the entry panel, the door opened into a hallway, and they got in an elevator.

"Apartment 802," Norm said. "Don't forget it. It's easy to get confused in these big buildings."

The apartment was spacious, much bigger than the scrappy trailer Ethan had been living in. It had two large bedrooms, two baths, a modern kitchen with an island and granite countertops, and in the well-furnished living room, a distant view of the much higher buildings in Manhattan. He wandered around, looked at the new furniture, and stared out the window, in awe, confusion, and increasing unease. Norm watched him with a slight grin.

Norm's phone rang. He looked at his screen, and said, "I have to take this." He rushed into one of the bedrooms and closed the door.

Ethan didn't hesitate. He picked up his pack, slipped out the door, and ran down eight flights of emergency exit stairs to the outside. He continued to run, tightening the straps on his pack so it wouldn't bounce as much. Like his sister, he'd never been in the city before, but he'd certainly studied the maps. The view from Norm's window and a general idea of how they had approached the city suggested he was possibly somewhere in the Bronx, but more likely, in the northern part of Queens. He formulated a plan of where he wanted to go, then added to himself that he wasn't up to it, at least not yet. With all the money he had, he would find a hotel somewhere.

He counted the street crossings, and after ten of them, turned a corner and stopped. The neighborhood had changed—no tall buildings, throngs of pedestrians, noisy, somewhat run-down, but with active storefronts. It was perfect. He wouldn't stand out and nobody would remember him. He passed a ratty looking motel, paid ninety dollars in cash he had in his wallet, and settled into a simple room.

The first thing was the money. He dug out one of the bundles but didn't tear off the heavy paper strap holding it together. He flipped through the edges of the bills and saw they were all hundreds. He counted fifty, examined how much space they took up, and compared it to what was left in the bundle.

"Holy shit. My God." He had three hundred thousand dollars sitting in three large bundles on his bed.

If that small amount was three hundred thousand, then the whole duffle bag must have had, what? Two million? Three million? Maybe more. And Norm made that remark about it being his money? Now he was terrified.

His phone buzzed with Norm's number. He didn't answer it.

He debated contacting his mom and decided whatever he did was potentially a bad idea. Instead, he texted her: I'm okay. In NYC. Have enough money until things cool down. Can hide. Feel terrible about Roy! Norm drove me. I ditched him. Don't trust him. Keep away from him. Don't tell anybody you talked to me. Nobody! Not Betsy. Especially Betsy. These guys are killers. I hope they think I died in the woods.

A half-hour later, he received a text from his mom: Roy is okay. Got knocked out. Are you sure you are?

Ethan sent back: So relieved!!! Don't worry about me. It's like woods and mountains here, only the opposite. I can take care of myself in rough places. Don't worry!

He sat on the bed, back against the headboard, and the entire experience, beginning the night before, flooded through him. Roy was alive and okay. He wanted to call him but didn't dare. Not yet. He used his phone to figure out where he was and develop a plan for how to get to somewhere new where he could hide. But not until the next day. He needed to sleep, he needed to chill, he needed to forget the gunshots, the terror, the sketchy ride with Norm.

Then Norm texted: I know you took the wrong bag. Walter threw yours in the snow and the police have it. But you said you had money with you. Where did you get it? Walter got his bag and said some of it is missing.

Ethan ignored the text. And he wondered, *if Walter really did get his bag why didn't he tell Norm exactly how much was missing?*

The next morning, Ethan left the motel, ate a big breakfast in a diner, and entered the underground world of the New York subway system. He knew where he wanted to end up but not how to get there. He made a few mistakes, getting off at the wrong station, going in the wrong direction, and didn't care. He kept mental notes and knew he wouldn't make the same mistakes again. He finished in a station in Manhattan he'd read about in a blog that had a way to enter an abandoned tunnel with a sizable underground population.

For the first few days, he kept to himself, sleeping away from his neighbors, only speaking when spoken to, and spending most of the daytime out on the street. Whenever he left his claimed spot, he lugged his pack with him but left behind his sleeping bag, a cheap pillow he'd bought, and a cook stove, pot, and plates. The bundles of cash always stayed in his pack and he hoped, prayed that he never got held up.

By the end of the first week, he had formulated a plan that included: joining a YMCA so he could take showers; opening two bank accounts so he could stash the money in separate safety deposit boxes; familiarizing himself with a few other underground communities so he could, if necessary, move from one to the other.

He went to a library a few times a week so he could sit at a computer and read the news. From the upstate newspapers, he learned about both Roy's and Lazrove's legal issues and prison sentences, and the details of the search for him or his dead body. He felt terrible about all of it, except for anything to do with Lazrove, and quietly cheered when he learned Lazrove was in jail for life.

A few weeks after he first arrived in the city, he sent an envelope to his mom's post office box containing two thousand dollars. The envelope had no note and no return address. He did this each month for the next six months.

Norm continued to text him at least once a week. The first one was an apology, a reaching out of sorts, requesting they meet somewhere so Norm could explain what had happened. The texts continued along those lines, always asking to meet. One directly referenced the missing money, stating that Ethan was welcome to keep what he took, but that Norm didn't trust anything Lazrove said, that Lazrove was stringing him along and would never tell him where he stashed the still-filled duffle bag.

One morning, as Ethan browsed on a library computer, a guy came in and sat at the station next to him. He was dressed in jeans and a t-shirt and looked to be in his mid-twenties. He tried to engage Ethan in conversation. "Hey, nice weather out there today, Not too hot."

Ethan didn't turn to look. "Yeah, it's nice."

"What's your name?" the guy asked.

"Uh, Jim."

"Oh yeah? Where're you from?"

Ethan stood, picked up his pack and turned to leave. "Ohio."

He left the library and hurried down the street. He stopped in a doorway and waited to see if the guy was following him. He decided he was being overly paranoid and continued on his way to the YMCA. He stuffed his pack into a locker, padlocked it, and hit the shower. When he got out, another guy was in the same locker row, staring at him. Ethan dressed and hurried back onto the street.

He turned around, and through the crowds, spotted a third guy, or so he thought. He walked a few hundred yards and the third guy was still behind him, talking on a phone as he walked.

I'm losing it. I'm making this up. He went into a subway station, hurried through a few tunnels, and found his current underground space. He rolled up his sleeping bag, stuffed his few belongings in his pack, and turned to leave. Four figures surrounded him, moving in close. One of them was Norm LaMarche and he had a gun.

Ethan spent the next two days locked in the barren room in Norm's other apartment, the dark place. Norm let him out, always at gunpoint, a few times a day to use the bathroom, and then locked him back in. Norm allowed him to keep his sleeping bag and a few clothes but took his pack with around twenty thousand dollars in it. Norm also took his phone, plus two other burner phones Ethan had bought to talk to his mom.

On the first day, Norm refused to speak or answer any questions.

On the second day, Norm asked where the rest of the money was that Ethan had taken. Ethan's one-word answer was, "Gone."

"I hope you sent a bunch to your mother. Somebody's got to take care of her."

Ethan didn't answer. He wondered how much Norm thought he'd actually taken.

Norm launched into his thoughts about Lazrove, how he most likely was going to get released from prison, how he said he'd taken the money from Ethan's car and hidden it but couldn't get it back until he got out.

Ethan didn't comment.

Then Norm dropped the bombshell. "The thing is, Ethan, I believed for so many years that you were actually my kid, my son. So, it made you special to me and I always treated you that way. Then, after we got down here, I did something I should have done years ago. When we first got to my apartment, I took a glass you'd drunk out of and had a DNA test done. And guess what? You're not my kid. Now that doesn't mean you're not important to me because you still are. Just not as much. You can't get away with as much. Fuck me over like your mother did."

"How did she do that?"

"Well, at the time, you were conceived, she wasn't even with your so-called father, my former friend, Doug. She was back with me. Sometimes. And then, she got pregnant. I didn't even know it until after Doug and her got back together—with my blessing, don't ever forget that. I let her go because I was done with her for a while. So, if you're not my kid, who else was she messing around with? I have a damn good idea."

Ethan sniped, "Why do you care so much about that? It was, like, nineteen years ago."

Norm paced around like a caged tiger. "Everyone who deserves payback gets payback. Don't ever forget that."

Ethan woke around one in the morning to the sound of a door slamming. He tried the door to his room and it was unlocked. He ran around the dark apartment looking for his pack and his phones. No luck, they were gone. He rolled up his sleeping bag, checked his pocket for the safety deposit box keys and his wallet, and left the horrible place. He ran down the street, into the group of abandoned buildings, and spent the rest of the night hiding behind a dumpster. The summer sun came up early and woke him out of a half-sleep. Two guys who looked like brothers stood over him.

"Hey man, you okay? You need help?"

Chapter 33

Ethan told the whole story, getting off the bed, pacing around the bare room in the shabby hotel, then sitting back on the bed. Betsy listened without interruption until, finally, she said, "Jimmy and Johnny, right?"

"How would you know that?"

"I talked to them. This morning. They woke me up, just like you. After I escaped."

"Aw no. Betsy. No." He pushed next to her, put his arm around her, and pulled her close.

Betsy let out a huge sigh. "I'm okay, you know. I really am. No way am I going to let those horrible creatures get the best of me."

"Creatures as in plural?" Ethan asked

"Well Skeet Burke is certainly a member of the club and Roy might be, too.

"Skeet Burke. It's hard for me to put him into the whole picture. And Roy. That's really a stretch. I hope so, anyway."

"So, this is what comes next," Betsy said. "I'm going to tell you as best I can everything that's happened to me since Roy got out of jail."

When Betsy finished, Ethan said, "Norm got Lazrove and Skeet together but Norm hates Skeet. He was most likely only using him because Skeet was a CO in Sing Sing, right? And Skeet doesn't like Norm much either. But guess what? I just remembered something, or at least I think I did, that's majorly disturbing."

"Huh? What?"

"Norm went on about me not being his kid, and way back then, somebody else was messing around with Mom and, well, use your imagination,"

"No, no way. I mean, if that's true then, wow, she sure knows how to pick the bad ones."

They laid in their beds and watched the TV until they fell asleep, leaving the volume to blare in the background. They drifted through dreams they wouldn't remember, and with daylight eventually peeking through a slit in the curtains, woke happier than either of them had been in a long time. Betsy claimed first use of the bathroom, took a long hot shower, washed away the dirt and grime of the last few days—and perhaps a touch of the mental and emotional stains—and put on clean clothes.

Ethan went next. Betsy watched a morning news show, heard the water run for a quick shower, and wondered what he was doing in there for another half-hour. He came out clean, with trimmed hair and beard, a happy smile, and his shining golden-brown eyes. Betsy stared wide-eyed, and choked out, "That's the guy I used to know."

Ethan lost his smile and his face drooped. "I hope I can be that person again."

She hopped off the bed and stood in front of him. "I was so pissed at you. That you took off, that you died, that you were still alive. Everything about it. And, when Roy showed up, God I treated him like shit. I get it now, I really do. I think I understand. Because we both had a full-on Norm LaMarche experience, and now I know." She sat down next to him. "But this is something that's going to change, that's never going to happen again. From now on, going forward, you can never lie to me. Not ever. Not about anything. No matter what happens down the road, I'm grown up enough to handle it. Let those other idiots lie to each other, but not us."

Ethan sighed, "You're right. We can't do that, act like that. But, holy shit, what a combo. Skeet, Lazrove, Norm."

"And Roy," she said, quietly. "Although..."

"Yeah," he mumbled. Then he brightened. "So, what're we up to today?"

"Let's not check out yet. Let's go get a big breakfast somewhere. But, uh, these glasses just don't fit with our current look so I was wondering if you have an extra pair on you."

"I do but they won't be strong enough."

She pointed at her face. "They have to be better than these."

Ethan dug through his pack and handed her a pair much like his.

She put them on. "Much better except now I can see just how grungy this place is. Almost as bad as the trailer."

They headed down the street, both with packs on their backs. Neither was trusting enough to leave them unguarded in the room. The sun shone down from a cloudless sky and delivered Betsy back to the cozier feel of early Fall. "It sure is warmer down here, isn't it?"

They passed a rough-looking man wrapped in an unzipped sleeping bag sitting on the ground with a cup in front of him. "Got anything for me?" he croaked.

Betsy took a twenty out of her pocket, put it in the cup, grabbed onto Ethan, and hurried away. "Now that was weird. I'm right now on welfare and I can actually afford to give somebody else something."

"It feels pretty good, doesn't it?"

She pointed across the street to a diner. "Let's go in there."

They crossed the street, Ethan opened the door for her, and she followed. When they passed through the door, she saw something out of the corner of her eye, spun around, and looked through the glass back at the street."

"What?" Ethan said.

"It's them. It's Skeet's truck. I know it is."

"Did they see you?"

"No." She took his hand. "Let's get out of here."

They ran in the other direction. A moment later, Ethan pulled Betsy behind a parked car, and pushed her into a squat. Another familiar car drove by. "That was Norm that drove by."

They continued, came to a subway entrance, and charged down the stairs to the platform.

Betsy said, "How can this be happening? It makes no sense."

Ethan looked at her, his face scrunched, thinking, examining. "It does make sense, actually. Skeet had your wallet, right?" She nodded. He said, "Let me see it. We have to do this, like, right now.

He went through each section of her wallet, handing her the contents. Behind her driver's license, he found a small square piece of plastic and showed it to her. "Now what about Norm? He could've done the same thing."

"Yes, he might've. I could have something in my pack. But he never believed I would get away."

"He stormed out of his hell-hole after he clubbed Skeet with that ashtray, right?"

"Yeah."

"He might have put something on Skeet's truck, you know, like in the movies. He might be just following Skeet."

Betsy shook her head. "We have to check my pack."

"Not here. Let's just get out of here."

He set the plastic piece under a bench, and they ran into a subway station and caught the next train. They stayed on for the next half hour, taking a roundabout route back to Ethan's vault. Betsy stayed silent the entire time and Ethan glued his attention to his phone, scrolling, looking for information. When they got back to the vault, Betsy laid down on the bed platform and closed her eyes. Ethan sat next to her. "We have to go through your pack. That phone tag thing doesn't make sense at all. It could track you really well in certain places but I doubt it could have found us over in Brooklyn. Or followed us underground. I mean, maybe if there were tons of people out with the right kinds of phones everywhere, it might work. I'm not sure."

Betsy barely paid attention, lost in her own thoughts. She sat up, her face wet. "I was so happy, so hopeful. This nightmare was finally going to be over. But it's not, is it? And it never will be. All I wanted was for you to come home and, and for Pepe to stay okay just a little longer. And Ma to stop being such a damn drunk. I just wanted to have a family again for a little while. But those assholes will never let up."

Ethan stood, paced around, sat again, and gave her a big smile. "You know what? I don't think I've seen you cry about anything since you were like six years old."

Betsy choked, laughed, and forced a small grin. "Go to hell, Ethan."

They started by going through all the pack pockets, looking for any slits in the waist and shoulder straps. Then they dumped all the contents of the pack on the floor into a pile. And there it was, staring up at them—their mom's purse.

"Isn't that Mom's old purse?" Ethan asked.

Betsy jumped up. "We have to get out of here. Right now."

Ethan didn't question. They shoved the clothes back into the pack and she put it on, Ethan did the same with his pack, and they jumped down into the tunnel. They heard voices coming from the way they needed to exit and ran in the other direction. Light from a flashlight bounced around the walls, close enough that it sometimes lit the tunnel in front of them.

"This is the police. Stop or we'll shoot," a voice yelled.

"Can we get out this way, the way we're going?" Betsy asked.

"It's complicated."

The rumble of an approaching train slowed them down. "No, we can't stop," Ethan said. "But the train will be really close in this part."

An instant before the train passed, Ethan twisted and hopped sideways. Betsy did the same. She faced the wall and the passing wind rattled her pack like it was trying to yank it off her back. After the train passed, Ethan took her hand and pulled her into a side passage. He had forgotten his flashlight and used his phone to see.

They came to a tee. Ethan took his mother's purse and heaved it far down the passage that turned right. They ran the other way until they broke out into an abandoned subway station filled with people who had made it their home. They hurried by meals being cooked, songs being sung, groups of old people, parents with children, and even a few pet dogs. Slices of daylight poured through a few skylights, but the majority of the illumination came from a dozen or so battery-operated flood lights.

Somebody said, "Hey Ethan, is that you?"

He stopped. "Hey Marvin. It's been a while."

Marvin looked about mid-fifties but it was hard to tell. He had a long beard and long hair, and wore a grey flannel coat that appeared relatively new and like it would stand up well to the outside weather.

"Where you been?" he asked

"Hidin' out."

"Still from that whack-job guy who thought he was your father?"

"Mostly, yeah."

"He came around a few more times after you left but we chased him off."

"Thanks, man," Ethan said. "I owe you one."

"You already did so much for me, I owed *you* one." He turned to Betsy. "Who's your friend?"

"My sister, Betsy."

"Thought so. She looks just like you. So, Betsy, this brother of yours, he's a good guy. We're all experts at scrounging things up but he's the best. Like this coat," he spun around like a model," he got it for me. And a few of those lights over there. All kinds of good things."

"Hey," Ethan said, "If any other weird characters come through here, can you tell 'em you haven't seen me in a long time?"

"Will do, my friend."

They hurried out of the main tunnel and into a smaller one. Betsy said, "If Norm was following Skeet's truck, he might try looking here."

"He won't."

"No, he probably will. And if he does, I think we should bait him and figure out a way to kill him."

"C'mon Betsy."

"No, I'm serious."

"Except he has a gun and we don't."

A flight of stairs led them part way out of the tunnel. At a concrete wall, designed to keep people out, they opened a side door and climbed another set of stairs. They came to another door and Betsy said, "I bet he's on the other side waiting for us."

Ethan slammed the door open and jumped back. The hallway on the other side was empty. They entered a busy street lined with stores and restaurants and Betsy slowed down and stared into each window.

"What are you doing? Let's get out of here."

They passed a deli and Betsy said, "There he is, sitting at a table." She opened the door to the deli.

"Betsy, stop."

She kept going and Ethan followed her. She charged up to the table, pulled out a chair, and sat down facing Norm. Ethan hurried to her side and stood next to her. Norm sat back in his chair so hard he nearly knocked it over.

Betsy leaned toward him. "Look who I found, Norm. And he has all the answers. Aren't you excited?"

Norm put his hand inside his coat. Betsy continued, "Take out your gun. Shoot us right here. See how that works out for you with all these witnesses."

"You're both coming with me right now," he growled. "I'm going to stand up and you're both going out with me behind you."

She laughed, sneered. "No, we're not. No way."

Norm pulled the gun out a little way so she could see it.

"Betsy, stop." Ethan whispered,

She ignored him. "Guess what Norman. I now know exactly what happened to the money. And the stupidest part is that you also know but just can't give it up. You just can't let it go."

His face clouded and his voice creaked. "So, what's the big theory?"

"Same as I said before. Lazrove took it and Lazrove is dead. Maybe someday in thirty or fifty years, some lucky character will find it."

"I'll never believe it," Norm said.

Ethan crouched down, finally joining in. "We're done with this, Norm."

"You'll never be done with this," Norm shouted.

Betsy shouted back, "Can somebody call the police? We have a man here with a gun..."

Norm tried to jump up but Betsy beat him. She tipped the little metal table up and pushed it into him so hard that he fell backward onto the floor. Then she and her brother ran out the door and down the street.

Ethan flagged a taxi and gave him an address. He said with a touch of anger, "Was that really worth doing?"

"Maybe not. But it sure felt good."

"Yeah, I guess it did."

"Where are we going?"

"Another place I stayed at a few times. This one is actually pretty nice."

"We have to come up with a plan. Make this thing stop," Betsy said.

"I agree. But killing people isn't for us. It can't be."

She didn't offer a comment, and for the rest of the trip stared out the window without speaking They pulled up to a pleasant looking hotel and settled into another room, confident now they were safe from followers. They stayed a few minutes and then went down to the somewhat upscale dining room and finally ate a huge breakfast

Betsy looked around in awe. "I've never stayed in a place like this. It's kind of strange."

Ethan frowned. "I only stayed here one time, but I felt guilty leaving the underground folks who have nearly nothing and I never came back."

"You didn't spend much of that money, did you?"

"No, I sent Mom a bunch, Norm got a lot of it, and, uh, well, I gave some away."

"I probably would have done the same thing and…wait. Wait. You only sent Mom like, what? Six thousand dollars?"

"I sent more later, too, another six thousand more."

"But she had a lot more than that, I think. Especially if she was spending it."

Ethan sighed. "It's not what you think, Betsy. She doesn't have the millions stashed somewhere. Just like Norm took my phones and answered my calls—or didn't answer and sent texts—he sent her money like he was me. And I know he texted her and called her. I can't even imagine the sick shit he said."

"It's gone, isn't it?" Betsy said.

"Other than what's in the safety deposit boxes, yes, it's always been gone."

Betsy said, "I think we should just give Skeet what's left of the three-hundred thousand. Pay him to leave us alone."

"I'd rather throw it all in the river."

"Or maybe split it with him."

"And then what? What about Norm?"

She didn't answer. Her only thought was that he would never, ever leave them alone until he was gone. Permanently.

Chapter 34

The next morning, Roy received a text from Betsy saying she and Ethan wanted to meet with him and Skeet and discuss splitting up the money that Ethan actually had, what was left of the money he'd taken from the duffle bag seventeen months ago. It was a lot, she said, a hell of a lot for people like them. She told Roy she had also texted Skeet with the same information and gave a proposed meeting site. It was up to Skeet to choose the time.

Roy texted back wanting to know how much they were talking about.

Betsy texted: Ethan took three bundles, three hundred thousand. He sent Louise twelve, gave away ten, spent twenty. Norm took twenty. Two hundred forty left to split four ways. Take it or leave it. If you take it, this whole stupid thing is over and you get lots of money.

Roy texted: What about Norm?

Betsy texted: Not invited. He was following Skeet's truck. We saw him. He has Skeet tagged just like Skeet had me tagged. Tell Skeet to get rid of it.

Roy read the last text three times. He could tell Skeet about Norm. It would be the safest, most sensible thing to do. Or maybe not. He could also follow a different plan, a new one rapidly forming in his head. Riskier, yes, but the outcome could be a whole lot better.

Three hours later, Roy sat in the front seat, passenger side, of Skeet's pickup, staring out the window as they drove north along the edge of Manhattan. He looked across the vehicle through Skeet's window at the gleaming Hudson River. Skeet's gaze stayed firmly pointed at the road in front of him, his face like a stone statue. If Roy asked him a question, he would only give him a one-word answer. Or ignore him.

Roy grappled with his annoyance, not wanting it to spill out his secret plan yet. If it was going to work, he had to keep himself under control a little while longer. He tried one more time to get Skeet to talk about something, anything.

"Hey Skeet. Like, right now, I'm riding shotgun in this seat. Where did that term come from?"

He answered in a monotone. "Stagecoaches."

Roy's annoyance level finally bubbled over. "Okay. But the thing is, I've got a stake in this whole operation, too. So, I need to know what the hell is going on with you." As soon as the words came out, he regretted saying them.

Skeet sighed. The quiet, sad, soft tone of what he said next was so far out of character from what Roy was accustomed to that it was actually scary. "Yes, I suppose you do. I'll tell you and then please don't mention it again. It's my wife. We're going to wrap this venture up and get right out of here."

It didn't last long. A minute later Skeet switched back to his normal self. Every thirty seconds or so, he started doing quick checks in his rear-view and side mirrors. He gripped the steering wheel so hard his knuckles turned white and he hissed, "This is a fricken disaster waiting to happen. It won't go down the way those two think it will." He sped up and began weaving in and out of the slower traffic.

Roy didn't bother looking behind him. He knew what was happening, what Skeet had seen. As the pickup continued to accelerate, he held on to the edge of his seat, and stole a scary glance out his side window at the whizzing road shoulder. When the pickup swooped into another lane, the cars to his right were moving so much slower, they looked like they were standing still. He didn't even notice the views of the rest of the glorious frigid Hudson River, the giant Palisades cliffs on the New Jersey side, or the approach of the George Washington bridge spanning the massive river divide. The pickup raced into the far-left lane for a few miles until Skeet yanked the wheel, forcing it across two lanes and onto an exit ramp. He slammed down the speed and slid into another northbound city avenue

Roy fought to keep a calm voice. "Aren't we way too early?"

"They will be, too. You can bet on it."

They entered a large city park that jutted into the confluence of the rivers surrounding most of Manhattan, and Skeet parked in a nearly empty lot. Roy got out and took his pack with him.

Skeet asked, "Why are you bringing the pack?"

"Gotta have something to put the money in."

"It's not that much. You could stuff it in your coat. But you can put mine in there, too."

Skeet looked at his phone, then scanned the parking lot. He pointed to a path. "Start up that way and it will come to a clearing. Just wait there. Not in the clearing, stay near the edge. I'll be there in a minute. I have to use the bushes."

Roy didn't question, happy he didn't have to say the same thing as an excuse. He hurried to the trail, took off his pack, pushed his hand down to the box he'd taken off the top shelf of his closet a few days earlier, and took out what he needed.

***

Skeet peed in the bushes, and then, like Roy, fished around under the back seat of the pickup to get something he needed. He also looked under the bumper of his truck, spotted the little tracking device someone had put there and tore it off. He said to himself, "Oh, Goddammit. This is about to be such a mess." He ran to the trail, and stopped and turned as another vehicle rolled in.

***

Skeet caught up with Roy and the two of them ambled into the clearing. A misty icy rain began to fall and Roy pulled his coat tight around him. His gloves were in his pocket and they needed to stay there. This was not the time to succumb to the cold, to shiver and shake. He bounced up and down on his toes, searching for some warmth.

Ethan and Betsy stood next to each other at the far side of the clearing, their packs and a duffle bag between them, a few feet from the edge of a small cliff overlooking the water. There he was, the actual real-life Ethan, no longer somebody who so many people had searched for, told stories about, speculated about whether he was dead or still alive. His oversized ragged clothes looked like throwaways after a bad yard sale, and the glasses were so strange. Nothing like he would have worn in the past, the opposite of hipster cool. But more was going on than just the clothes and the glasses and Roy spotted it. Ethan's body language, stiff and straight, and his stricken face looking like he was seconds away from running off, put it out there for anybody who knew him from before, that the last seventeen months had damaged him, the same as everybody else.

Skeet and Roy hurried toward them, toward the money. About fifty feet away, Ethan yelled, "That's far enough. Stop there."

Skeet slowed but didn't stop and Betsy hoisted up the duffle bag and hung it over the cliff. "You have to stop. We talk first."

Now Skeet halted. "No, we can't. We have to get out of here right now. You come with me, we get in my truck, and we all go."

"No," Betsy yelled.

Skeet scanned the woods behind and beside him. He pulled a gun from his pocket.

Roy backed away, pulled out his own gun, held it in a crouch, and said, "Drop the gun, Skeet."

Skeet turned, looked at Roy, and stopped. "Oh, come on. Not now. We don't have time for this."

"Drop it now or I'll shoot you."

Skeet dropped the gun. "This is a big stupid mistake, Roy."

Roy stayed in his crouch and fired a shot at the pistol, sending it skittering back another few feet. Skeet jumped back and fell on his rear, stunned. Roy looked up at Betsy and Ethan and caught the mood and direction of their faces: fear, panic, and staring into the woods. He spun around as Norm LaMarche charged at him like a mad cowboy, waving a gun around his head like it was the end of a lasso. Roy fired two more rapid shots. The first one missed, but the second one whammed into Norm's gun-holding hand. He screamed and fell to the ground, rolling around, clutching at the damage.

Roy ran toward Ethan and Betsy, still holding his own gun. Ethan yelled, "Stop, what are you gonna do, shoot us now?"

Roy stopped. "No, no, we have to run."

The rain changed to sleet and came down harder, slick and blinding.

Norm sat on the ground hunched over, moaning.

Skeet picked up his pistol, examined it, and threw it back on the ground. He balled his hands into fists and stomped toward Betsy, Ethan, and Roy. Betsy pushed the duffle bag so that it was right on the edge of the cliff. "Any closer and it goes over the edge."

"Does that mean your money is in your pack?" Skeet asked.

Norm forced himself up, and with his gun in his undamaged hand, stumbled toward all of them. "It's my money and I'm taking it all."

Ethan grabbed both packs and Betsy lunged for the duffle bag. Before she got her hands on it, she slipped on a patch of ice and slid into it headfirst, knocking it over the edge of the cliff. She jumped back up, Ethan passed her pack to her, and they raced into the woods. Roy followed close behind.

At the edge of the clearing, Ethan looked back and said, "Hey, stop a second. Look."

They turned and watched, too far away to hear the actual words. However, just like an old silent movie, from watching the actions, they could follow the general idea of what was happening. Skeet and Norm stared over the edge, Skeet calm, subdued, and Norm frantic, still waving his gun around. When Skeet knocked Norm's gun out of his hand, Betsy said, "Time to go."

Roy said, "Wait, wait. What is that?" He ran back a few feet into the clearing, picked something up, and they all tore off through the woods.

As they ran, Ethan asked, "What did you find?"

Roy showed them both a bright red key fob. "When you have a newer vehicle, not some old piece of shit like we would drive, this is how you start it."

They surrounded Norm LaMarche's gleaming white SUV, debating for a moment whether they were actually going to do what they all wanted to do.

Roy unlocked the vehicle, climbed into the driver's seat, and said to Ethan, "Let your sister ride shotgun, okay?"

They likely had lost all the money, every bit of it, and the two whackos would likely find a way to continue to harass them, but at that moment, Roy felt better than he had in a long time.

***

The duffle bag never made it to the water. A bushy growth about five feet below caught it and was still hanging on. Skeet and Norm stared down at it and Norm said, "You have to get it, I can't."

"It's probably empty, maybe a few rocks inside."

"You don't know that. It could have millions,"

"Gimme a break, Norman. A hundred-and-twenty tops. Those kids aren't that stupid, you know. If you hadn't come and messed it up, it was almost a good plan. A good way out for them."

"That asshole, Roy, is the one that messed it up."

"Yes, he did. Good with the gun, though."

"What, so they're your good buddies now?"

"Hardly that. But let's just say I don't dislike them nearly as much as I dislike you."

Skeet saw it coming. Norm swung his good hand around, the gun still in it. Skeet slammed his fist into Norm's arm, the gun fell to the ground, and Skeet kicked it over the edge. The gun avoided the bushes and made it all the way to the water.

Norm backed away and screamed, "Jesus Christ, I wasn't gonna shoot you."

Skeet reached behind him, pulled up his coat, and pulled out another gun stuffed in his pants. "Just making sure. Now this is what's going to happen. You're going to back way up and I'm going to step down on a branch sticking out of the dirt down there. Then I'm going to toss the bag up here. And, if you try to grab it and run, I'm going to shoot you in the back of both knees. And that will hurt about ten times as much as your hand,"

Norm turned and walked away. "I'll be in my car in the parking lot."

Skeet let him go. He would get the duffle bag, do an end run around Norm before he got another gun out of his SUV, and a Wild West shootout would be avoided. But, with his swelling and bleeding hand dripping a trail of blood behind him, Norm began to run, and in seconds, had sped up to a full-on sprint.

Skeet needed to get out of there, get on the road, get back to his home as fast as possible. His world up there was rapidly falling apart and he didn't have time for Norm LaMarche's ongoing idiocy. He began a wide loop through bushes, another parking lot, and around a few buildings.

Norm's voice echoed in the distance, yelling something about his car. Skeet circled around to the entrance of the lot where he and Norm had parked. The lot now had only one vehicle in it—Skeet's pickup. And one person standing next to it—Norm LaMarche.

Skeet came up behind him, the duffle bag in one hand and a gun in the other. "What's going on?"

Norm spun around. "They stole my car."

Skeet started laughing. "Quite a bunch of characters, huh Norm? You just have to love 'em."

"I need a ride."

Skeet unlocked his pickup and threw the duffle bag on the passenger seat. "So, call an Uber."

"Wait. What's in the bag?"

"One-twenty, like I said."

"You can't take that. It's mine."

Norm charged the pickup, but Skeet had the door closed and locked before Norm got his first punch on the glass. Skeet backed up, nearly knocked Norm over, and roared out of there.

Chapter 35

Ethan's phone had the only maps feature that worked well so he directed from the back seat. The other two stayed silent, focused on an escape, blocking out the reality of what they were doing. Once they were out of the city and on one of the northbound highways, Betsy said to Ethan, "Is this your first ride in the kidnapmobile?"

"I sat right back here in the middle, a guy on either side holding a gun."

"Oh God, I'm sorry. I was knocked out so I don't remember any of it. Let's switch seats."

"No, I'm okay. Stay there."

"How about you, Roy?"

"I'm glad you're sitting where you are and not me."

"We have to ditch this anyway," Betsy said. "He'll call the police or somebody and then we're screwed. We should do it right away."

"How much gas is in this thing?" Ethan asked. "We don't want to stop and have a security camera record us at a gas station.

"It's half full."

"I'll figure something out. We'll get rid of this and take a train or a bus or something."

Ethan stared at his phone, scrolling and hammering in searches. A few minutes later, he said, "Roy, real soon, you're gonna see a sign for the Taconic Parkway. Get on it and we can go to Rhinebeck. It will take about an hour, maybe longer, and then we can take the Amtrak train to Plattsburgh. It leaves at about 12:15. You all okay with that?"

"That's too far," Betsy said. "The cops will be all over us. Looking for us."

Roy chimed in, "Maybe not. Norm's hand is a mess. He might be in the hospital or, or…"

"Or what?" Betsy said. "Just say it."

"He could rent another car, or even hop on a plane," Ethan said. "And calling the cops might be the last thing he wants to do."

"And then there's Skeet," Roy said.

Ethan leaned forward between the front seats. "You know, the bag didn't make it all the way to the water. I saw it catch on some branches."

"What? What are you talking about?"

"That means Skeet got it all." Roy said.

"He got a hundred-and-twenty-thousand. That should keep him happy. We have the rest with us in our packs."

Roy's happy mood began to evaporate. "Oh. Really? I guess he got my share then."

"We'll split what we got with you," Betsy said.

He wasn't sure he believed them. He looked over at Betsy and then in the mirror at Ethan. Both were with him, both were alive, but even though he might have just saved their lives, they probably still didn't trust him. He tried changing his tone back to pleasant and happy and said, "Actually, thank you both. I would greatly appreciate it if you would split it with me."

A little while later, Ethan said, "You know, from where I stood, it looked to me like Skeet was trying to protect us from Norm. I mean, if it wasn't for the fact that he whapped my sister with a billy club, I would've thought he was an okay guy."

With a big dose of sarcasm, Betsy added, "Yeah, right. Good old Skeet." Then, seriously, "You don't have any idea. We know. He puts on a good act and then he goes fricken nuts."

Roy added. "Don't ever forget this. I watched him blow somebody away and act like it was nothing. And then I spent the last three days with him and, you know, the guy will never give up. He still believes the big money is out there and he still thinks he can find it. And he's acting weirder than ever."

"I don't know," Ethan said. "Maybe you're reading him wrong."

Roy didn't answer. He stared ahead at the road and tried to imagine he was in the car by himself.

Other than Ethan giving directions, nobody spoke until they arrived in Rhinebeck. They parked the SUV on the street with the red fob still in it and hurried to the Amtrak station to buy tickets. The train was running late so they went to a nearby coffee shop to load up on muffins, donuts, and caffeine.

They brought their orders to a circular table and sat, still not speaking. Finally, Betsy said, "All right, enough of this crap. Let's talk, let's be friends, we're all in it together and all that."

She stared at Roy, then turned to Ethan and started to laugh. "Hey Roy. Be honest. I'm wearing the same glasses as him. Do I look as ridiculous as he does?"

Roy cracked a smile. "You both need a makeover. I guess I do, too."

Ethan shook his head, no grin, eyes cloudy, still silent.

"Ethan?" Betsy said. "It's your turn. Smile, laugh, say something funny."

He lifted his head. "I can't go back there. I have to turn around."

"Why?"

"What am I going to do up there? People are gonna stare at me. Ask me stupid questions. Treat me like I'm a freak or something."

Betsy gently put her hand on Ethan's arm. "Yeah, well, first off. You are a freak, just like me and Roy here. So just deal with it. And what you're going to do up there is you're going to become your mother's son again and your grandfather's grandson and your sister's brother. And maybe even Roy's best friend."

"But, if I'm there then it becomes way more dangerous for everybody."

"Hey," Roy said. "We all know we're possibly about to reenter the big nightmare. It started in the warehouse and still hasn't ended. Whether you're there or not, that's not going to change anything. But, more of us are better than less of us, right?" He paused, then continued, There's something else you should know, something your sister said to me the other night. I asked her something. I asked her if there was anything in the world she's actually afraid of. And she said two things."

"Roy, stop," Betsy said.

"No. He needs to hear this. The first thing she said she was afraid of was she would find proof that you really were dead. And second, she'd find out you were still alive and there was no good reason you didn't come home. Wish I had a sister like that."

Ethan took it in for a moment, then grinned and looked at Roy. "What's this about the other night when you were with Betsy?"

Betsy took Roy's hand and raised it up in Ethan's face. "We're a hot couple now so you can deal with that, too."

Roy nearly choked on his donut.

They boarded the train for the five-hour trip to Plattsburgh. Betsy insisted on sitting by herself across the aisle, because, she said, Ethan and Roy needed to be together, get reacquainted, and work out their differences. Roy agreed, but he wished he was sitting next to her, holding her hand, and watching the scenery shift.

Ethan broke the ice and dove right into the frigid depths of his doubts. "Hey, man, I am so sorry. So, so sorry. About everything."

"No worries. I mean, I didn't understand for a long time but I get it now. I think I do, anyway."

"It was rough, really rough. Everything was. And I freaked out. I just fell into this whole new thing, and to be honest, I'm really scared right now. Not even about guns and money and all that. It's just that, I want to be who I used to be, and it ain't gonna happen, man."

"So, we don't be who we used to be. We try to be something else."

Ethan lightened. "Maybe I'll be like you were, you know, work on cars, fix anything, worry about everything, and you can be me, the laid back guy. Like everything's always fine, a big adventure, dare me to do anything, and I got it planned and covered."

"Yeah, sure. But none of it sounds too realistic anymore."

"But you'll still fix my car, won't you? I loved that piece of junk and Betsy says it's still there at the trailer."

"Yeah, yeah," Roy said. "Probably the alternator's gone so I'll fix that. And that damn heater. Winter's on its way so that's got to get fixed. And, I'm sure it needs new brake pads. Maybe new rotors, too."

"And what about the spare? You still have it, right?"

"The spare? Sorry. I forgot about that. I guess it's still in my mom's garage."

The train stopped at the Plattsburgh station and they got off and stood for a minute, huddled together on the platform, looking around. The sun had begun its descent and the air chilled down. They could see flashes of Lake Champlain through the trees and a faint moon coming up over it.

"Betsy put her arm around Ethan. "It was less than a week ago for Roy and me but, my God, it must be weird for you."

"We could walk through downtown," Ethan said. "But I'm not ready for it yet."

They went up a flight of steps to the front of the station and got in a taxi. They didn't know the driver—his accent suggested he was somebody who was not from the area—and were thankful he didn't recognize them. They stayed silent the entire trip to Roy's house.

The taxi left and Roy said, "I'm going inside to tell my mom I'm back. She's really pissed I just took off and I gave her quite a line of bullshit about why I left. So maybe you two should wait out here."

"What about the bruise on your mouth?"

"I have to lie. I have a good story ready."

They sat on the front steps, looking up at the night sky at Venus and what they thought might be Jupiter, and identifying some constellations. Ten minutes later, Roy came back out, sad face and droopy shoulders, carrying a small day-pack. "I have to do better than this. She was worried sick about me."

They got in Roy's car, Roy driving, Ethan in the front, Betsy in the back. Roy turned on the radio, loud enough that Betsy couldn't hear their few snippets of conversation very well. She didn't mind and stared out the window to distract herself from her mounting unease about what was coming next.

Roy had his own distraction—how Ethan and Betsy had no working vehicles and how he was going to fix Ethan's car the next day. He ran through all the problems, immediate and potential, and mentally itemized them by level of importance. He'd have to find the spare tire in his mom's garage. He hoped it was still there, that she hadn't gotten rid of it for some reason.

Another idea began to take form in Roy's head. A number of small unconnected rivulets, gradually merging into wider streams and finally meeting as an overflowing torrent. It couldn't be. It wasn't possible. No way.

His hands shook on the steering wheel, his body twitched, and he barely got the words out. "So, tell me something. Whenever we got in your car and went anywhere, you didn't ever have a spare tire, right?"

"No, because you never fixed it."

"Like even when we went to the warehouse that night?"

"No. I didn't have it."

"Wow."

Roy made a quick sharp turn off the main road, onto a small side road, and pulled onto a wide shoulder. He leaned over closer to Ethan. His voice trembled, "Where did you put the bag with the money that night? Where in the car?"

Betsy leaned forward. "What are you doing? What are you guys talking about?"

Ethan turned to her. "Where the spare goes. It wouldn't close so that's why I took three bundles instead of one." He looked at Roy. "Why? Oh no, c'mon Roy. I'm sure Lazrove checked it out. He definitely took it."

"It was a whiteout snowstorm and you shot him. He might not have looked there. You know, opened up the big flap over the spare well."

"Then Betsy or my mom would have found it."

"Hey, stop it." Betsy said. "What are you guys talking about?"

Roy looked at her. "Did you know there's no spare in Ethan's car? Hasn't been for years."

"I didn't know, but so what?"

"I put the duffle bag where the spare would be," Ethan said. "Did you ever look in there?"

"No. Why would I? I mean, uh, somebody would've looked there. Like Norm. Or Mom. No, not Norm. Probably not unless he snuck around when nobody was home. And Mom? Holy shit! You don't think it's possible, do you?"

"And the police?" Ethan asked.

"They never checked it. They hardly even talked to us, just focused on Roy."

"Maybe somebody just found it at Trombly's when it got towed there."

"But Mom got it towed back to the trailer before Trombly's worked on it."

They all leaned in closer to each other. Betsy put her hands on each of their arms. They didn't speak, just stared.

Roy said, "Is that just me or are we all shaking here?"

She whispered, "I drove that damn car. Twice I drove it. And, if it hadn't broken down, I would've driven it all the way to the cabin in the Catskills. It had more than three million dollars sitting in it and I didn't even know it."

Ethan and Roy spoke soothingly, trying to calm her and themselves. "We don't know that's true. Really, we don't know."

"But, in another few minutes, we're going to find out."

Chapter 36

Skeet left the city, got on the interstate, set the cruise at seventy, and headed back to the North Country. He left Norm LaMarche in the deserted parking lot, seriously injured and stranded. Except that, no matter what condition Norm was ever in, he always managed to find a way to keep going, to continue to disrupt and disturb the lives of so many others. He had access to loads of money, all gotten—Skeet was positive—through illegal and morally repugnant ways. He imagined Norm calling somebody, bringing him to an airfield, and hiring a private jet to take him upstate. And he would be able to afford it. He would, at least, call on some of his goons to come pick him up.

He was sick of it. He wanted it to end. He wanted Norm LaMarche permanently removed from his and everybody else's lives. For Norm, the money mattered mostly because it represented a failure, a way that others had gotten the best of him, conned him, made a fool of him. And Norm always had to get revenge. Skeet didn't care about the money anymore. He had gotten some, not enough to do much to fix his problems, but at this point, those problems had grown so far out of control that no amount of new financial input was going to make them go away. And the bulk of the millions was gone anyway. He was positive of that now. Skeet's motivation to race back home and do what he planned to do, was fueled now by a raging desire for his own need for revenge.

As he drove, he reflected on how it had all started. The trouble with Norm went way back. Two sports stars from different high schools on opposing teams, both loud theatrical showmen wanting to impress everybody, needing to put on a good act. And then that next round many years later. Skeet had also acted in a few high school plays and secretly liked it more than sports. Secretly because his parents didn't approve and had no interest in paying for their big macho son to go to some downstate school and waste his time acting in plays.

To please his parents, Skeet joined the marines. He did his four years, came back home, and when he saw a write-up in the local newspaper about a summer theater group, he joined right up. What a shock when, at the first meeting he attended, one of the potential big stars was Norm LaMarche, newly returned from a downstate college with an acting degree. An even bigger shock was when he met Norm's girlfriend, Louise Bennet—later to become Louise Racine. Skeet tried out for the lead role opposite Louise in the first play they did and beat out Norm for the part. Louise swept him away, or that's what everyone else in the group thought, but he was never sure if his infatuation was because he truly liked her or because he was simply overjoyed that he'd so thoroughly pissed Norm off. Probably a combination of both.

As Skeet got further away from the city, he couldn't decide if he was in a rush or should take his time. This was a new sensation—he was always in a rush, always had way too much energy, even now as he approached middle age. Maybe that was the problem, he was just getting old. Maybe he would get sick like his wife and finally slow down and die. No. No way. He pulled into a rest area, went through a drive-thru, bought an extra-large coffee, and roared back onto the highway, this time setting his cruise at eighty.

Now that he was revved back up, he ran through scenarios of how the approaching scene was going to play out. Although all of them qualified as bad, and some were downright terrible. He needed to coordinate, to get and give input, to have at least a little bit of information in advance. The first phone call he made left him feeling good. The second one, with an update on his wife's condition, gave him a serious punch in the gut.

Chapter 37

As they approached the trailer Betsy said, "Don't pull in yet. Just drive by slowly. And try to spot any vehicles parked in the woods."

"Does your mom even know you two are coming back?"

"No. And I hope she's not there. I hope she's with Pepe."

Betsy's car sat in the driveway exactly where she'd left it, the trailer was dark, and no other vehicles that she could see were hidden in the woods. But something was missing.

"I didn't see Ethan's car."

"It might have been parked further back in the woods," Roy said. "Should I turn around?"

"Yeah."

They jumped out of the car and ran to the far end of the trailer. The car still hugged the trailer, just like before but was back a few feet, hidden in the brush. Ethan tried the door and it was locked. He yanked on the back gate and it popped upward and opened. It should have also been locked. He pulled up the cover to the tire well, and except for a small jack and hex bar, it was empty.

Betsy lifted the jack, picked up a thin slip of sturdy paper, and handed it to Ethan. "One of the bundle straps."

Roy shone the light from his phone on the rear gate latch. "Somebody busted this. It wasn't like that before, was it, Betsy?"

"No, definitely not. It would have flown open when I took the car."

"I think somebody just did it," Roy said.

"Which means, either they took the money and ran off with it or it wasn't there and they'll be back."

"We need to get out of here."

The sound of a car engine and the crunch of tires on dirt and rocks traveled up the driveway and around the corner of the trailer. Four car doors slammed. Somebody groaned. A hand slapped onto a body. Betsy motioned to the woods behind them and started running. Ethan and Roy followed.

They stopped a few hundred feet back from the trailer, stayed still, and listened. Chipmunks and squirrels rustled through the underbrush. The wind shifted their way and a light but steady rain tapped their coats and the fallen leaves around them. The trailer door opened and shut. The smell of the woodstove wafted over. A few back windows lit up.

Betsy pointed forward. "Mom's having a party," she whispered.

"Let's go look," Ethan said.

Powerful lights came around each end of the trailer, bouncing up and down as their owners raced through the woods in their direction. The three took off in the blackness, slipping, smacking into trees, sliding down inclines.

They broke out of the woods at the clearing with the pond. A third blinding light rose up from the edge of the water and a commanding voice said, "Do not move."

The three stopped and stood close together.

"I left my gun in my pack in the car," Roy whispered.

"Skeet?" Betsy said.

Enough light shone on the gun holder's face that Ethan recognized who it was. One of Norm's bad guys from the city. "Not Skeet." He walked slowly toward the figure. "I'll show you where the money is right now. All of it."

"Ethan, stop," Betsy yelled.

A noise like scraping rocks came from the woods on the side of them. The figure turned his head and Ethan charged. He dove at the figure's waist and they both flew into the frigid water. They disappeared under the surface, their outlines briefly illuminated by the flashlight until the water snuffed it out.

Betsy ran over, about to dive in, when another light shone on her and another commanding voice said, "You go in there and I'll shoot you. Now, turn around slowly and let me see your hands."

Betsy did as she was told. Still not Skeet. Roy sat on the ground, another flashlight towering over him. Who were these guys? Three of them altogether. And Ethan acted as if he knew at least the one. She had to help him.

She sat on the ground, cross-legged, submissive. "Is this okay?" she choked. She started to cry.

Behind her, the unseen water battle raged with splashing, punching, choking, and groaning. Ethan's opponent screamed, "Somebody help me with him. Take him out. I'm freezing."

As the one with the gun on Betsy ran by her, she grabbed his legs, and using his momentum, flipped him into the pond. She dove in on top of him, landing on his back. She grabbed on.

When Roy's keeper tried to rush the water, Roy pulled the same move, but this one landed on the ground. He flipped back over and lunged at Roy. They wrestled in the dirt, the guy's gun a foot from their struggling hands.

Betsy turned on her back dragging her combatant with her under the water. She knew the pond as well as any piece of earth anywhere. She knew where it was shallow enough that she could stand if needed. She also knew where it was deepest and coldest and that was her plan. This guy she had latched onto would either drown or freeze or hopefully both. However, he was a lot bigger, and with his now surging fear of losing the air in his lungs, a lot stronger. *No. He's not a lot stronger because I have something to gain that he doesn't. I'm going to get rid of this guy, then move a few feet over and save my brother.*

She got an arm around his neck and pulled until he opened his mouth and his last stash of air bubbled out. His body softened and his motion stopped. She surfaced where she could stand, dragged him to the shore, and plopped his upper body on the dirt, leaving his legs still in the water.

She spun around, looking for Ethan. Looking without her glasses. She picked up one of the flashlights, still on, and shone it on the pond and around the shore. The blur on the other side was him. She hoped.

"Help Roy." Ethan yelled. "I'm okay."

Roy and his dance partner were still going at it, except now Roy was on the bottom. The guy's fingers finally reached his gun, his index finger pulling it closer. Betsy stamped on his hand a few times and picked up the gun. The guy screamed and Roy slid out from underneath him.

Roy stood and pushed next to her. Red spots splattered his face and hands. He sat back down, laid on the ground, and groaned.

Betsy pressed the gun into the guy's chest. "Don't worry, Roy. I got this asshole. I'm gonna blow him away if he moves."

Out of the corner of her hazy eye, Betsy saw a shape fly in behind her. She heard a whack of flesh on flesh, and out of the corner of her other eye saw a mass of tumbled bodies and a fist slamming into a head. Then a large shape loomed over her and a familiar voice said, "Betsy please, give me the gun. Please"

"No way."

"Can you at least give the damn thing to Roy? You can't see shit without your glasses and you really don't want to kill this guy."

"How do you know what I want?"

Ethan yelled over, "This guy's waking up and I need some help."

Skeet said to Betsy, "Well, then shoot him in the head if you have to. I'll be right back."

A half-minute later, a line passed by—Ethan's guy holding his head and choking, Skeet, holding a shotgun, and Ethan at the back, stumbling and wet and also with no glasses. What was that thing in Skeet's other hand? Betsy couldn't tell.

Skeet ordered the two guys to lie face down in the grass with their arms out. He dragged the third guy, the one he'd punched and Betsy had almost drowned, over next to them. The mystery object in his hand was a fat stick. He kneeled down so his knees were a few feet from their heads and tapped them, one by one, on their faces with his stick.

In his most menacing voice, he said, "Don't do what I say, then you get the stick." He switched from the stick to the shotgun. "Don't do what I say a second time and you get this. Now, you will all lie there motionless while we talk."

Betsy said to Skeet, "Is there any way you can just go away and never come back?"

Skeet handed her his club. "Here, hit me good and hard, and then we're even. We move past it."

"But why are you here?"

"Because I think your mom is in the trailer with Norm LaMarche and we have to get her out of there."

Chapter 38

For the last few days, Louise knew Bud had been leading up to a final question to ask her. It was obvious that even he had had enough of her. He took her to Marcotte's, bought a couple of drinks, brought them over to her table, and asked, "Are you just using me because nobody else wants anything to do with you? You know, like for rides or free drinks or sex? Although you seem to have lost all interest in that."

She answered a simple, "Yes. That's probably true."

He stormed out, leaving the drinks on the table, and she took a sip and decided she was also done. She put on her coat, wrapped a scarf tight around her neck and lower face, and pulled her knit hat far over her ears.

She said to Dewey, the bartender, "There are two full drinks over there on the table. Give 'em to somebody. I don't think I'm coming back here for a while." And she walked out into the cold.

But now she had no ride home. She could always walk, of course, it was only about three miles. Or she could go back inside until she found somebody to flirt with, although she knew there was likely nobody left who would have any interest in her in that way. The best option would be to reach into her new purse, which she'd just bought the day before, and slip somebody a ten or possibly a twenty. That strategy usually worked best if she went outside and asked the right person as they were walking out.

Other than the faint sound of the mist-filled wind, the parking lot was silent, barren. She counted ten parked cars but no living creatures. Maybe she would walk home. It would be fine. She was sober for a change, so she would have the presence to move way onto the shoulder when she heard a car racing up behind her. Yes, she was going to leave.

A van drove into the lot and parked at the far end. Two young men got out and hurried toward her. As they passed her, one said, "Any action going on in there tonight?" She didn't answer and kept walking. Rough hands grabbed her shoulders, spun her around, and dragged her back in the direction of the van.

She got one hand free and tried to punch one of them in the face. They laughed and their grip tightened. "You'll do better if you don't resist."

The sliding back door of the van opened and the two guys pushed her in. One climbed in next to her and pulled the door shut and the other hopped in the driver's seat and started the vehicle. A third sat in the front passenger seat. And a fourth one, whose face was hidden in the dark, sat on her other side.

She felt strangely calm and unafraid. "Who are you? What do you want?"

A voice from the shape in the darkness said, "Hello, Louise. It's been a long time. Too long."

She had always known this day would come, and in her infrequent sober and coherent moments, even ran scenarios in her head: how she would act, what she would do, how far she would be willing to go. Now that it was happening, she wondered if the timing was all wrong, it shouldn't be that night, or even that week. But she didn't have a choice, so it had to mean the timing was perfect.

She touched his hand in the dark, only a slight swish, and said, "Hello Norman. Yes, it has been a long time. Too long. And, guess what? I didn't drink tonight, even in a bar. I'm sober. Guess I'm on the wagon. Is that all right with you?"

He didn't answer, only put his bandaged hand in his lap for her to see.

"What happened to you? Your hand."

"A dog bit me."

As they approached the driveway, Norm said to his cohorts, "Look for other vehicles in the woods."

"Are you expecting somebody?" Louise asked.

"No, no."

"Then why do you have these boys with you?

The van swung into the driveway and the headlights revealed another car already there, one Louise didn't recognize.

"Whose is it," Norm barked.

"I really don't know."

They all got out of the van and stood in the driveway. Louise checked out the car, at first couldn't place it with anybody, and then remembered. It was Roy's car. She hoped he was in the woods somewhere, ready to run. And Ethan or Betsy or both of them? She wouldn't let herself think that. It wasn't possible. No way could they be out there, too.

Louise turned to Norm and said with a hint of confrontation, "Does this car belong to one of your friends? Because it doesn't belong to one of mine."

Norm ignored her and said to his guys, "Cover this entire area. Make sure nobody is out there. Two of you split and go around either side of the trailer, then head straight through the woods. You'll come to a pond. And you," he turned to the third one, "go back down the driveway, turn left on the road until you see a small open space. A short trail will lead to the same pond. Hurry, run."

Louise said, "Is this really necessary?" She slowly walked up the steps to the front door, fished a key from her new purse, and unlocked the door. Norm followed her in.

She opened the door to the woodstove, pushed down the coals with a poker, and loaded it with a few pieces of hardwood and as much softwood kindling as she could stuff in. She closed the door and left the temperature controlling vents open.

Norm backed away. "What are you doing? It's already roasting in here."

"I haven't been staying here and I don't want the pipes to freeze. And the oil tank is low and too expensive to fill."

"Where were you staying?"

"With Bud. But we're done now. He's not a good one to hang around with if I'm going to get sober."

Louise sat on the couch and motioned Norm to sit next to her. She pushed close to him. "Now tell me, Norm, what is it you want here? With me?"

"I want the money. All of it. The millions."

"And why would I be the one to know anything about that?"

"Because nobody else does. You're the only one left."

She raised her voice, let out more anger than she wanted. "Lazrove knows exactly where it is."

"Lazrove is dead."

It was a surprise. And a relief. "How did that happen? Did you kill him or something?"

"I think Skeet Burke did."

She gulped down what she wanted to say, forced herself back into her act. "I guess that's too bad."

"We came by here earlier and broke open the back gate to Ethan's car. Just to see. Just to make sure. Did you ever look in there? In the spare tire well?"

"Of course, I did."

"And?"

"I found the same thing you did. Nothing."

He stood, paced around the room, and for the next five minutes, went into a stream-of-consciousness rant about Walter Lazrove and what he knew and didn't know. How Lazrove was his friend who betrayed him. Or maybe he didn't but Skeet killed him and now he'd never know.

Louise acted like she was listening but her now alert mind began to formulate a coherent plan of what to do next. She accepted that it was a long and shaky shot, yet if only part of it worked, it would be a quick way out and might be good enough. However, if she could make the whole vision play out, the symbolic poetic justice of the scene would be glorious.

She stood and walked into the kitchen. "You want me to make you some coffee, Norm?"

He followed her in, grabbed her arms, and turned her toward him. "Lazrove tore this place apart, didn't he? What did he find?"

"He didn't find anything. He just trashed the place."

"Maybe he didn't look hard enough."

As her response flew out of her mouth, the lightbulb lit and the final piece of the plan revealed itself. "Norman, what could you possibly be thinking?

That I took the money out of the car and stuffed it in the walls of the trailer?"

Norm didn't answer, his face morphing from an inquisitive stare to a vicious glare. He stormed down the hall and into her bedroom, then Pepe's room, the bathroom, and finally Ethan's room. She could tell where he was by the volume of his footsteps and vocalizations. He'd be back in a minute, and she opened the stove door again, grabbed an old leather and wooden bellows from behind the stove, and blew a hard wind inside it to fan the flames. The blaze roared up and the sides of the stove began to glow.

She hurried over to the hallway just as Norm rushed out of Ethan's room. Her plan spun out of control, thrown way off course. In his uninjured hand, he held a small pickaxe Ethan had used for his occasional rock climbs. She should have been holding the ax or something like it, not him. Still, she had no choice but to keep going.

He lifted the axe toward her. "Where is it? Which room?"

She pointed to her room and he went in. She followed him and closed the door.

She pumped up her courage and yelled, "Norman. Now sit down on that bed and listen to me! You want the truth? Then I'll give it to you. And if you don't believe me then you can just go to hell."

He sat down and stared at her. "What is wrong with you?"

"You're what's wrong with me. I mean, do you actually think I have millions of dollars hidden in here and am still living like this? Who the hell would ever do that? Why wouldn't I be living in someplace nice?"

He continued to stare, confused.

"Answer me."

"I don't know. I just…it's the only thing left to think."

"Give me that damn thing in your hand. I'll show you where the money is."

She took the pickaxe from him and swung it over her head at the closet shelf, knocking it onto the floor. "Ethan sent me some money. You already know that."

She took another swing at the paneling above where the shelf was. "And this is where I placed it. All twelve thousand dollars of it, most of which I spent to stay alive."

She swung again and pulled hard downward so that a large section of the paneling broke off. A wad of hundred-dollar bills was wedged between the remaining paneling and a horizontal beam it was attached to. "Oh look, I found some more that fell down in there."

She turned around and handed the pickaxe to him. "Have at it, Norm. I'm sure there are at least a few thousand more in there. Maybe you'll find some of what you sent me, pretending to be my son."

He turned his back to her and raised the axe to the wall with his uninjured hand. She didn't hesitate. She picked up her ceramic table lamp, lifted it high, and smashed him over the head. He fell forward and dropped the pickaxe. She grabbed it, began another downward swing, and at the last moment, twisted the ax so that the pointed parts didn't make contact. Even so, the part that hit him was heavy enough to knock him out cold.

Then she went outside, hid behind some trees, and waited.

Chapter 39

Six combatants clustered around the edge of the pond, accepting orders from the drill sergeant, either because they were commanded at gunpoint or were too battle-spent to object. Skeet shouted for order from the guys on the ground, and when one of them couldn't stand, hauled him upright with one hand. He used the shotgun, seemingly attached permanently to his other hand, as a concert tool to point, direct, and intimidate. With the other three, Betsy, Roy, and Ethan, his approach switched to asking instead of demanding, concern instead of brutality.

He created a line with him at the back, then guy one, Roy with a gun, guy two, Ethan with a gun, and guy three. He kept Betsy by his side because, he said, without her glasses, she couldn't see well enough to hit the shit out of a tuna casserole. The plan was to march across the clearing, down the trail, turn onto the road, and into the driveway.

"And then what?" Roy dared to ask.

"They try to run and we blow them into a whole new world."

Skeet left the line, commanded them not to move, and walked about twenty feet away. "Now here's what you three goons need to know. Early this morning, this character here, Roy Collins, is the one that nearly blew the hand off of your leader, Darling Norman. Just like this." He mimicked Roy's earlier movements exactly, except he dramatically used his shotgun instead of a pistol. "And me, I'm called Skeet because I'm really good with a shotgun and, you know, can do skeet shooting. You run and Skeet will shoot you like a skeet. Now, I know you three goons are starting to panic, wondering if there's a way out without dying. And, guess what? There is.

When we get to that driveway, you even get to run. Right into your van and right out of here. And you will never, ever come back."

It went on for another five minutes with Skeet talking about his position as a Sergeant in the prison system and his work history at Sing Sing and other prisons. Then he ramped it up a few notches, taking it into the land of wild fabrication. He claimed he had worked undercover with the NYPD for the last ten years and had deep connections with every aspect of New York State law enforcement.

"Now, if you try to get back into this mess with any of these people, I will track you down and pull strings so that, for the rest of your life, you will wake each day hoping it's your last. Now, let's go soldiers. Hup two three four. I'm back in the Marines and I'm loving it."

***

The unlit silhouettes of the silent troop magically appeared at the bottom of the driveway. A tall rifle-holding figure at the back broke ranks and ran to the front, stopping at the side of the van. Three others staggered over and climbed in. The motor started and the van backed out and drove away. From her safe spot in the woods, Louise watched in awe.

Another three stood still, cautious, observing. Their outlines were enough. She knew who they were. She thanked Skeet as she ran by him and nearly fell on top of them, her blessed brood. Her son, her oldest, held her gently as she broke open. Finally, finally. And Betsy and Roy, clinging to each other, holding each other up.

"Are you hurt?" She gently touched Roy's face.

Betsy let out a happy sigh. "I think we took care of things, Ma. I think we did."

Skeet broke the mood. "Where's Norm, Louise?"

"He's inside. I'm going back in. To finish this."

Roy had a gun in his hand. She swiped against him, took it away, and ran toward the trailer.

Betsy caught her, firmly put her arm around her, and held her back. "No way, Ma, you're not the one to do this. Give me the gun."

A loud pop and a sound like a high wind came from the trailer.

"Sounds like there's a nasty chimney fire going on in there," Roy said. "Is the stove too hot?"

"I'm going in to check," Louise said.

"No, Ma, "Betsy said. "It's my turn."

Skeet swooped in. "Both of you, listen to me. Please. Louise, we talked about this."

Betsy let go of her mom and tried to push Skeet out of the way. "You talked about this? You two are talking about things?"

Skeet stepped back. "Please stop, just hear me out. The thing is, Betsy, my life is already trashed. It's completely screwed. So, it doesn't matter what I do here next. But if you go in there and do what we all know you want to do, then you'll end up being as bad off as me. And you're too young for that."

"What are you, my damn counselor now?"

But he was right. She stood still and put her arm around her mom.

Skeet went into the trailer and ran back out a minute later. "The whole back of the trailer is smoking and I think it's all about to go up."

"What about Norm?"

"The room is filled with smoke. I think he's already gone."

Nobody knew what to do. They all stood, looking at each other.

"We have to get out of here right now," Ethan said.

"Yeah," Betsy said, "but if somebody calls the Fire Department and they come, they'll find Norm."

Skeet broke in, "This is what happens next. The four of you get in Roy's car, Roy, you drop them off at a hotel I'm going to book for them. Then Roy, you go home, do your parole meeting in the morning, then pick 'em up and go someplace else for a while. Until this all gets sorted out. If the place burns, you weren't here."

"What about Norm?"

"I'll take care of him right now. I'll get my truck and be back in a minute." He turned and ran off into the woods.

A minute later, the pickup roared up the driveway and stopped next to the front porch.

Skeet jumped out, ran over to Roy, and handed him an envelope. "Your share of the money. Now, I'm going in and you all don't need to know what happens so get in the car and get out of here."

Roy backed out onto the dark silent road, Betsy next to him, and Ethan and Louise in the back. He chugged down the route they had just done their soldier march on, past the trail to the pond, and finally by the house of their nearest neighbor.

"Speed up," Betsy said.

"I don't want to hit a deer. Or a moose."

Ethan said from the back seat, "Imagine hitting a moose, and after what we've all been through, that's what takes us down."

"A good way to go."

Betsy looked at her mom. "Ma, you're not talking. What's up? Tell us something."

"Like what?"

"Like what is going on with Skeet Burke? What happened to him?"

"His wife just died, his daughter took off from the rehab facility she was in, and he thinks he'll never see her again."

"What?"

"And he's really, really sorry he whacked you on the head, Betsy."

"He gave me my share of the money," Roy said. "I don't even know what to think about it."

"So, what's going to happen, Ma? He's going to take Norm's body out of there and hide it? Do you actually believe that?"

"Yes, Betsy, I do. I believe it's exactly what he'll do."

Chapter 40

Early the next morning, Roy had a nice sit-down breakfast with his mother and filled her in on a few more of the details of where he'd been for the last four days. He only told her the good parts: hanging out with Betsy, hunting down Ethan, and bringing him home. He didn't mention Skeet Burke, Norm LaMarche, the hunt for the millions, or that Skeet had handed him sixty thousand dollars. He would have to wait until later to share those parts of the story. He went to his parole hearing, gave a fabricated version of what he'd been doing for the last few weeks and why his face was such a mess, and left with a pass until the next meeting two weeks later.

***

The Racines also woke early. Betsy brought coffee and cereal from the breakfast bar into their room, and then she and her mom took a taxi to a rehab facility where Pepe was still recovering. Ethan stayed behind, not yet wanting to be recognized by local gossips, or worse, by somebody from the local media. They all agreed it was too soon, and were also worried about creating too much excitement for Pepe. They did tell him they had found Ethan, that he was okay and would be coming home soon. Pepe cried and laughed as best he could with the oxygen attachment.

Roy picked them up from the rehab facility and they arrived at the hotel to get Ethan just before the eleven am checkout time. Louise had borrowed some of Betsy's clothes and they were dressed exactly alike, in tee shirts, old jeans, dirty hiking boots, and stained parkas. Ethan walked around them and looked them up and down. "The fashion queens," he said.

They were hungry but didn't want to eat anywhere in Plattsburgh where somebody might bother them, so they took a detour into the mountains to Lake Placid where they could dine out unnoticed. The route took them by the entrance to the Whiteface Mountain Ski Center, not yet open but the high upper peak already sporting a white collar of snow.

"I'm going to take you there," Ethan said to Betsy. "Teach you how to snowboard. "You, too, Roy, if you want."

They parked on the main street in Lake Placid and went to a café for lunch. After they ordered, Betsy asked. "Who's paying?"

Ethan laid a hundred on the table. "My turn."

Next, they raided a grocery store, stocked up on everything, and slowly drove out of the town. Again, Roy drove, with Betsy in the shotgun seat, and Ethan and Louise huddling in the back. The still wind and the bright sun in the cloudless sky made the day feel warmer. Patches of snow adorned the tops of the surrounding high peaks like shining jewels.

Ethan said, "I can't believe I left this place for so long. I forgot how beautiful it is."

The road wound its way through the wilderness. They passed steep cliffs, shimmering lakes, and forests of spruce and pine dancing on the slopes. When they reached the interstate, it straightened out some but the peaks still made their presence known in the distance.

Betsy fiddled with the radio, found a station, and sang along with many of the songs. Nobody else made a noise. She looked at Roy who was focused on his driving and then in the back. Ethan and her mom both had their heads back against their headrests, eyes closed, breathing softly.

Betsy turned the music down and whispered, "Look back there, Roy. They're asleep. Both of them. They look so cute. And peaceful. I can't believe it."

Roy took her hand and held it. He didn't let go for a long time.

Every five minutes, Betsy turned to check on them, to make sure they were still there and she wasn't dreaming.

Ethan opened his eyes, caught her, and said, "What are you staring at?"

"Just making sure you're all right."

Ethan poked Louise, "Hey Ma, You good?"

Louise also woke up, looked at her two kids, and put on a big grin, "Oh yes. Most definitely."

Betsy asked, "Will you still be all right later? You know, with no drinking and all that?"

"No guarantees there. And I apologize now if it gets bad."

"We'll deal with it," Ethan said.

Betsy had their attention and figured now was the time to strike, to ask the big question. "So, Ma. I don't know if Ethan's asked you this yet…"

He broke in and took over. "I haven't. Now Ma, Norm had this strange idea for some reason that I was his kid. And, when he figured out that I wasn't, he said I was Skeet Burke's kid. Is that true?"

"Oh my God." She shook her head. "Yes, it's true. But only if I'm the Virgin Mary and you're her son, the Savior."

"Huh?"

"He couldn't be your father if I never slept with him. It's so stupid. You don't even look anything like him."

"Then where did he ever come up with the idea?"

***

After Louise and Norm graduated from college in New York City, Louise followed Norm back to his childhood home in upstate New York. They had met in the theater three years earlier and soon after began a relationship. Both majored in acting and aspired to continue with it in some form after they graduated. They contemplated staying in the city or venturing out to Los Angeles, but neither of them had any money left, their parents were tapped out, and they needed to find jobs before going off on any new and exciting adventures. Norm had a job waiting for him with an uncle who ran a car dealership and Louise knew she could find a waitressing job, so they headed north with the idea that it would only be for a short while.

To keep their acting interest alive, they joined a loosely structured summer theater group run by an eccentric and lively grad student, and with their honed skills and good looks, they quickly made a big impression on the group. Especially Louise. The grad student/director steeped his followers in a style of acting involving full immersion in the character one was picked to play. The process demanded that, when Louise received one of the lead roles in a play as a drunken, unstable, yet lovable wife of a comedic hyper-active obsessive husband, she had to become the character—all the way, not just while in rehearsal—from the time she woke in the morning to the time she went back to sleep. And maybe even then.

Norm told Louise the director had given him the role and he'd declined it. He said he disliked the play, was no fan of the director and his immersion teachings and abhorred Louise's character. "It's not who you are," he said. "Why would you ever want to play such a terrible role? And now Skeet Burke's got the lead? Why would you ever want to play opposite him?"

However, Betsy loved the role and thought Skeet was a perfect fit. She was not about to let it go. One night after a practice, many from the group gathered in a local bar, and in Norm's opinion, the two leads from the play carried their personas way too far into real life. Louise downed a shot of whiskey, just enough for a slight buzz, and launched into a few of her lines. Skeet went to the bar and returned with a cup of coffee, chilled enough with ice so that he could also chug it. They floated through a scene, spinning the lines off of each other, the rest of the group egging them on, and then went into full improvisation mode, wearing their characters like a second skin.

Louise's slurring speech, slumped and nearly passing out mannerisms, and pathetic attempts at bad jokes put Norm way over the edge. Worst of all was the fact that the crowd of adoring fans paid no attention to him. He slipped out unnoticed and fixed in his mind that Skeet and Louise surely had spent the night together. The next day, he gave Louise an ultimatum—quit the group like he was going to do, or they were finished.

***

"So, that was that," Louise said.

"And you never slept with Skeet? Ever?" Betsy asked.

"No. Never. Your dad came along and Norm encouraged it. He didn't want to get back with me, but even more, he really didn't want me to get involved with Skeet. And real soon, Norm had a new girlfriend, anyway."

"Do you ever miss acting, Ma?"

"Yeah, sometimes. But you know, one time a few years ago, I was in

Marcotte's, pretty wasted, and Skeet was all hyped up and he pulled me aside and said that he thought both of us played those characters so well it was who we were now. We were still playing them."

***

South of Albany, they left the interstate and Louise passed her phone up to Betsy because hers had the most intelligent map app. Betsy pressed up the volume for Roy to hear and reflected on the oddity that, of all of them, Louise's phone was the most functional. Maybe it was a good sign for the future. For the next half hour, they drove on backroads into the northern part of the Catskill Mountains. They went through a number of small towns, some cute and quaint, others ragged and vacant, until they turned onto a small, empty road.

They passed a few driveways with whatever was at the end of them obscured by thick evergreen woods. The trees changed to leafless oak, maple, beech, and locus and Louise told Roy to slow down so she could spot the correct turnoff. On her command, he turned left onto a rutted dirt path, just wide enough for the car, and a hundred or so feet later, they arrived.

Betsy had had an image in her head of what they would be going to and this wasn't it. Not at all. Rough around the edges would be a compliment. Her first impression was that it was nearly falling down, but once she got out and ran around the whole building, she decided it wasn't so bad and possibly had potential.

Ethan caught up with her in the back as she examined the foundation. "Better than anywhere we've been living for the last five years."

"Do you think you actually want to live here?"

His face transformed into something like it used to be. He took her hands and spun her around. "It's perfect for me. Right smack in the middle of my two worlds. You know, like the city in one direction and the borderlands in the other."

"The money won't last. It's a crazy amount but it will still run out."

"You don't think I could find a job out in the woods here?"

They went around to the front. A porch with a full overhang ran the length of the house. Much of the flooring was rotten and the lattice work had big chunks hacked out of it. Betsy looked underneath, stuck her hands through the holes, and felt the framing. A lot of rotten beams would need shoring up.

Roy and Louise came out of the woods from opposite sides of the yard.

"Doesn't the toilet work?" Betsy asked.

"We have to start the generator to get the pump working," Louise said.

"We didn't bring gas."

"Oh, there's still gas here," Louise said.

Unlikely.

Louise unlocked the simple wooden door and they entered a large wooden-walled living room. Roy spotted a pile of small logs, kindling, and an old newspaper and went to work on getting a fire started in the wood stove. As he crumpled up a few pieces of the newspaper his eye caught the date on one of them.

"Hey, what's the story on this paper?" he said. "It's the Plattsburgh paper and it's only two weeks old. How did that get here?"

Louise looked at the paper. "Oh yes, I brought it when Bud and I were here."

Ethan and Betsy looked at each other, then at Louise. "Why were you and Bud here?" Ethan asked."

Betsy chimed in, "And why didn't you tell us?"

"What's the big deal? I was trying to clean some of the stuff out of the trailer and this seemed like the best place to put it. We were going to stay the night but Bud got all pissed off at what a mess this is and we turned around and left."

"What stuff are you talking about?"

"Mostly your things, Ethan, and a lot of mine. I didn't go into the camper, Betsy. I didn't touch anything in there."

Betsy raised her voice. "So, you were already planning to burn down the trailer like, what? A week ago?"

Louise sat down in a wicker chair with a frayed cushion and hunched over, her hands across her chest. "I didn't plan anything. I just knew." She looked up and her volume also increased. "I knew something was going to happen." Then much quieter. "And I needed a place to escape to if it did. And I figured, if any of you came back, you might need that, too."

Betsy put her hand on her mom's shoulder and whispered in her ear, "I'm sorry, Mom."

"Where is all the stuff?" Ethan asked.

Louise pointed across the living room. "That far door. Where you stayed the last time we were here."

Ethan opened the door and looked around. The room was in the corner of the house and had two windows, both looking into the woods. The walls copied the siding in the living room. Except for a simple bed, a wooden dresser, and four large boxes in the center of the floor, it was empty.

Ethan went over to Louise. "You did good, Ma. Thanks."

She tried to stand and plopped back down in her chair. She put her hand on her forehead.

"You all right?"

"I'm not used to this. I'm going to lie down."

"It's freezing in the bedrooms. We'll wrap you up in our sleeping bags."

Roy stayed by the stove, working to get it going, and Ethan and Betsy built a cocoon out of the sleeping bags. They tucked Louise in, Ethan went out into the living room, and Betsy laid down beside her. She whispered, "It's okay. You're going to feel like crap for a while but we're going to take care of you. We're gonna do whatever it takes to get you back into this world."

Louise said, "I'm getting warm now. Why don't you go out and do something with Roy? He's such a nice young man. And he sure does like you."

Betsy laughed some. "Whoa, that's a little bit of pressure there, Ma. But I am glad you approve."

"I don't want you to make the same mistakes I did."

"Don't worry about that. I'll have my own list of mistakes to make."

She went out on the porch and joined Ethan and Roy in a conversation about their futures. They were already deep into it, covering topics like how much longer Roy would have to show up for his parole meetings, whether he wanted to continue working on cars again, and if he would ever want to move somewhere away from Plattsburgh.

Ethan had to do it. "So, what about you two?"

"Why are you being such an asshole, trying to embarrass me?" Betsy asked."

Roy jumped in, "And what about you, Ethan? You stay hiding out here in the woods and you'll never find a mate, ever."

Betsy looked at Roy, caught his eye, and pushed back a grin. "He's way too weird, anyways. He'd never find somebody who was his type."

Ethan poked Roy in the arm. "You told her what I said that night, didn't you? Some friend you are."

They all started laughing.

"But seriously," Ethan said, "I've been thinking about trying to become some kind of outdoor guide. I could do caves, mountains, urban, wild outdoors, pretty much anything."

For the next half hour, they sat close, trying to catch the remnants of warmth from the fading sunlight and from each other. They dove all the way into Ethan's fantasy, assigning different roles to each of them, imagining locations, determining a base location—or possibly two, with one being where they currently sat. They even covered the look and feel of a website and social media, and at some point, sending Ethan public with his strange but interesting story to attract clients.

"I guess we have enough money," Roy said.

"We'll have to give some to our mom," Ethan said. "But there's enough that it shouldn't matter."

"That much money, it's so crazy," Betsy said. "But it might be the perfect amount to slide it into a business when nobody's looking. We're probably lucky we didn't end up with all the millions. I don't think we could handle it. It would end up doing bad stuff to us."

Roy started the generator on the side of the house so they would have a few lights and they went inside to get warm. Betsy quietly opened the door to her mom's room. Louise was sitting up, staring out a window, a bottle of whiskey in her hand. Betsy came in, closed the door, and walked over to her.

"Whatcha looking at, Ma?" she said.

Louise turned around, shaky, cloudy-eyed. "I guess you caught me," she slurred. "And now you're disappointed."

"Yes, I am. But I understand. After what we've been through, if I was a drinker, I'd be lying on the floor right now." Betsy hugged her and continued, "but dammit, Ma. You are going to go get some help."

"I know. But not today."

Ethan unpacked cans of soup to heat up on the top of the woodstove and bread to attempt to toast. Nobody objected. This still qualified as a decent meal for all of them. Betsy let on that Louise was drunk and they agreed to not make a big deal out of it. They pulled an old couch and a few chairs over near the stove, found a few ancient bowls and plates in a crooked cupboard, and sat by the fire, enjoying the quiet, the food, and each other.

When they finished, Ethan said, "I think tomorrow I want to go to a place not far from here that has some caves. Anybody want to come?"

They didn't answer?

"Well then, anybody want to help me go through those boxes so I can see what our dear sweet mother rescued for us?"

"Sure," Betsy said. "But I'm going to bring a few more things in from the car." She turned to Roy. "You want to help me?"

They went outside to the car and she said, "Can we sit in here for a minute?"

They got in and she took his hand, squeezed it tight.

He couldn't read her face in the dark. "You okay?"

"Yeah, I just wanted to talk to you for a minute. Like, alone. Just you and me."

"Are you cold?"

She leaned across the console between the seats and hugged him. "Yes. But I have to ask you something. Why did you do everything you did these last few days? It was…I appreciate it so much. But I don't understand. Why do you like me so much?"

"I don't know. But I've felt that way for a long time. Something about you."

"But I can be such a pain in the ass. Just awful sometimes."

"Really? I never noticed."

She caught the sarcasm and laughed. "You know what. I finally realized on the trip down here that I like you a whole lot, too. And not because you impressed me with all the stuff you did. Although you did impress me a whole lot. I mean, wow! But that's got nothing to do with it. You're just a damn good guy."

They stayed close for a while longer.

"We've just hugged for a whole minute," he said. "We're getting somewhere."

"And you're funny, too."

The cold had seeped in and a light snow was falling. Roy said, "I didn't go in the third bedroom. Is that where I sleep or should I crash in the living room?"

"I don't even know if there's a bed in that room. Definitely no sheets. But we're going to need each other's warmth. You know, like close together."

They left the car, arms around each other, and slowly headed toward the cabin. The door opened and Ethan came flying out, his movements exuding panic. "You guys have to come inside. Something just happened."

Betsy charged toward him. "Is Ma all right?"

He didn't answer. He turned, ran back into the cabin and into the room with the boxes. Roy and Betsy followed.

The four boxes laid empty in a heap in the corner of the room. The contents of the boxes—Ethan's clothes and belongings and some of Louise's clothes—were mounded up into a great pile in the center. Eight small cardboard boxes, the kind found for free in any United States Post Office, sat in two neat stacks next to the messy pile. They had never gone through the mail and only sat there because they were the perfect size for what was in them. One of the boxes was partially opened.

Betsy and Roy stared, at first not understanding. Then, "No. No way."

Betsy picked up a box, felt its weight, opened it, and looked inside.

Roy did the same. He pulled out a bundle of bills.

Ethan whispered, "I think it's all here. Every bit of it."

"And Ma? We have to get her up."

"Let her sleep. She's the one who did this. Has to be. She might not even remember."

Betsy grabbed onto Ethan and Roy, pulled them close to her. She laughed but almost cried. "Three million dollars. No, more than three million dollars. Now what are we supposed to do?"

* 9 7 9 8 9 8 9 1 1 7 9 1 8 *